# PIA
### AND THE
# SKYMAN

# SUE PARRITT

ODYSSEY
BOOKS

Published by Odyssey Books in 2016



www.odysseybooks.com.au

National Library of Australia
Cataloguing-in-Publication entry

Author: Sue Parritt
Title: Pia and the Skyman / Sue Parritt
ISBN: 978-1-922200-52-5 (pbk)
ISBN: 978-1-922200-53-2 (ebook)
Dewey Number: A823.4

Cover designed by Elijah Toten

# CHAPTER 1

Long after the familiar face had faded, Pia continued to stare at the screen, her hands suspended above the communication console as though a sudden movement could shatter her fragile composure. Her interior world ran riot, bitter memories racing to the surface, swiftly overshadowing Line Leader Zira's disturbing message. A stranger's voice swirled through her head, one minute welcoming, the next evasive, ultimately a direct response for truth, the news of her mother's fate relayed in a single sentence Pia would never forget: 'The death penalty was carried out last night before the rescue team could reach her.' Time unravelled; once more she witnessed Kaire's quiet collapse against the Sky-ship console, heard her own impassioned reaction. Hands flew up to cover her ears in an attempt to silence spinning screams and the woman's shouted warning as the Sky-ship careered towards an Aotearoan mountain.

How could she impart this latest appalling news, destroy confidence, today of all days?

It was one year to the day since she'd promised to rise above her own grief and work to secure a future free from oppression for the thousands still suffering back home in apartheid Australia. Safe at Kauri Haven, a farming community established forty years earlier on the northwest coast of Aotearoa, Pia had laboured long and hard not only to fulfil her promise, but also to keep herself occupied and prevent images of her mother Sannah's last weeks from pushing to the forefront of her mind. Initially she had joined a group of former political prisoners building a ship for the Women's Line, the clandestine group that worked to undermine the tyrannical Australian government. Sawing timber, hammering nails, varnishing decks—physical activity that along with sweat had brought anger and grief to the surface, slackening the tension pervading her young body.

Two new ships capable of transporting prison escapees from Australia to Aotearoa had now been built, a considerable feat for those previously unskilled in such work. Several Aotearoan shipbuilders had provided expert advice, but most of the credit had to go to the Australians. So far the ships had only been used to bring over the three hundred political prisoners freed when members of the Women's Line, youth workers and local villagers had sabotaged a train transporting them to new prisons built beneath the desert sands. The former prisoners, predominately White men, had been in hiding for months since being liberated and were relieved to be leaving the country. Democratic Aotearoa offered a new life free from the constraints of apartheid Australia, the government being sympathetic to those fleeing persecution, especially former political prisoners. So far, the Australian government, although aware some prison escapees had made their way to Aotearoa, remained ignorant of the Women's Line's existence.

After a nine-month stint shipbuilding, Pia had wanted to return to her homeland, believing she would be more useful working on the inside. Over in the Brown Zone, the Women's Line was developing a Truth Network, its mission: *'To banish ignorance and lay the foundation for revolution.'* In villages from the northern tip of the Brown Zone to the Asian Zone border, both women and men were being recruited and trained, a fitting tribute to her mother, Sannah, whose initial attempts at public truth-telling had led to her death.

Kaire had persuaded Pia to stay and channel her energies into organising a Truth Network group at Kauri Haven. For several months now, Pia had provided initial training, using drama, song and dance to teach the group what would have been second nature to their Pacific island ancestors—the oral tradition. If the truth of their people's history were to be spread covertly, the group had to be competent performers. It wouldn't be an easy task, this re-moulding of minds saturated with myth and led to believe inherited traits justified their low status in Australian society. Week after week Pia had listened to her mother, an official Storyteller, regurgitate government rhetoric in the village community dome, ensuring the villagers' continuing compliance. But Pia had been fortunate; from a young age she had also heard the other side of the story. She came from a family long-versed in Truth-tales: her maternal grandmother co-founder of the Women's Line in 2355; her father a tireless worker for justice and equality throughout his short life. Pia had never known him—he had died just before her birth, from disease deliberately injected by a government medical officer.

Most members of the Kauri Haven Truth Network group were descended from the first settlers and their partners, local Pakeha and Maori women. They could pass as White, which would make travelling around the Brown Zone less problematic. The remainder, three young men of eighteen years and one girl of seventeen, had been among the Brown Zone youth workers that had participated in the train sabotage. Brought to Aotearoa in a small Asian fishing boat soon afterwards, they had volunteered to spread the word throughout the northern Brown Zone islands. Far from the prying eyes of government officials, they could simply blend in with the local population, troopers being fairly lax in remote communities.

Footsteps in the corridor prompted swift action. Pia keyed a brief message to Kaire as Sami, the burly Tasmanian, entered the room.

'Refreshments for the hard worker,' he said brightly, handing her a glass of juice.

She tried to smile her thanks but failed utterly.

'Would it help to talk?' Sami asked, gently squeezing her shoulders. 'We all know what you're going through today.'

Pia took a few sips before answering. 'Thanks, Sami, but right now I must push grief aside. Zira's just communicated. I need to talk to Kaire.'

'Bad news?'

She nodded. 'Last night troopers raided all the villages along the southern Brown Zone border.'

Sami looked aghast. 'Any arrests?'

'Five.'

'The troopers aren't usually that competent.' Sami removed his arms and stood beside her chair, a frown creasing his broad forehead. 'Could someone be feeding them information?'

'It's possible.'

'Where are the detainees now?'

'En route to the desert prisons, Zira thinks.'

Sami's fist struck the desk, sending the communicator skidding towards the screen. 'The one place we can't penetrate,' he said bitterly, 'even with Kaire's superior equipment.'

Pia retrieved the communicator and shoved it in her pocket. 'No need to take it out on the furniture.'

'Sorry, I just feel frustrated, stuck over here unable to help.'

She rose quickly and placed a hand on his arm. 'You are helping, Sami. Look at the hours you put in building the new ships and the work you do servicing and repairing the settlement's machinery.'

'Guess you're right.' He managed a brief smile. 'Want me to take over here?'

'Thanks, it won't be for long, my shift finishes in an hour.'

'No problem.' Sami slipped into the seat she had just vacated.

The well-insulated engineering workshop where Kaire worked was located far from the residential area. Pia entered her code in the wall pad next to the main door but there was no response. A glance at her timepiece confirmed lunch had finished, although Kaire could still be in the main dining area. Apricots, fresh from the orchard, had been available today and Kaire could never resist fruit. From his first days among her people, he had taken great pleasure in food, tasting everything that came his way regardless of its origin or appearance. *Making up for lost time,* she supposed, thinking of his distant home where the population swallowed Sustenance tablets instead of preparing and eating food, a custom that certainly didn't appeal to her.

But there was no sign of Kaire in the main dining area either, so Pia made her way to his small brick house adjacent to the settlement's northern perimeter, where she noticed the front windows were closed and blinds drawn. A knock on the door elicited a swift response from the external audio-box: 'Kaire is not available today unless the matter is urgent.' Pia keyed in her personal code plus the code for urgent and waited for the door to open.

Inside she found the living room deserted and thought maybe the door lock had malfunctioned. 'It's Pia,' she called, before crossing to the closed bedroom door. The door opened as she approached. Peering inside, she saw him lying on the bed fully clothed, staring at the ceiling.

'Are you all right?' she asked anxiously.

He shifted slightly. 'Yes.'

'Then why didn't you answer me before?

'Silence suits my mood. Conversation would seem frivolous today.'

She recalled the overwhelming grief Kaire had displayed in the months following her mother's death, difficult to comprehend considering he had only known Sannah for a short time.

'I haven't come for a chat,' she retorted. 'Have you read the report I sent a few minutes ago?'

'No, is it urgent?'

'I wouldn't be here if it wasn't.'

'Okay, give me the details.' He sat up and swung his long legs over the side of the bed.

Pia quickly related Zira's message.

'How long will it take for the authorities to transfer the women to the desert prisons?'

'Twenty-four hours at most, but that should give you sufficient time to fly over. Most likely local line leaders are already devising a plan to sabotage the vehicles transporting them. It's not as though they can travel to the desert by train.'

'The Sky-ship hasn't been used in months. I need at least thirty-six hours to run all the pre-flight checks.'

'Couldn't you just run the important ones?'

He leapt to his feet and stood facing her, hands on hips, green eyes flashing. 'No way, we only have one Sky-ship! I don't want to find myself stuck in the middle of hostile Australia.'

Pia backed away. 'So what's the alternative?'

'I propose we monitor the situation for a few days.'

Brown eyes blazed. 'A few days! The women will be underground by then.'

'Forget the desert prisons for now, Pia. With five simultaneous arrests from a small area, I imagine the troopers will be keen to demonstrate what happens to those caught trying to undermine the government. There's bound to be a public trial before long so we can arrange to …'

'Fly over and pluck the prisoners from the court chamber during the trial,' Pia interrupted, her tone sarcastic. 'A mission bound to fail just like the one to rescue my mother.' She struggled to suppress tears but Kaire had already noticed her moist eyes and the slight quiver of her lower lip.

'Go easy on yourself,' he said softly, moving to her side. 'You shouldn't even be working today.'

She tried to wipe away tears with her fingers, and sniffed loudly as he enfolded her in his arms.

'Let the tears fall, Pia. I have. It's perfectly normal to grieve, especially on this first anniversary.'

'I was coping just fine until I heard Zira's news,' she cried, raising her head. 'But now I feel as though I'm reliving everything that happened during those last weeks in Australia. Arrest, interrogation, fire, escape, trial, death. It's doing my head in, Kaire.'

'Try to focus on the present, we can't alter the past.'

'I'll try I promise.'

He smiled down at her and loosened his hold. 'Good, I suggest we go and see Mac now. Apart from KAL needing to know what's going on over there, he'll react rationally, which I'm not sure either of us can do today.'

She nodded, waiting while he straightened his clothes and put on the sandals lying beside the bed.


KAL, acronym for the Kauri-Australian Line, had been established the previous year to formalise Kauri Haven Council's support for the Women's Line's work in Australia. For years, the council, of which Mac was presently chairman, had endorsed missions to transport political prison escapees to Aotearoa as well as supplying information useful to the Women's Line, obtained through infiltration of Australian government databases. The decision to officially acknowledge those involved had been prompted by Kaire's offer of the Sky-ship's superior technology to assist future assignments, soon after his and Pia's arrival. Ever since, the craft's computer had proven invaluable, both for obtaining information and providing a secure communication link with Women's Line leaders, whose equipment was suspected of having been compromised.

The chairman's office door was open, Mac having noticed Kaire and Pia walking across the grassed area in front of the main building and presumed they were heading his way. Mac, a White Australian of fifty whose youthful appearance belied the appalling treatment he had suffered at the hands of prison troopers decades earlier, always welcomed the opportunity for conversation with the young man from a distant space station and the girl he had rescued from certain imprisonment in Brown Zone Australia.

'Come in,' he called, swivelling around in the chair, but his smile faded when he noticed their sombre demeanour.

'We have disturbing news from the Brown Zone,' Pia announced tersely as she entered the office, closely followed by Kaire.

'Take a seat.' Mac gestured towards the chairs arranged in front of his desk, before pressing a floor button to lock the door behind them.

Throughout their short but helpful exposition, Mac listened carefully without question or comment, and only when certain both had finished speaking he asked, 'So apart from alerting KAL, how do you think we should respond?'

'The council should also be informed,' Pia answered quickly.

'I agree, but what I meant was, have you any suggestions for immediate action?'

Pia and Kaire exchanged glances, neither prepared to propose what would be a dangerous mission.

'We would prefer to leave complex decisions to others at present,' Kaire replied.

Mac was about to ask why, when he remembered Kaire's request for a day of quiet contemplation to mark the first anniversary of Sannah's death. 'How about I convene an urgent council meeting?'

Kaire nodded. 'Most appropriate.'

'Fine by me,' Pia added.

Mac turned to his screen and issued an urgent communication.

Within an hour, council members were taking their places at a large oval table in the conference room situated further down the corridor from Mac's office. The current council, gender balanced as required by long-established protocol, comprised ten mainly long-term settlers. Three of them, including Mac, had fled Australia two decades before following a purge of White Zone activist groups working to erode government power. The assistance of supporters not then known to the Australian Security Department had enabled all three to escape from separate prisons and make their way to Aotearoa. Eventually, after undergoing stringent medicals and the prerequisite quarantine period, they had arrived at Kauri Haven.

As older members of the council, Meras and Dove, the former White Zone political prisoners, represented the interests of elderly settlers, while Dona and Tuva, the adult daughter and son of former Brown Zone activists, dealt with youth matters. The five remaining councillors had been born at Kauri Haven, but regardless of birth country, all members were in agreement that efforts to assist others in undermining the brutal Australian government must be given priority over mundane issues.

Discussion centred on ways to secure the release of the five women, all Line members. Once they were transferred to the high-security Brown Zone prison complex beneath the northwest desert, gaining access from ground level would be almost impossible given there was only one well-guarded entrance. However, recent information had advised that tunnels from lower levels led to a uranium mine, recently recommissioned to provide useful employment for long-term prisoners.

'Why don't we use Kaire's scanner to see if there are any mineshafts *outside* the prison complex?' Tuva suggested after lengthy debate had failed to achieve any conclusion. 'I believe it has a range of two thousand kilometres.'

'Not a good idea,' Dona countered, disagreeing as usual with her brother. 'Scanning would have to take place in Australia, and given the current situation we shouldn't expose either Kaire or the Sky-ship to danger.'

Meras leaned forward. 'I suggest we postpone any action until the five women are brought to trial, presumably at the Border Court dome or possibly in their home villages.'

The others agreed but felt the least KAL could do was to try to discover what had precipitated the arrests.

Mac glanced around the table. 'We may have not reached unity but I sense there is a way forward, so I propose a first step. If we're to find out why the women are being held, we need to gain access to prison records. The best and probably the only way to accomplish this is to get someone from outside into the prison. I was thinking a mining or engineering expert would be suitable. It would have to be someone who hasn't been used before to prevent any likelihood of exposure. Any ideas?'

Dona looked across the table at Mac. 'Why don't we go a step further and create a situation where the five women *have* to be brought to the surface? Then we'd stand a better chance of getting them out.'

'What have you in mind?' Mac asked.

'How about a highly infectious disease that would require isolation in the prison hospital?'

Mac frowned. 'And how do you propose to infect the women?'

'There wouldn't be any need for genuine infection. A medical specialist could forward a report to the prison administrator detailing the women's recent exposure to a new strain of, say, respiratory disease. It's well known the Brown Zone authorities are fearful of such diseases as they reduce workers' productivity.'

Mac leaned forward. 'Do we know anyone over there with suitable status who would be willing to take this risk?'

No one spoke and Mac was about to veto the whole idea when Meras thumped the table with his fist. 'Why don't we speak to Sami? I believe his partner Kela is a doctor of some standing in the White Zone.'

'That's correct,' said Mac, 'but she hasn't made any attempt to join him here so we can't be sure of her allegiances.'

'Sami often talks about her,' Dona advised. 'My guess is they're in contact.'

'I see no harm in sounding him out.' Mac looked down at the message-board on which he'd been making notes throughout the meeting.

'With your agreement I'll postpone writing a minute until we reconvene in, say, two hours?'

Heads nodded around the table.

'Thank you, I'll go and speak to Sami now.' Mac pressed the side of his message-board with his thumb.

Councillors rose at once and filed out of the room, the usual post-meeting conversation abandoned.

# CHAPTER 2

Kaire and Sami sat side by side facing a console divided into panels of varying size. Sami felt cramped in the small seat he'd installed at Kaire's request as there hadn't been much space between pilot seat and capsule wall, the Sky-ship originally designed for solo voyages. A convex window wrapped around the capsule nose giving a spectacular view of the night sky. Enthralled, Sami gazed at winking stars and a clear outline of Earth's moon. This was his first flight, and having no knowledge of space other than that gained from school history discs he had assumed the Sky-ship would travel at immense speed in order to overcome the force of gravity and leave Earth's atmosphere. So when Kaire announced they would not be venturing into space, Sami had struggled to hide his disappointment. Kaire had gone on to explain that a sub-orbital space flight would use far too much fuel and was also unnecessary, Australia being only a short distance away. After a brief ascent, the craft would fly at optimum altitude for a few minutes and then descend directly over the central desert, landing in an area remote from mines or any other form of human activity. The remaining journey to the rendezvous with Kela would be by the land transporter stored in the rear module.

Sami longed to see his partner again. It had been five years since their comfortable life in a southern White Zone village had been terminated by his arrest and imprisonment for crimes against the government. For nearly four years, Sami had had no contact with Kela and could only speculate on whether she'd been implicated in his crimes or had managed to convince the authorities she had known nothing about them. Only since his arrival at Kauri Haven nine months earlier had Sami been given the opportunity to communicate with Kela through the Sky-ship's secure link and learned that her innocence had been believed. She was now a senior medical researcher.

As an engineer, Sami had been allocated on arrival to the engineering workshop where he was introduced to Kaire and asked to work with him on the vehicle referred to as a land transporter, which lay in pieces on the floor. For some time Kaire had been struggling to repair damage to the engine sustained months before in Australia and welcomed the assistance of an experienced engineer, his own skills in that area being limited. The two men worked well together and had soon effected repairs plus improved the thrusters' performance. After a few weeks, they had begun to meet after work, initially sharing meals in the communal dining room where they discovered a mutual liking for the wine produced from grapes grown at Kauri Haven. Meals at Kaire's home had followed, the younger man keen to demonstrate his newly acquired cooking skills. Over interesting, if unusual combinations of ingredients, Sami learned of Kaire's extraordinary heritage as a descendant of scientists that had colonised an abandoned space station known as Skyz59 in the 2220s. Ever since, the inhabitants had made it their mission to search for another less-spoiled planet capable of supporting human life. Kaire had been one of hundreds of pilots that departed at regular intervals in small spacecraft to undertake galactic exploration. The explanation for Kaire's presence at Kauri Haven had proven even more fascinating, triggering Sami's admiration for his host's resolve to make a pilgrimage to Earth and subsequent decision to assist the Women's Line. As a result, Sami had felt his own history of seditious activities, imprisonment and liberation from a train transporting prisoners to high-security desert prisons would seem tame by comparison, but Kaire had relished the tale.

After a few months, their conversation had turned to more intimate subjects and Sami had revealed his longing to communicate with Kela, prompting Kaire's offer to try to locate her using the Sky-ship computer. This had been accomplished with relative ease, the technology far superior to anything Sami had ever seen before, but wisely Kaire had insisted he speak first to make certain Kela wished to resume contact. Sami smiled as he recalled the day Kaire had interrupted work on the land transporter and taken him into the Sky-ship for that first communication.

Kaire looked up from the console and noticed a smattering of stars. 'Night sky, so beautiful, so enticing,' he said wistfully. 'Sometimes I long to leave Earth and its myriad problems, spend my life as I intended exploring galaxies untouched by humankind.'

'There's no reason why you can't leave, surely?' Sami replied, grateful for conversation to help pass the time until reunion.

'No reason at all, but to leave now would seem like desertion, the abandonment of hope.'

'Did you promise Pia you'd stay?'

Kaire shook his head. 'No, but before I go, there are tasks I must undertake in memory of her mother.'

*His former lover,* Sami thought, recalling a late night conversation. 'And after that, will you resume space exploration?'

'That depends on my commander. He may insist I return my ship to Sky so a more reliable pilot can make use of it.'

'You don't strike me as unreliable.'

'I've broken the rules, Sami. I should have left Earth months ago. Commander Breta has been very understanding, but for how much longer, who knows?'

'Just don't up and leave me in the middle of the desert, mate.'

'You have my word.' Kaire turned his attention to the console. 'Prepare for landing,' he advised the computer. 'Commence deceleration.'

Sami waited until Kaire had raised his head again before asking, 'How long will it take to reach the rendezvous?'

'A few hours.'

Sami sighed loudly.

'Anyone would think you were in a hurry to see Kela,' Kaire remarked, digging Sami in the ribs with his elbow.

'Thank the moon the council agreed to my accompanying you. For a while there I thought they'd refuse.'

'Me too, but my portrayal of love enduring despite long separation managed to sway even cynical Mac.'

'Thanks, mate,' Sami replied, his voice wavering.

Kaire nodded and turned to address the communication screen. 'Sky 323 to Kauri 378.'

After a slight delay, Pia's face materialised. '378 connected.'

'Descent in progress, suspend communication until advised.'

'Understood. Connection closing.'

Her image dissolved but Kaire held it in his mind, savouring not for the first time the vision of dark curls framing a friendly face, soulful brown eyes, and lips that puckered when she concentrated. A moment or two passed before he registered that the exterior view had altered and all he could see now were desert sands turned ghostly grey by the night vision camera. A slight bump and the Sky-ship had landed and was taxiing towards an immense sand dune.

'Apply reverse thrust,' he advised. Red sand spewed like a blizzard, covering wings and fuselage. 'Initiate cessation.' Moments later the craft shuddered and was still. Kaire double-checked the location coordinates to make certain the Sky-ship had landed as planned in the southern part of the desert, far to the west from the rail tracks and paths that linked Brown Zone villages.

Over the past few centuries, the central arid region had crept steadily seaward, swallowing pasture and cultivated land until, at the beginning of the twenty-fifth century, only a narrow green rim remained arable and habitable. Huddled around the edge of their vast continent, Australians could only hope climate change would stabilise before they were pushed into the ocean.

After shutting down all computerised equipment, Kaire directed Sami to follow him into the rear module where the land transporter—a cylindrical vehicle topped with two dome-shaped 'bubbles' one behind the other—was stored. Before engaging the thrusters, a smaller version of those that powered the Sky-ship, Kaire programmed the navigation panel and gave the command to open the rear door.

'Prepare for exit,' he advised Sami as the transporter began to move slowly towards the opening.

Despite the safety harness, Sami felt impelled to clutch the sides of the seat.

The din intensified and the transporter blasted away from the

Sky-ship, sand billowing in its wake like scarlet waves.

Near the eastern perimeter of the desert, a small egg-shaped car with wide wheels stood behind Kaire's much larger vehicle. Thanks to Sami's engineering skills, the land transporter had performed well on the journey from Sky-ship to rendezvous. Prior to the engine rebuild, Kaire had been reluctant to use the vehicle except on short journeys, fearing a recurrence of the thruster problems experienced as he and Pia had sped across open grassland in their escape from the Brown Zone one year earlier.

Inside the transporter, Kaire checked the console timepiece before retrieving a small parcel from a storage compartment. Tucking the parcel under one arm, he lifted the front bubble and climbed out onto hard-packed sand littered with small rocks. Sami and Kela stood beside the car, arms around each other's waists, lips locked.

'Time's up I'm afraid,' Kaire called.

Reluctantly the pair moved apart. 'Separated for five years and you give us ten minutes!' Sami retorted.

Kaire hurried over. 'My apologies, but it's too risky to hang about, we could be within security beam range here.'

Kela, a tall, slim woman of twenty-seven with the blonde hair and blue eyes of her Swedish ancestors, gestured towards the parcel. 'Is that for the added diversion Sami mentioned?'

Kaire nodded. 'We thought it advisable to have more than the five women brought to the surface.'

'Can I take a look?'

'Of course.' He opened the box and held it towards her.

'It looks just like one of my vaccine phials.'

'Your diagrams were perfect,' Sami told her proudly.

Kela swivelled around and flashed Sami a brilliant smile before turning back to Kaire. 'So what do you want me to do with it?'

'Insert the liquid with a syringe into various exterior walls as close to ground level as possible.'

'Prison medical dome or the main building?'

'Both if you can.' Kaire closed the lid and handed over the box. 'How long will your vaccines take to work?'

'Seven to ten days, it depends on the body mass of the recipient.'

Sami hurried to Kela's side. 'Does that mean you have to remain within the prison complex all that time?'

'Yes, but that won't be problem, I have a perfectly legitimate reason for being there. I must be available in case there's an adverse reaction.'

'Which of course there will be,' Kaire added.

'Provided my calculations are correct.'

Sami frowned. 'Shit, I didn't realise there was any doubt.'

'This is the first trial on humans. I can't guarantee the results.'

'So the recipients will be at risk?' Sami persisted, his frown deepening.

Kela sighed. 'I don't know.'

'Let's presume all goes as planned,' said Kaire, anxious to depart. 'What's the anticipated timeframe, Kela?'

'At the first indication of a problem, I'll have the prisoners brought to the medical dome, which will give me the opportunity to view their files. If there's no improvement after a week they'll be transferred to the isolation dome. Apparently, I have limited jurisdiction there, so I'll head home.'

Sami clutched her arm. 'Can't you find some excuse to stay in the Brown Zone? We'll be returning for the women in a few weeks if all goes well. Come back with us.'

Kela shook her head. 'I must be seen to return home.'

'But won't there be trouble from your superiors when you report the vaccine trial went wrong? You could be hauled off to prison for incompetence!' Sami's voice resounded like thunder through the still night air.

'Unlikely, my report will state the phials were contaminated.'

'But if they don't …'

Kaire raised his hand. 'Enough Sami, just be patient. Kela has promised she'll join you before too long.'

Sami bit his lip and looked down at his feet.

'We must leave now,' Kaire said firmly. Turning around, he headed towards the transporter, leaving Sami and Kela to say farewell in private.

All through the night Kela drove at high speed along the eastern flank of the desert, a plume of red dust fanning out behind the car. By the time she turned onto the super-path leading to the prison complex, pale fingers of dawn were creeping over windswept dunes. Prior to the construction of these top-security jails, no paths had crossed this remote and desolate landscape, although it was rumoured a train track had once run from a northern city to a central town, cutting the desert in two like a wire slicing cheese. Sand storms had long since covered all traces of rails, cement sleepers and track ballast. The new super-path failed to live up to its name, being narrow with no guiding path-side lights or rest areas to recharge vehicles and give drivers a short respite from the tedium of travel through such a monotonous landscape.

After an hour's drive, the car's inbuilt navigation system indicated a further ninety kilometres to the prison, so Kela pulled over and got out to stretch her legs. Hot wind blew stinging grains of sand over the bare skin below her calf-length white robe and despite protective eyewear she blinked in the harsh sunlight. *A few body stretches will have to do,* she thought, *there's no point in risking heat stress.*

Back in the air-conditioned car, glaring morning light subdued by tinted windows, she set cruise speed to maximum and turned her thoughts from Sami to the forthcoming meeting with the prison administrator. It had been relatively easy to organise a visit to the complex, but she would need her wits about her when dealing with a senior security officer. She pondered his experience with medical matters and whether he would insist on accompanying her to the medical dome. In spite of the cool environment, perspiration beaded her forehead as distance diminished and she experienced a strong desire to turn around. Only the promise of a future with Sami kept her heading north.

As the car approached the prison complex gates, a camera emerged from an opening box fitted to the top rail, swivelling on the end of a stalk like a single cactus flower blowing in a desert wind. Kela waited for the flash, making sure to look straight ahead. Subsequently, an electronic voice emanating from the car's communicator granted her permission to enter the complex, indicating her identity had been verified. The gates swung inwards and she drove at low speed up a gravel path to an area marked with numerous parallel lines of white rocks, as though the inmates were expecting a rush of visitors. She parked close to a set of glass doors, behind which a trooper could be seen sitting staring at a monitor.

The doors slid open as she approached and the trooper, almost reluctantly it seemed to Kela, raised his head and slowly got to his feet.

'Greetings, Professor,' he said, ushering her inside. 'Please follow me.'

She returned the greeting, pondering the absence of other staff; several stools were visible behind a counter at the rear of the foyer. The young trooper led her to the right of the counter and down a long corridor, at the end of which a red light band pulsed around a door panel. To the left of the door, beneath a sound-grill, a light strip illuminated the words 'Administrator Jurt'.

'Professor Kela to see you, sir,' the trooper advised, bending slightly to address the sound-grill.

'Welcome, please enter,' a deep male voice replied.

The door panel opened as Kela turned to the trooper standing behind her. 'Thank you for escorting me.'

'My pleasure.' He smiled and stomped back down the corridor, his boots ringing on the polished concrete floor.

The long narrow chamber Kela entered was sparsely furnished with a white work-module at the far end and several cream-coloured chairs positioned around a small table close to the right-hand wall. The walls were pale and devoid of decoration, the lighting dim, and the man who rose to greet her seemed out place in such an insipid environment with his florid complexion and flaming red hair.

'Greetings, Professor Kela,' he said, walking towards her, his left hand extended.

'Greetings, Administrator Jurt,' she replied, placing her bag on the floor before taking the proffered hand.

'I trust your journey from the train terminus wasn't too onerous,' he said, a half-smile playing around his generous red mouth. 'That so-called super-path is appalling.'

'I've seen worse, sir.'

'Please, call me Jurt, we can dispense with formality within this chamber.' He gestured towards the chairs.

She smiled. 'And please call me Kela.' She bent to pick up her bag.

'Allow me.' Stepping forward he grasped the strap with tapering white fingers, then deposited the bag beside the nearest chair.

Sinking into the low chair, Kela was surprised to find it more comfortable than it appeared. Beside her, Administrator Jurt leaned forward and, lifting a small jug from a tray on the table, carefully filled two tumblers. 'Orange and ginger,' he remarked, handing over a tumbler. 'Most refreshing.'

'Thank you, Jurt.'

Sipping the juice, she listened carefully as he commented on the file she had submitted a week earlier outlining her research project and the need to trial the new drug as soon as possible. Jurt had accepted without question her choice of the desert prison complex for the trial despite the presence of a juvenile detention centre within a short distance of her workplace. When permission for the trial had been granted without the usual delay, she'd wondered if he felt isolated out here with only troopers and a few administrative staff for company and relished the thought of someone new. She was well aware family or partner quarters were not available for prison staff in remote areas, regardless of rank.

She finished her drink, noted his attention was now focused on her breasts and deduced he had contemplated a brief affair. If he had read her personal file, he would have known her age, which by her reckoning was at least twenty years less than his. Dismissing speculation, she began to address the question of the new drug's side effects, stressing the odds, albeit slight, of lasting health problems.

Jurt considered this for several minutes, pale blue eyes half-closed, long fingers bunched into a fist beneath his jutting chin. 'I appreciate your candour,' he said finally, opening his eyes and looking directly into her face. 'It's rare to find a researcher prepared to admit there could be a risk.' Smiling, he uncurled his fingers and smoothed the dark blue tunic over fleshy thighs. 'However, I don't foresee any post-test recriminations. My prisoners have forfeited any right to, shall we say, humane treatment.'

Kela nodded. 'I do have one request, Jurt.'

'And that is?'

'I realise the majority of your prisoners are males but it would be helpful if I had access to some females. It's important my research is gender balanced.'

'Of course. I can easily arrange for some females to be brought to the surface.'

Kela smiled. 'A mixture of Asian and Brown-skins would also be most useful.'

Jurt scratched his head. 'No problem with Asians but I've only got five female Brown-skins at present.'

'Five will do.'

He leaned back in his chair. 'Good, then I suggest we adjourn to my private quarters for a meal. You must be hungry after your long journey.'

'Yes I am, the food on the train was appalling.'

'It usually is, but I can assure you this prison administrator eats well.'

Kela smiled and bent to pick up her bag.

'You can collect that later.' He jumped to his feet. 'I'll escort you to your chamber after the meal.'

'Thank you.' She followed him to the door, which opened silently as they approached.

Late that afternoon before the prison population awoke to another night of labour, Kela made her way to the medical dome, situated a short walk from the main building. Just before reaching the entrance, she deliberately tripped, sending her communicator flying from her hand. It landed on a ridge of sand blown against the wall near the door. After regaining her balance, she stepped off the path and made a show of searching for it. With her back to the path, she quickly unfastened her bag, extracted Kaire's phial and filled a syringe. Bending down, she injected the contents into the mortar between the bottom two rows of concrete blocks. In her practiced hands, the syringe took only seconds to refill, so she shifted a few metres to the right and repeated the procedure. Then she reached out, collected communicator and bag, straightened up and walked back to the entrance.

After keying in the code supplied by Administrator Jurt, the door panel opened and Kela stepped into a cool chamber with beds lining the curved windowless wall. Only one bed appeared to be occupied, while in the centre of the chamber, a solitary medical worker slumped in a chair in front of a screen.

'Greetings,' Kela said in an officious tone.

A head jerked upright, hands grasped the chair arms, and the young man struggled to his feet. 'Er, greetings,' he answered and, taking note of her doctor's robe, quickly raised his right hand level with his shoulder.

'Professor Kela,' she announced, 'and you are?'

'Medical Worker Yohan.'

'Well, Medical Officer Yohan, no doubt you've been briefed on the drug trial so I won't bore you with the details.'

He nodded and gestured towards a door panel between two beds at the rear of the chamber. 'The doctor's chamber is through there, Professor.'

'Thank you, Yohan.' She swept past him in a cloud of lightweight cotton, a supercilious smile on her lips.

Towards midnight, an assorted group of fifteen prisoners were brought to the surface and given a thorough examination at the medical dome before being injected. After a brief rest, they were returned below ground with a warning to report any unusual rashes or other health issues occurring over the next few nights. While Kela waited for the expected side effects, she kept herself busy in the doctor's chamber, studying the prisoners' files. At night's end, she dined with Jurt in his private quarters, acknowledging his overtures with coy remarks and the occasional touch of her hand, but on returning to the guest chamber decided to seal the door panel, at least for this first day. No knock on the door roused her from sleep, so she presumed Jurt was content to proceed slowly.

After seven nights, three young Whites, two males, one female; two middle-aged Asians, one male, one female; and the five Brown-skin women recently arrested in the border villages had been admitted to the medical dome. The remaining five participants in the drug trail remained unaffected, Kela having injected them with saline solution only. Throughout the week, she kept Administrator Jurt informed as each patient presented. None were seriously ill, so he didn't feel it necessary to visit the medical dome until the seventh night when an urgent message flashed on his communicator.

Kela was bending over a patient when the entrance door panel opened and Jurt strode into the chamber, startling Medical Worker Anue, engrossed in administrative work at the computer.

'Greetings, Administrator Jurt,' she called, rising quickly and walking towards him.

Jurt grunted a response as he kicked off his lightweight boots. Anue stepped to one side, bowing her head as he passed.

Kela met him halfway across the chamber. 'Greetings, Administrator Jurt. I do apologise for interrupting your meeting but I felt it imperative you see the new patients before the day medical worker begins his shift.'

'No need to apologise, Professor, I appreciate the need for caution.' Jurt turned to a nearby shelf and grabbed a pair of disposable footwear.

Kela stood aside while he pulled the tight socks over broad feet and thick ankles. 'I had thought the adverse reaction was confined to females,' she continued once he had straightened up, 'but the latest three are male, one White, two Asian.'

He frowned. 'Same symptoms?'

'Similar, although blistering is confined to the abdomen this time. Come and take a look.' She led him over to an older Asian, who lay on his back, a sheet covering the lower half of his body. His abdomen was covered with red blisters.

Jurt moved closer to the bed, took a quick look and stepped back a pace. 'Any pain?'

'A little, sir,' the man answered in a submissive tone without turning his head.

'When were you first aware of these blisters?'

'Two nights ago, sir.'

'So why did it take you forty-eight hours to report it?'

'I thought it was something I'd eaten, sir.'

Jurt nodded and turned to Kela. 'Show me the next one.'

She took him to a bed opposite where a young White man lay propped on several pillows, his forehead wet with perspiration and bright patches shading pallid cheeks.

'This one has a fever as well,' Kela advised. 'He was brought in an hour ago. Apparently he collapsed in the tunnel leading to the mine.'

Jurt glanced at the man's abdomen from a safe distance. 'Were you on the way to or from the mine?' he asked the patient.

'To, sir.'

'Then we can eliminate dehydration,' Jurt remarked to Kela.

'Certainly. And there's no sign of toxic ingestion.'

Jurt signalled Kela to move away from the bed. 'How are the women responding to treatment?' he asked in a low tone.

'No change in seven, three show slight improvement.'

'Inform the day medical worker the new cases are allergic reactions to food,' he said quietly. 'We don't want to alarm staff unnecessarily.'

Kela nodded.

'And come to my chamber when you've finished here, we need to discuss this matter in private.'

'Of course, Administrator.'

They crossed the chamber to the entrance, Anue hurrying over with Jurt's boots as the door panel opened.

'Thank you, Medical Worker Anue,' said Jurt, removing the socks and dropping them on the floor before taking the boots.

'Goodnight to you, sir,' Anue answered with a slight nod of the head.

Jurt pulled on his boots and walked away briskly. As the door panel closed behind him, Anue scowled, picked up the soiled socks and, holding them at arm's length, deposited them in the nearby bin.

# CHAPTER 3

The temporary removal of ten prisoners from the workforce marked the first in a series of problems that would beset Administrator Jurt during the next few months, but sick prisoners were far from his mind the following morning as he relaxed in his private quarters after several hours spent in the delightful company of Professor Kela. When his communicator began to flash and hum, it took him a few moments to register the unwelcome intrusion. Grabbing the machine from the bedside table, he blocked the visual display with the tip of his index finger before pressing the answer panel.

'What is it?' he demanded curtly. 'Don't you know it's the middle of the day?'

'I apologise for waking you, sir,' said Trooper Gord, a senior member of the prison maintenance team, 'but we have a structural problem in the administration building.'

Jurt sighed. 'I'll meet you in the foyer in ten minutes.'

'Very good, sir.'

The communicator slipped from Jurt's hand as he swung his legs over the side of the bed. Hurrying to the adjoining bath chamber, he splashed cold water over face and neck, more to dislodge the image of voluptuous breasts than refresh his skin. Back in the sleeping chamber, he retrieved the tunic tossed on the floor earlier and slipped it over his head before pulling on his boots.

Once they were outside Trooper Gord related his findings in his usual brusque manner. 'Damage appears to be confined to the administrative building, sir, both inner and outer walls. This small pile of dust alerted me and then I noticed a crack in the lower rows of block work.' He pointed to the evidence. 'After scanning the area to determine the depth of the fracture, I entered the building and examined the internal walls on the ground floor. Result—four cracks in the synthetic skin covering the concrete. To double-check the scanner readings, I descended the stairs and inspected the exterior walls of the store chambers located directly beneath the ground floor. Apart from a few minor ceiling cracks, I found no sign of structural damage and judging by age and discolouration, concluded these were unconnected with the ones above.'

'Thank you, Gord, a most comprehensive report.' Jurt peered at the damaged wall, grateful Gord had alerted him first. This was a serious situation, details of which must be communicated on a need-to-know basis only. 'We could do with expert advice,' he said, turning back to Gord. 'The only problem is it could take at least three nights for a senior engineer to be sent from down south. Have we anyone here with highly developed engineering skills?'

Gord considered the question. 'There's Judd 37, sir. Mining engineer before he got mixed up in subversion. He's been most helpful dealing with minor problems in the tunnels.'

'Bring him to the surface and get him to undertake a preliminary inspection. We need to determine whether our own workforce can make repairs.'

'Yes, sir.'

'Inform his supervisor the maintenance team needs Judd's expertise for a short time. Let's find out what we're dealing with before making it public.'

'Right, sir.'

'Report to me directly the inspection is completed.'

'Yes, sir.' Gord looked down and scattered the pile of dust with his boot before following Jurt back to the administration building.

In the middle of the path leading from main entrance to medical dome, Trooper Gord stood under a portable sun-shield watching Prisoner Judd 37 press a scanner against yet another crack. It had been a long morning and apart from needing a cold drink and sleep, Gord felt extremely uncomfortable in his sweat-dampened tunic and heavy boots. He hadn't dared leave the prisoner alone in case Administrator Jurt appeared. After checking the reading on the scanner, Judd stood up and stretched cramped limbs. Pulling a dirty rag from his tunic pocket, he wiped perspiration from head and neck.

'Finished?'

'Yes, sir.'

'About time too, I'm frying in this bloody heat.' Collapsing the sun-shield, Gord tucked it under his arm and headed up the path towards the entrance.

'If you don't mind, sir,' Judd called after him, 'I'd like to take a look at the medical dome before I compile my report.'

Gord stopped abruptly and pounded the path with the sun-shield's metal tip. 'Whatever for? It's at least a hundred metres from here.'

'Yes, sir, but its entrance runs parallel with admin's rear wall where we saw that large crack. If there's no sign of damage, we can rule out seismic disturbance.'

The sun-shield fell to the ground. 'That's all we need, the fucking ground shifting under our feet!'

'Just a theory, sir.' Judd ran to pick up the sun-shield.

'Okay, get moving.'

Outside the medical dome, Gord stood in a patch of shade, having refused Judd's offer to re-erect the sun-shield. Nearby Judd ran the scanner up and down the concrete blocks, his long limbs moving rhythmically, bare feet creating sand patterns at the base of the wall. He was almost out of sight when the door panel opened and Kela emerged, bumping into Gord as her eyes adjusted to the bright sunlight.

'I'm sorry, trooper,' she said, stepping aside quickly. 'Are you sick?'

Gord shook his head. 'Just a routine building inspection, Doctor. Much more accurate to do it in daylight.'

She nodded. 'Will you be inspecting inside as well? I've just settled some new patients and would prefer they weren't disturbed for a while.'

'We can come back this evening, Doctor, if that would suit?'

Kela smiled. 'Thank you, evening will be fine.'

Lifting the head-cloth from her shoulders, she carefully covered her hair and neck and was about to close the fastener when she saw a man wearing prison garb back away from the wall and glance down at a small device he held in one hand. As she stepped onto the path, he looked in her direction. Her fingers fumbled with the clasp. Quickly recovering her composure, she turned back to Gord. 'Why don't you slip inside and get a drink from the water cooler? It's in the alcove just to the right of the door. I'll keep an eye on the prisoner for you.'

'Good idea, thanks.' He moved towards the door.

Kela waited until Gord was safely inside before walking towards the prisoner and, pushing the head-cloth away from her mouth, whispered, 'Judd, it's Kela.'

Halted mid-stride, Judd stared for what seemed an age. 'My dear friend, what the sun are you doing here?'

'Research project.'

'Where's Trooper Gord?'

'Gone to fetch a drink.' She checked the trooper was still inside before moving closer. 'You'll be coming back this evening to inspect inside. I'll talk to you then.'

Judd looked puzzled. 'I'm supposed to do it now.'

'Change of plan.' She leaned towards him. 'I'll be with the new patients, beds against the rear wall near the door to the doctor's chamber.'

Judd nodded. 'Any news of Sami?'

'He's safe over ocean.'

'Thank the moon.'

Reaching up, Kela kissed the grimy cheek and hurried away, leaving Judd standing on the path, a broad smile creasing his pale face.


An unscheduled meeting with Jurt delayed Kela's arrival at the medical dome that evening and she was concerned Judd and Trooper Gord might have already carried out their inspection.

'Has anyone from the maintenance team called?' she casually asked Medical Worker Sandi, who had been on duty for several hours.

'No, Professor, are we expecting someone?'

Kela nodded. 'Something about the walls, I believe. A Trooper Gord mentioned it earlier.'

'Will Trooper Gord be visiting this evening?'

'I expect so.'

Sandi smiled and turned away, but not before Kela had noticed her almond-shaped eyes were shining, her cheeks flushed.

Before long, Trooper Gord entered the dome, followed at a respectful distance by Judd. Kela was busy examining Fern, one of the new patients, so merely looked up, waved to Gord and continued with her work. She heard Judd pad towards her but kept her head bent over the patient until the footsteps stopped at the foot of the bed.

'Excuse me, Doctor.'

She looked up. 'Yes, prisoner?

'I need to inspect this wall when it's convenient,' he answered, keeping his eyes focused on the floor.

'Go ahead.' Kela glanced across the chamber. As she'd hoped, Gord had stopped to chat with Sandi. She stepped away from Fern and pretended to be studying the small monitor attached to the bedside cabinet.

'Thank you, Doctor.' Judd moved to the head of the bed, took out the scanner and held it against the wall.

After a few moments, Kela walked around to the other side of the bed, where she stood staring at the scanner running up and down the wall. 'I trust you won't be long, prisoner,' she said brusquely. 'I don't want my patients disturbed any more than absolutely necessary.'

'Nearly finished this section, Doctor,' he answered, still facing the wall. 'Only one crack here.'

Kela stepped forward, pushed past Judd and peered at the wall. 'Doesn't look too serious to me,' she remarked. Then lowering her voice she said, 'I'm leaving tomorrow night, I can take you to safety.'

'Not possible,' Judd whispered, staring at the scanner readings. 'I must remain to supervise the repairs. Six hundred lives could be at risk.'

Kela bent towards the scanner as though she too were interested in the readings. 'I'll work something out. Speak to Fern, bed on my left, before the repairs are completed.'

'I understand.' Judd raised his eyes from the scanner. 'I'll make sure there's minimal disturbance. Goodnight, Doctor.' Stepping aside, he walked across the chamber to where Gord was still engaged in conversation with Medical Worker Sandi.

'All done?' Gord asked.

'Yes, sir, for now.'

Gord frowned. 'What do you mean, for now?'

'More cracks, sir,' Judd said quietly. 'One floor to ceiling.'

'Shit.'

'Everything okay?' asked Sandi.

Gord smiled. 'Sure, see you after your shift.' He turned to Judd. 'Let's go, it's time you were below ground.'

By the time Prisoner Judd 37 returned to the medical dome, huge spotlights had been positioned behind the building to facilitate night work and a barricade erected between it and the small dome housing the power plant to impede any escape attempt. In Judd's opinion the barricade was a total waste of time and effort, prisoners being unlikely to abscond and risk certain death in the desert.

Repairs to the administration building had been given priority and taken forty-eight hours to complete, so he'd had no opportunity to see Kela before she left. Now, Judd wished he'd taken up her offer, the structural damage not being as serious as first thought and posing no risk to the prison's inhabitants. Pushing thoughts of escape aside, he watched several prisoners manoeuvre equipment close to the wall, and frowned when he saw a young man kick a cylindrical machine balanced on a low trolley.

'Easy there, Romi,' he shouted. 'That's a delicate piece of machinery. Treat it gently.'

Romi looked up. 'Imagine it's a woman, shall I?'

Judd sighed. 'Whatever you like, just take care.'

Romi stroked the handle. 'Come on darlin', we're going walkies.'

Judd shook his head and walked over to the power plant dome where Trooper Gord stood drinking from a flask. 'Excuse me, sir. I need to take some internal measurements. May I enter the medical dome?'

Gord belched before answering with a nod of the head.

'Thank you, sir.' Judd gave a small bow.

Medical Worker Sandi quickly responded to Judd's call through the sound-grill, releasing the door panel and handing him disposable footwear the moment he entered the chamber.

'Here again, Prisoner Judd,' she remarked. 'I thought the repairs were being carried out externally.'

Judd smiled. 'They are. I'm just going to take measurements.'

'Make it quick then, the patients are resting.'

Judd nodded and hurried over to the row of beds arranged around the rear wall either side of the doctor's chamber. He quickly located Fern and, slipping between two beds, made sure to bump into her bed as he extracted the scanner from his tunic pocket.

Fern opened her eyes. 'Judd?' she queried, staring straight ahead.

'Yes.' He held the scanner against the wall.

'Would you mind passing me a tumbler of water?' She turned her head slightly.

'No problem.' Pocketing the scanner, he walked around the bed to the bedside table, poured water from a jug into a tumbler and placed it in her outstretched hand.

'Thank you.' She lifted the tumbler to her lips. 'Meet me Friday after the midnight break at the rear of the power plant. Five women are leaving. I'll be the last.'

Judd's eyes met hers and blinked understanding. Then he returned to his work, grateful to be facing a blank wall as a burst of joy threatened to escape his lips.

By Friday afternoon, repairs to the medical dome were almost complete and Judd queried whether there would be sufficient work to keep him occupied until midnight. Fortunately, one of the spotlights flickered and went out, halting work on the upper block work and requiring his expertise to fix the problem. He took his time, walking back and forth to the power plant to check the power supply and remarking on the complexity of the problem to Trooper Gord. Work had only just resumed when Gord announced he was going back to admin for lunch, leaving only one trooper to guard the prisoners.

'You might as well have a break too,' Trooper Victa called to Judd the moment his colleague disappeared around the dome.

'Thank you, sir.' Judd inclined his head. 'Shall I turn off the equipment?'

'No, I just meant for you and me to have a break. The others can finish what they're doing.'

'Right, sir.' Judd walked back to the wall, related the instructions to the hungry men and retreated hurriedly, their curses ringing in his ears.

Trooper Victa, a stout individual known for his voracious appetite, retired to the low chair Gord had vacated a few minutes earlier and, opening a cooler box lying against the barricade, extracted a large slab of cooked meat, a hunk of bread and a small flask containing his favourite liquor. He had planned to drink this should Gord leave him alone. Saliva dribbled over fleshy lips as he ripped off chunks of meat with large square teeth. He chewed with relish, alternating between bread and meat, pausing occasionally to take a swig from the flask.

Several metres away where the dome wall curved into darkness, Judd sat on a patch of dry grass behind a spotlight, eating his meagre rations with total indifference, his mind focused on the forthcoming escape bid. He had no idea how the five women planned to break out or why they would choose a night when the dome was surrounded by workers and troopers. Perhaps they figured the noise of machinery would drown their attempts to disable the entrance door panel. But first they would have to deal with the medical workers to ensure they couldn't call or message for assistance. He found himself hoping no harm would come to those who in his experience nursed troopers and prisoners alike with equal diligence and care.

A slim cone of light spilled over dark ground a few metres ahead as a small door opened a fraction. Puzzled, it took Judd a few moments to remember this was the rear entrance to the store where pharmaceutical supplies were kept. Glancing sideways, he saw a figure emerge and carefully close the door. He could see it was a woman from the outline of breasts visible as she pressed against the white wall, and presumed she was the first to attempt escape. As she slid along the wall towards him, he longed to call out, warn her to head away from the spotlight. She kept advancing, so he got to his feet, walked in front of the light and squatted as though checking something. After waiting a couple of minutes, he straightened up but a glance at the shadowed wall revealed she was still there. Ambling towards her, he scratched his balls through the coarse fabric of his tunic.

'It's Fern,' she murmured, showing no reaction when he lifted his tunic and urinated close to her feet. 'Make an excuse to go to the power plant. I'll see you there. Ten minutes max before we must leave.'

He nodded, and watched her streak across open ground and disappear behind the isolation dome situated a short distance from the power plant. He marvelled at the women's daring, their ability to flit from dome to dome without alerting anyone to their presence. Four other women must have passed within metres of his lunch spot, yet he hadn't heard or seen a thing.

In the centre of the work area, a large circular drum vibrated, churning mortar. Judd nudged an operating panel on its base with his big toe as he passed by on his way to speak with the men smoothing mortar over the cracked wall. The drum began to swing violently from side to side but he kept on walking, turning around only after he heard a loud crash. Mortar was spilling over the ground; as expected the drum had fallen from its metal sling.

Over by the barricade, Trooper Victa replaced his flask in the cooler and struggled to his feet. 'What's up now, Judd?' he shouted.

'Not sure, sir, it was fine when I checked just now.'

Suddenly both spotlights went out.

'Not again,' said Trooper Victa crossly. He walked over to Judd, kneeling by the drum. 'I thought you fixed the light problem?'

'I did, sir. Want me to take a look at them again?'

'No, get over to the power plant. The problem's gotta be over there.'

'Yes, sir.'

Inside the brightly lit power plant, Judd leaned over the control panel, frowning as he concentrated on what was proving a difficult task. After several agonising minutes, he managed to cut power to the rooftop solar panel and override the back-up system. Slipping out of the darkened doorway, he crept down the side of the building to where Fern stood like a statue, her white robe melding with the painted blockwork behind her. One behind the other, they crossed the patch of hard-packed dirt between power plant and perimeter fence, where to Judd's relief someone had disengaged the security alarm before cutting a large hole in the wire. Smoke began to billow from the power plant's roof vents as the two figures vanished into black desert night.

# CHAPTER 4

Inside the pilot capsule, Pia exchanged smiles with Kaire before fastening her safety harness ready for take-off. He had asked her to accompany him on the mission, concerned the five women could become anxious in the presence of a White man. The Sky-ship alone could cause unease, any form of air travel being unheard of in the Brown Zone. Deprived countries like Australia could not afford to purchase, let alone operate and maintain a fleet of aircraft. Pia had readily agreed to his request, eager to assist in the rescue mission but also, if she were honest, longing to step on home soil again even for a few minutes. Life at Kauri Haven might be secure and the inhabitants friendly, but she still felt like an outsider.

Behind her, six passengers sat on the floor, crammed into the narrow space separating pilot and storage module, normally reserved for pilot sleeping quarters. The addition of a male escapee had initially triggered suspicion, Kaire refusing to allow Judd aboard until both Kela and Sami had confirmed his identity. Pia hoped all six escapees would comply with Kaire's instructions to remain seated during the ascent. Once the thrusters reached maximum revolutions, unrestrained passengers could easily sustain injuries.

One passenger troubled her, a young Asian woman named Yuki, who according to Kaire hadn't uttered a word since being rescued. Pia turned her head slightly and smiled, hoping to evoke a reaction, but Yuki continued to stare straight ahead, her small hands tightly clasped around raised knees.

*Traumatised or indifferent?* Pia pondered as a flicker of fear played around her mind.

'All systems engaged,' Kaire announced, 'prepare for take-off.'

Conversation ceased immediately. The escapees faced forward, eyes riveted to the seats in front, hands clutching the rail used to hold the pilot's bed in place when it unfolded from the wall. Control panels flashed, powerful thrusters roared into life. Golden light spilled around the Sky-ship as it moved away from the shadow of the huge sand dune, prompting an audible sigh of relief from Kaire. Although the landing place had proven a safe refuge from the prying beams that had swept nightly across the desert sands ever since the prison breakout, he couldn't wait to be airborne. It had taken several trips to ferry six escapees to the Sky-ship, despite doubling up in the transporter's rear seat when possible. On reaching more solid ground, he increased speed, sending a plume of red sand high into the dawn sky. Soon the Sky-ship ascended gracefully, a silver bird shimmering in the growing light.

They were over the ocean before anyone spoke again. Judd was the first, praising the creators of such an amazing machine and expressing a desire to learn the technology necessary to build another one. Kaire promised to show him the thruster bay sometime but chose not to reveal the Sky-ship's primary function. Experience in the Brown Zone had taught him to be wary when meeting Australians for the first time. Any explanation of inter-galaxy travel would be deferred until more was known about this friend of Sami and Kela.

Unexpectedly, it was Yuki who spoke next. 'Where are we going?' she asked in an anxious voice.

'To Kauri Haven,' Pia answered, loosening her safety harness so she could turn around.

'Is that a safe dome?'

'It's a village.'

'Which zone?'

'None, it's over ocean.'

Yuki burst into tears.

'No need to get upset, you'll be safe there.'

'But how will my son ever learn what happened to me? He'll grow up thinking I abandoned him. I promised him I'd return someday.'

'You were foolish to promise him anything,' a middle-aged woman named Cheva remarked. 'If we hadn't escaped, we were facing life imprisonment. Surely you realised that.'

A plaintive cry filled the module.

'We can get word to him, Yuki,' Pia said quickly, 'tell him you're safe.'

'No you can't, he's only three.'

'So who's looking after him?'

'His grandmother.'

'Problem solved then,' said Cheva.

'That's not possible, his grandmother is White!'

'You stupid woman,' Cheva retorted.

Fingers fluttered over a flushed face, settled on tear-stained cheeks.

'A bit of compassion wouldn't hurt,' admonished the woman on Yuki's left.

'Facing facts would do more good,' Cheva muttered.

'Cruel bitch!' Yuki shouted, making a fist with her right hand.

Pia grabbed Yuki's wrist before her knuckles could make contact with Cheva's face. 'Enough, I don't want to hear another word out of either of you.'

Cheva sat back against the wall, arms folded. Yuki blubbered.

'And you can stop that noise, Yuki.'

Silence settled over the capsule as Pia twisted around in her seat and tightened her safety harness. 'How long before we reach Aotearoa?' she asked Kaire in a low voice.

'Five minutes,' he murmured, glancing at the console.

*Thank the moon for that*, she thought.

'We'll be landing at Kauri Haven shortly,' Kaire announced officiously. 'Passengers are to remain seated until the thrusters have disengaged and I give the command to disembark.'

Six heads nodded, six bodies braced for landing.

The new arrivals were immediately taken to the village medical centre and examined for any obvious signs of illness, particularly those respiratory and skin diseases prevalent in northern Australia. Saliva, blood and hair samples were also taken to test for underlying health problems and confirm DNA matched that obtained surreptitiously from the Australian National Database. Peni, once a highly regarded Australian government official employed to update the database, had managed to access DNA records without detection in the five years she'd lived at Kauri Haven. She also used her skills to alter records should former prisoners returning to their homeland for seditious purposes require false identity.

After medical examination, the five women and Judd were interviewed by a council member to determine whether they wished to remain in Aotearoa or preferred to take their chances in the wider world. All six elected to return to Kauri Haven after they had completed the mandatory quarantine period in an isolated camp further south.

Six weeks after landing, Judd moved in with his old friend Sami who shared a house with two other men, while the five women were housed in the dwelling reserved for new settlers. They would remain there until arrangements were made for them to join other households, a group of singles or a family offering a spare room. Following a brief induction into village practice and procedure, all six were found employment in areas appropriate to their skills and experience, if at all possible, so Judd soon joined Sami and Kaire in the engineering workshop.

Throughout the weeks following their return from quarantine, Pia kept an eye on the five women, especially Yuki, whose sullenness deterred others from offering companionship, making sure they had opportunities to meet other settlers socially as well as at work, and dealing with any problems that arose. Adjusting to a society lacking the rigid strictures of Australian life, be it village or prison, sometimes proved difficult and required patience on the part of established settlers. Homesickness also had to be addressed; once the initial glow of liberty had faded, some found it distressing to realise family and friends were forever beyond their reach. Although attempts could be made to bring family members to Kauri Haven, the risks involved were great and this was only contemplated when children or partners back home were deemed to be in a life-threatening situation.

Family reunion wasn't an option for Pia. Her mother Sannah's death had marked the final disintegration of what had always been a small family unit. There had never been any contact with her father's family either before or after his early death. Perhaps it was this loss of loved ones, both recent and long ago, that led Pia to befriend Yuki; but whatever the reason, she felt compelled to spent time with the young woman.

A few months after the rescue mission, Pia decided to organise a picnic lunch beside the village lake in an attempt to engender at least understanding between Yuki and her remaining housemates. Two of the women had already joined other households leaving Yuki, Cheva and Milda, another testy individual, sharing the new settlers' house. According to Cheva, Yuki and Milda had almost come to blows the previous week over the allocation of household chores.

When Pia and Yuki reached the grassy slope leading down to the lake, they spread out a blanket, opened one of the two baskets and began to set out plates and glasses.

'The others are taking their time,' Pia remarked to Yuki.

'I bet it's that Milda holding them up,' Yuki replied, screwing up her button nose.

Pia looked up. 'Why don't you like her, Yuki?'

'She's an old fraud.'

'Why do you say that?

Yuki scowled. 'Line Leader for twenty years, says she's devoted her life to helping our people but she hasn't got a kind word for me. Always telling me to get my emotions under control and be thankful I'm free. Of course I'm thankful, who'd want to spend their life locked away beneath desert sands? But that doesn't stop me crying when I think about my little boy so far away and I can't help it if I keep having nightmares and scream sometimes.'

Pia recalled her own childhood nightmares following the death of her adored maternal grandmother in a bushfire. 'I'll see if I can get you moved into a house with some young people.'

Yuki grasped Pia's hand. 'Oh, Pia, I'd be so grateful.'

'I'll have to speak to Dona first but don't worry, she's very approachable.'

'A council member!' Yuki's sulky mouth widened with surprise. 'You sure move in the right circles.'

Pia smiled and turned to the second basket, which contained their lunch.

'You seem to spend a fair bit of time with that pilot, too,' Yuki continued. 'How do you manage that?'

Pia's fingers hovered above the basket's woven handle. She had no desire to reveal her late mother's relationship with Kaire or her own flight from Brown Zone prosecution. 'Kaire and I share more than a common cause,' she answered wistfully. 'We share a legacy and live by its light.'

Yuki looked puzzled but had no opportunity to ask for an explanation as the other women were approaching. 'Bad timing, you bitches,' she muttered.

Pia ignored Yuki's scowl. 'Set out the food, would you? I don't know about you but I'm hungry.'

The picnic passed without incident, both Cheva and Milda making a great effort to include Yuki in conversation and praising the cake she had baked for the occasion. Pia felt hopeful the three women had at last put aside their differences and would endeavour to be, if not friendly, at least tolerant of one another.

During the following week, Pia was too busy with Truth Network training plus regular shifts monitoring the main communication system to pay much attention to relationships in the new settlers' house. But as promised, she had spoken to Dona about Yuki and was hopeful arrangements would soon be made to transfer her to a household of young people.

Pia's final shift for the week at the communication console was nearly over and she had just finished a message to Kaire suggesting they meet for dinner, when movement in the corridor caught her attention. Hours earlier, she had opened the door panel, the breeze having dropped making the communications office even more stuffy than usual. Instinctively she saved the text and blanked the screen before turning around. Yuki stood in the doorway, twisting her long black hair with thin fingers.

Pia smiled. 'Hi Yuki, what can I do for you?'

A curtain of hair fell to thin shoulders as Yuki padded across the polished concrete floor, her tiny feet encased in embroidered slippers.

'I've been thinking about our network in the north of the Asian Zone. Only a single line leader remains to cover the area from Second River to the Brown Zone border.' She sidled close to Pia's chair.

'That's right.'

'An unsatisfactory situation, don't you think?'

'Definitely, but we can't do much from this end.'

'I think we can.'

Pia looked down at the screen, suddenly perturbed by the hazel eyes riveted to her face. 'You'd better sit down.'

Yuki picked up the chair leaning against the wall and positioned it close to the console.

'So what did you have in mind?' Pia asked when Yuki had finished smoothing her short skirt over her skinny knees.

Yuki leaned forward, her hair brushing Pia's bare arm. 'I have a friend who lives just inside the Asian Zone. If I were provided with false ID, I could help monitor the area until we have replacement line leaders.' She raised her head and, cradling her face in her hands, said in a low voice, 'I'm a split like you, but I can pass as Asian anywhere in the Zone.'

Pia shivered. She hadn't heard that hated term since arriving at Kauri Haven. The ruling Whites in Australia reviled splits, especially half-Whites who were a constant reminder not just of past illegal unions but that pale skin could be subsumed by darker flesh.

'There are advantages in mixed parentage, despite the law,' she answered, remembering stories of her light-skinned father's frequent forays into White society, 'but have you thought this through? Even with fake ID it would still be dangerous work.'

'I'm prepared to take the risk.'

'But if your real identity is uncovered, you'll never see your son again. Can you face that?'

Yuki shifted her position, bracing her back against the chair's hard plastic. 'It's time I thought of others beside myself,' she replied in a forthright tone that to Pia seemed forced. 'Children are very resilient. Max will cope without me. His father and grandmother love him dearly.'

At the mention of a father, Pia started; most Whites did not acknowledge their mixed-race offspring. 'Is Max registered as White?'

Yuki nodded.

'So who does he think you are?'

'His carer.'

Pia looked up. 'Under the circumstances your plan might just work.'

'I can go then?' Yuki exclaimed in a high-pitched voice reminiscent of a child offered a special treat.

'Yuki, I'm in no position to make that decision. KAL will have to agree to your proposal before any arrangements can be made.'

'Of course, I don't know what I was thinking.'

'I'll speak to Dona this afternoon.' She patted Yuki's arm.

Yuki's thin arms tightened around Pia's chest. 'You're the best person here. I don't know how I'd have managed these past weeks without your friendship.'

Pia recalled her mother's best friend Fley, an important role model during her childhood. Did she fulfil a similar role for the immature Yuki? More than a year after another fire had claimed Fley's life, Pia still couldn't think of her without a deep sense of sorrow welling up and threatening to destroy her equanimity. Despite her misgivings, Pia considered perhaps she had misjudged the young woman.

After careful consideration and extensive communication with several line leaders, KAL members agreed in principle to Yuki's proposal. Since the raids on Brown Zone villages bordering the Asian Zone and the subsequent arrests, the Women's Line had been reluctant to try to recruit new members or attempt to manoeuvre any transfers into the district. At present, a large area encompassing twenty villages relied on the work of one experienced line leader, Neene, an elderly woman who would no doubt welcome assistance from someone much younger. All concurred with Yuki's suggestion she stay with her friend Vina in Asian Village 2. As a precaution, Dona, currently KAL director, warned Yuki not to cross the border into the Brown Zone under any circumstances.

Prior to Yuki's departure, a Women's Line member visiting the northern Asian Zone for a cousin's end of life ceremony, called on Vina, supposedly with a message from Yuki about her forthcoming visit, but primarily to obtain a DNA sample. Following analysis of hair taken from a comb lying on Vina's bath chamber basin, results were checked against the Women's Line database listing those Asian and Brown Zoners known to collaborate with the White authorities. No match was discovered.

A small ship slipped into northern Asian Zone waters and deposited its female passenger on the banks of a wide river shrouded in early morning mist. In her robe pocket, Yuki, now Kiwa, carried an identity disc authorising her temporary transfer from a distant Asian Zone village to gain experience teaching young children. She waited until the ship was out of sight before setting off to walk the ten kilometres through windswept scrub to the nearest riverboat terminal. The riverboat would carry her upstream as far as Asian Village 3 from where it was only a short walk through fields and orchards to Vina's house, adjacent to the school in the next village.

The ship did not return directly to Aotearoa. Instead it travelled south, taking care to evade coastal surveillance equipment by keeping to the route far out to sea once taken by container ships bringing goods from distant countries. These days, only Australian ships transporting goods from zone to zone frequented the eastern seaboard and they tended to hug the coast, but in case another vessel should appear, the ship displayed an Australian code on her bows.

Midway down the eastern White Zone, the ship veered towards the coast. The rendezvous with an old ferry that usually carried passengers across a broad coastal inlet took place under cover of darkness, lights dimmed on both vessels. As the ferry's tender bobbed alongside the ship, the single passenger stood up and grabbed a ladder draped over the ship's side. Then, taking care not to slip on the sodden rope, Professor Kela climbed aboard.

# CHAPTER 5

Evening light filtered through the thin curtains drawn halfway across the large window facing Kaire's rear garden. He never tired of the view, flowers and trees a joy to one raised in the artificial environment of a space station, but Pia had asked him to shade the table near the window, concerned sunlight would spoil their meal. Tonight he had prepared a simple dish made from the produce of his garden, vegetables he had not encountered during his brief stay in the Brown Zone. Unfamiliar with the concept of preparing and cooking food, he had earlier welcomed Pia's offer of lessons after his initial attempts proved almost inedible.

They sat side-by-side on a worn but comfortable sofa, empty wine glasses cradled in their hands. On a nearby table, smudges of tomato sauce congealed on plates, the remains of a delicious meal.

'What a change in Sami since Kela arrived,' Pia remarked, leaning forward to place her glass on the table.

'Yes, Sami lives up to his nickname every day now.'

'Sunshine Sami, smile as wide as the ocean,' Pia mused, settling back on the sofa.

Kaire turned and placed his hand over hers. 'I wish I could make your smile bright as the sun.'

She smiled fleetingly.

'No, that's only a tiny smile peeping out from behind a bank of grey clouds. Try to sweep the clouds away.'

Her mouth split in a cheesy grin.

'That's better.' He pulled her closer with his free hand and kissed her smiling lips.

The kiss delighted and something shifted inside her. 'You're right,' she said when he raised his head. 'It's time to lighten the load. Grief has weighed us down these past fifteen months.'

He nodded and bent to kiss her again.

Over the next few months, Pia shared many meals with Kaire, delighting in the variety of foods he prepared to tempt her taste buds. At first their absence in the communal dining room was noted with wry comments, but as the relationship progressed, most acknowledged a positive change in both partners. The usually reserved man from an environment the others could hardly imagine now joined in social events even if Pia's duties prevented her from accompanying him. For her part, Pia had lost all trace of the melancholy previously observed when she thought no one was around to see slumped shoulders or eyes filled with tears.

Late one afternoon, Pia sat behind the console in the communication room, idly pushing her message-pad from one side of the desk to the other. Bored stiff, she couldn't wait for the shift to end and the hours spent with her lover begin. To pass the time, she had been reading text on her message-pad, a weak, long-winded narrative that after hours failed to absorb her. She rubbed her tired eyes; they felt gritty as though sand from the nearby beach had blown in through the open window. Glancing up at the console's blank screen, she willed a face, any face to appear and shatter the boredom of an unproductive shift.

Eyes half-closed, body slouched over the console, she failed to notice Kaire had entered the room and was creeping towards her. The kiss on the back of her neck startled her and she swung around. 'I'm on duty you know.'

He stepped forward and leaned against the desk. 'Only for another ten minutes.'

'Thank the moon for that.'

'Busy night?'

She shook her head. 'I've been reading most of the shift.'

'Anything interesting?'

'No.' She yawned, raised her arms and wriggled stiff fingers.

'Then it's time you had some exercise.' He watched breasts strain against taut fabric.

'What had you in mind, Skyman?' she asked coyly.

Leaning forward, he brushed her face with his fingertips. 'To begin with, a brisk walk to my house.'

'And then?'

'Warm-up exercises on the sofa.'

She kissed the tip of his nose. 'And after that?'

'Strenuous activity in the bedroom.'

'That sounds like an excellent work-out.'

Pale fingers travelled down her neck and began to burrow under her shirt. 'We could begin now if you set the system to automatic.'

Pia grinned and turned back to the screen. 'Commence manual logout,' she ordered and without waiting for visual confirmation, stood up and stretched sensuously.

He reached for her but she stepped aside and skipped down the room like a child, pausing in the doorway to drape honey-brown arms either side of the door in a mock-embrace. Laughing, he strode towards her, grabbed her small waist and twirled her into his arms. Behind them a face materialised on the screen.

'KiwaAZ2 to Kauri 378,' said a barely audible voice.

There was no response.

'Kauri 378, are you there?' Yuki cried. 'I must speak to you urgently.'

Pia lifted her head. 'Oh shit.' She dashed to the console. 'Override manual logout.' The screen flickered as she slipped into the chair. 'Kauri 378 receiving you.'

'Sweep of the villages along the Border River this afternoon,' said Yuki, the words coming in short sharp bursts as though she were struggling to breathe. 'Brown Zone side. Six women arrested. Not line leaders.'

'Is their location known?'

'No, the message from Neene cut out. I suspect interception.'

'Is *this* communication secure?'

'I don't know.'

Pia glanced back at Kaire before answering. 'Stay calm, we'll run tests this end.'

'I'll try.' Thin lips quivered, hazel eyes blinked rapidly.

'Kauri will contact tomorrow. 378 terminating.'

Yuki's face faded as Kaire moved to Pia's side. 'Should we alert KAL?'

'There's no point in causing alarm until we know for sure the system's been infiltrated. Can you run tests tonight?'

'Sure.'

'Change of venue then.'

Kaire frowned. 'What?'

'A brisk walk to the Sky-ship will be the first item on our exercise routine now.'

A fleeting smile passed over Kaire's sombre face.

Next morning Kaire presented his findings at a hastily convened KAL meeting, explaining the tests had been inconclusive. Communication over ocean remained secure but he couldn't be certain about intra or inter zone within Australia.

'Have you managed to contact Neene?' Dona asked.

'No, but Pia is convinced Neene's daughter would have risked sending a message to Yuki if her mother had been arrested.'

'I agree,' said Dona, after conferring with Mac in a low voice. 'The one I'm concerned about is Yuki, she's far too volatile. If she panics the Women's Line could be in even deeper trouble.'

'Do you want me to get her out?' asked Kaire.

'Not yet. We need to find out where the women are being held. Yuki has more chance of finding out as she's outside the Brown Zone.'

'My guess is the Border Court dome,' said Mac. 'It's the closest place with high security prison chambers. I doubt the troopers would take them to the desert at the moment.'

'Still having structural problems out there, are they?' Peni queried, suppressing a smile.

Dona nodded.

'Kela did a great job,' Peni added. Several others murmured in agreement.

Dona raised her hand. 'To return to the current problem, I suggest we play it safe for the moment and keep communication with line leaders to a minimum, regardless of where they're located. However, we must keep trying to contact Neene. Mac, would you take over this task please?'

'Sure.'

Dona looked over at Kaire, sitting opposite. 'When you contact Yuki, don't reveal the results of the tests. We don't want her stressing out unnecessarily. Keep conversation to a minimum but impress on her the need to find out quickly where the women have been taken.'

'Your directives have been noted,' Kaire replied in the formal manner he still used when asked to perform a task.

'Thanks everyone.' Dona glanced around the table. Some KAL members stood and left the room at once while others remained seated, talking in low voices.

Kaire was halfway to the door when he paused and turned back to the table. 'I've just had another thought about communications.'

Dona and Peni, still seated, looked up.

'When I contact Yuki, I'll link with another line leader at the same time, say Maris on Island 1. If I run a test while the three-way link is in progress, I should be able to prove if inter zone communications are secure.'

'Excellent.' Dona smiled. 'Could you do something similar for intra zone?'

'That should be possible.'

'Good, keep us informed.'

Kaire nodded and turned to leave but as he reached the door someone touched his shoulder.

'If further tests prove communications have been compromised,' Dona whispered into the back of his neck, 'I fear this is the end of the Women's Line.'

He continued walking, conscious of her footsteps behind him, but when they reached the corridor, he waited for her to fall into step beside him. 'Have faith in your people, Dona,' he said quietly, 'they will find another way. The path to liberty is never straight.'

She raised her hand to wipe away a tear.

Later that morning Pia sat with Kaire in front of the Sky-ship console. Unable to concentrate on anything other than the latest Brown Zone arrests and communication issues, she had cancelled Truth Network training for the day. Kaire was attempting to contact Maris, the line leader for Island 1, situated off the southern Brown Zone coast in the middle of an immense bay. The island was familiar territory to Pia, who as a child had visited on several occasions with her mother, and she knew Maris well.

A flicker on the monitor drew Pia's attention away from island memory and she watched intently as a middle-aged woman's face filled the left-hand side of the split screen.

'LLM receiving you.'

'Security check only,' Kaire announced, quickly activating the test module and a second link. 'No further response required, but please remain online.'

Maris looked puzzled.

'SkyZ59.323 to KiwaAZ2,' he said, eyes fixed on the blank half of the screen.

The screen flickered.

'Please respond, KiwaAZ2.'

Yuki's face slowly materialised. She looked extremely agitated. 'Make it quick.'

'Location?' asked Kaire, puzzled by the ripple effect visible behind Yuki's head.

'Border River.'

*What the sun is she doing there?* Pia thought, but knew better than to voice the question.

Kaire looked at Pia, his own thoughts echoing hers. 'Are you okay, Kiwa?'

'No.' Yuki's mouth opened but the sound of angry voices prevented any response. Her eyes stared unblinking.

'What's going on?' Kaire shouted at the screen.

'Get me out of here!' Her image vanished.

Both Kaire and Pia stared at the screen, oblivious to Maris's worried face. Minutes passed before either remembered the link with Island 1 was still open.

'LLM please disconnect,' Kaire said finally.

'But I heard everything,' Maris protested. 'What's going on down there, and who is Kiwa?'

'I cannot reveal, security issue. I'll communicate later.' Kaire pressed a pad on the console and sighed with relief as Maris's face faded.

Kaire went straight to Mac's office, preferring to speak one to one than risk the inevitable delay should another KAL meeting be convened. After relating the latest dilemma, he informed Mac the Sky-ship could be launched in less than two hours, having been fully tested prior to the previous rescue mission three months earlier.

'But you don't know Yuki's exact whereabouts,' Mac replied, reluctant to act right away.

'I'll try to contact her before I leave.'

'And if there's no response?'

'Her friend Vina may know what's happened.'

'Determined to go, aren't you?'

Kaire nodded and stepped away from Mac's chair.

'I'm well aware I have no authority over you, Kaire, but I wouldn't want you to put your life at risk.' Mac drummed his fingers on the arm of the chair. 'I fear Yuki may be overstating the immediate danger.'

'It's possible given her temperament. However, in this instance I believe her fear is justified.'

'Then go with my blessing.' He got to his feet and, hurrying across the room, threw his arms around Kaire. 'You remind me of my son,' he said in response to Kaire's puzzled expression. Arms slackened and he retreated, leaving an appropriate space between them.

'Your son is in Australia?' asked Kaire, sensing the older man's distress.

'White Zone.' Mac looked up, his eyes focused on the wall above Kaire's head. 'I haven't seen him for decades.'

'Couldn't you arrange for him to come here?'

Mac smiled ruefully. 'I can't expect him to abandon his wife and child.' He ushered Kaire to the door. This was no time for further conversation of a personal nature.

# CHAPTER 6

Pia insisted on accompanying Kaire to Australia, dismissing his fears for her safety by reminding him she was fully conversant with Brown Zone life and had many friends to call on should she need assistance. Besides, she had no intention of sacrificing either life or liberty to save Yuki. Selfish though this unspoken thought might be, Pia was convinced her future lay with Kaire's and nothing on earth or in space would alter that belief. Likewise, the possibility her lover could perish on this mission did not enter her mind. After more than a year on Earth, his skin had lost the almost translucent appearance that had marked him as different on arrival, so he could easily blend in with other Whites. But as an added precaution, both Kaire and Pia made slight alterations to their appearance in the brief time remaining before departure. Kaire now sported the short haircut favoured by White men working in the Brown Zone, his black curls consigned to a rubbish chute; while Pia, keen to avoid detection as a split, had applied a tanning agent to darken her skin. False identity discs had also been prepared but with any luck would not be required. The mission would be brief: locate–retrieve–depart, no time or need to linger in hostile territory.

During the flight, Kaire managed to contact Yuki and arrange a rendezvous some distance upstream from the most westerly Asian Zone border village where she had found refuge since her previous communication. This stretch of the river was too shallow for riverboats and, according to her hosts, troopers rarely intercepted small local craft.

After learning of her predicament, the family had offered Yuki the use of an old flat-bottomed punt to enable her to travel upstream and make her escape.

The Sky-ship landed several hundred kilometres west of the Border River on the edge of the desert. After a brief but heated argument, Kaire relented and allowed Pia to travel with him in the land transporter to within a few kilometres of the river, where he left her in charge of the vehicle and proceeded on foot to the rendezvous.

The navigation aid on his communicator guided his steps, taking him across dry ground littered with stones and then through a patch of low scrub to a narrow strip of bush bordering the river. Treading lightly on grass and soil, he wove his way to the riverbank, avoiding the numerous fallen twigs and branches that littered the ground. On the muddy shore, he climbed onto an overhanging branch and scanned the river for the punt. Beneath the branch, sluggish brown water lapped exposed mud, while beyond the blue-grey leaves brushing the surface halfway across, deeper water hugged the opposite bank. There was no sign of a punt or any other craft; the river as deserted as the land he had walked through, a few clouds gathering in the early evening sky the only evidence of activity.

Sliding back along the branch, he lowered his feet to a broken limb embedded in the mud before leaping onto solid ground where he rechecked the coordinates. The results confirmed what he already knew: he was six kilometres upstream from Asian Zone Village 5 on the Brown Zone bank, exactly as Yuki had requested. Concerned, he sat down and considered whether to try to communicate with her or simply wait a while longer in case she'd had problems with the punt. He was about to retrieve his communicator from the money-belt fastened around his waist when a light breeze stirred nearby foliage and a flash of red caught his eye. Rising quickly, he pushed through thick undergrowth and emerged close to the bank a few metres downstream. At his feet a length of red rope snaked across muddy ground towards a dense bush. He picked up the rope and tugged hard. Branches and leaves parted easily, but the rope slithering towards him had no punt tethered at its end.

He located the punt a short distance away, pulled up on the bank, its red painter recently severed, dangling over the bow. A quick heat scan showed no large living beings within a five hundred-metre radius. Although Kaire felt relieved that whoever had cut the rope and presumably taken Yuki away had already departed, there remained the possibility he was being watched, perhaps from another craft further downstream. He had no idea what surveillance equipment troopers possessed, other than the electronic devices implanted in the wrists of all prisoners and scanners to search coastal waters for unauthorised shipping. Wading into the river up to his knees, he walked upstream until he reached the overhanging branch, swung one leg over and, after washing mud from his feet, propelled himself to the bank. By standing up and grabbing another stout branch, he was able to leap onto a patch of dry grass from where it was only a few steps on dry ground to tangled foliage.

When Kaire communicated from his hiding place with news of Yuki's failure to turn up Pia felt deep disquiet, which intensified on hearing he planned to visit Vina. She tried to convince him to return immediately but soon realised he would not be swayed. 'Take care, my love. You're worth ten of Yuki.'

'So are you, but I can't just abandon her.'

'What do you want me to do?'

'Go back to the ship, you'll be safer there. I'll communicate when I get to the village.'

'A good thing you taught me to drive the transporter last month.'

Memory surfaced, the two of them alone in the forest east of Kauri Haven, lying on a bed of leaves at the base of a tall tree. Sunlight filtering through a green canopy, her golden skin smooth, malleable, a honey feast for his fingers. 'That was a magic day,' he murmured.

'Promise me you'll get out at the first sign of trouble.'

'I promise.'

'And don't forget to keep me up to date on your progress.'

'Yes, Commander.'

'Sorry, I'm being bossy again, aren't I?'

He refrained from giving an honest answer. 'Just a fraction, my love. Communication terminating.'

Pia lifted the passenger bubble and climbed out, her sandalled feet sinking in sandy soil. Opening the driver bubble, she levered herself forward, balancing on the transporter's smooth side to shake her feet before sliding inside. Her mouth set in concentration she leaned over the console and pressed the ignition panel. To her relief, the thrusters started at the first attempt, showering the surrounding scrub with earth. The transporter moved forward, responding to her light touch on the control panels and gathering speed once stunted trees gave way to open ground. Pia relished the sensation of speed, a new and exciting experience for a Brown Zone girl accustomed to walking everywhere. Inside the Sky-ship, even though Kaire had remarked on the vehicle's optimum velocity, there was little sensation of movement. High above land or ocean it seemed to float, a silent silver creature surrounded by billowing clouds or touched by shimmering sunlight. But here, alone in the transporter, connected to solid ground by wide wheels and with only a thin layer of metal and glass between her and the air rushing past, Pia felt a freedom powerful and addictive. Nothing could touch her as she sped across the dusty plain towards the desert, nothing could subdue her innate control.

On the banks of the Border River, Kaire plastered face, hands and legs with mud before venturing downstream in the punt, a darker complexion less likely to attract attention from any trooper he might encounter. Soon buildings began to appear on the Asian Zone side. Unlike the domes of Brown Zone villages, these houses were square and flat-roofed with small windows shaded by canopies. He recalled seeing similar images in the Sky data hub as he studied history programmes during his quest to learn everything possible about the world of his ancestors.

A glance at the navigation aid confirmed this was the first (or last depending on the direction travelled) of the five Asian Zone villages strung along the southern bank of the Border River. At this early hour there was unlikely to be much movement on the river, so he planned to pass two more villages before abandoning the punt. Unlike the Brown Zone, where under the Nocturnal Life Project villagers would be scurrying to complete tasks and return to their domes before morning curfew, Asian Zoners would be just waking.

A short distance from Asian Zone Village 2, Kaire steered the punt to the southern bank and concealed it amongst the reeds growing there in abundance. After washing the caked mud from his skin, he set off towards the village, hoping to reach Vina's house before she left for work. Not far from the river, he emerged from thin scrub into a field planted with a crop he hadn't seen before, waist-high with broad green leaves and sturdy stems. Paler green leaves attached to the stems enveloped what he presumed to be cylindrical fruits or vegetables, but he had no time to investigate. Sustenance tablets would have to suffice until he returned to Kauri Haven.

A narrow path made of hard-packed earth ran alongside the field and led to a row of concrete houses, uniform in their construction and colour. No one opened a door or window as he passed, for which he was thankful, even though his White skin warranted travel in any zone provided he possessed the correct permits. These, along with fake ID, were safely stored in a pouch attached to the inside of his loose-fitting shirt. As befitted an Inter-Zone Security Officer, baggy cotton trousers and leather sandals completed his outfit, while his backpack contained a change of clothes plus the standard issue Security Department communicator and stun gun.

The firearm bothered him.

Apart from the fact he had never used a weapon of any kind or even taken part in a fight, Kaire recoiled at the very concept of physical violence. An upbringing on Skyz59 where violence was anathema had taught him alternative methods of conflict resolution, such as deep listening and cooperation. His months in the Brown Zone, where he'd witnessed first-hand an oppressive and brutal regime, had both shocked and repelled, but also confirmed his belief in the value of non-violence. He shuddered at the thought of the gun wrapped in a shirt at the bottom of his backpack and hoped the situation would never arise where he felt compelled to use it.

At the end of the row of houses, the path widened and then divided into two, the left-hand fork leading away from the river towards more dwellings, clustered in groups of three. Kaire took the right-hand path and soon reached the long low building that housed the village school. An unlocked gate at one side opened into a playground comprising various activity frames and low benches protected from heat and sunlight by colourful sun-shields. Skirting the play equipment, he made his way over to a small house on the playground's northern periphery. The blinds were drawn back and music filtered through an open window, so he stepped onto the bare concrete pad in front of the door and looked around for a sound-grill or audio-box. Finding neither, he announced his arrival by knocking on the door.

'Chief Instructor Vina's dwelling,' an automated voice declared from somewhere inside. 'Please state your business.'

'Security Officer Kapor, educational establishment audit,' Kaire answered in what he hoped was a suitably officious tone.

The door opened revealing a child-size woman wearing a white wraparound robe. She stood facing the doorway, her eyes screwed into slits, her mouth a rigid line. As he waited for her to speak, she raised her right hand in the traditional gesture required when greeting a White superior and with the left hand signalled for him to enter. Inclining his head slightly, he stepped into the room taking care to leave appropriate space between them.

'Greetings, Chief Instructor Vina,' he said, noting the communicator poking out of her robe pocket and the tremor in her tiny hands as she lowered them to her sides.

'You are not expected,' she said curtly, her lips scarcely moving. 'I need to sight your authorisation.'

'I was expecting Kiwa,' he replied, looking directly into her face. She crumpled to the floor without a sound.

He carried her over to a small sofa and deposited her gently, making sure to elevate her head on a cushion. As he straightened up, he looked out of the window behind the sofa. A swathe of grass led down to a stand of eucalypts where patches of water shimmered between the spindly branches. *Direct access to the river,* he thought, turning back to the woman he presumed was Vina. She stirred, pale eyelids slowly opening to reveal amber eyes.

'Kiwa,' she murmured, so softly he barely caught the name.
'Where is she?'
'Taken by troopers.'
'From the river?'

Eyelids slowly closed and he heard the sound of her breathing, deep inhalations followed by long slow exhalations as though willing herself to slip back into unconsciousness. He tried to rouse her by shaking her narrow shoulders, calling out, even slapping her pale cheeks as a last resort, but she remained comatose. Moving away from the sofa, he pulled out his communicator and was about to key in the transporter's code when a warm current of air wafted against his bare ankles. He looked up, noticing the rear door panel was slightly open. *Faulty closure mechanism,* he thought, crossing the room to press the manual override button before the atmosphere became uncomfortable. But the button appeared stuck; he would need a thin-bladed tool to affect its release. A large dirty thumbprint on the shiny metal doorframe caught his attention, so he pushed the panel further open and slipped outside.

Pia answered immediately, her delight at hearing his voice quickly tempered by unwelcome news. 'Most likely a trooper administered the drug in order to gain more information regarding Kiwa,' she told him, pondering how the authorities had learned about Vina's visitor.

'I agree, but I intend to remain here until she regains consciousness, it's the least I can do.'

'No, they could return at any moment to check on her.'

'I can't leave her in this state.'

Pia took a deep breath to steady her nerves. 'Our mission is to rescue Kiwa, not Vina. Get out of there, I beg you!'

'I'll contact you later advising my location. Communication terminating.'

Pia assumed he would make his way back to the riverbank hiding place, stay there overday and retrieve the punt once darkness fell. The Border River was navigable for at least another fifty kilometres, enough to see him past Asian Village 1 and into uninhabited country.

A short distance from the water, Kaire stepped between two thin trees whose branches cast a flimsy shadow over bare earth and began to follow the river's lazy passage downstream. The blow came without warning, striking the back of his head and sending him flying down the muddy riverbank.

# CHAPTER 7

The Sky-ship's rear door opened as the transporter drew near, the sensors having registered its proximity. The entrance was only just wide enough to accommodate the vehicle, so Pia selected minimum speed, her fingers hovering over the controls in case a slight change of position should be needed. A jolt indicated the front wheels had locked on to the guide strip. She held her breath as a grey shadow slid over the bubble leaving her encased in a metal cocoon. Hands trembling, she waited what seemed an age for the rear wheels to lock into position and the door to begin its descent.

Light suddenly illuminated the module, so she disconnected the thrusters and released her safety harness. There was insufficient space to open the bubble completely, so she twisted around and slid out feet first, taking care not to trap her hair as it resealed. Making her way along the narrow walkway to the door, she thought of Kaire hidden in foliage waiting for the camouflage of night and hoped he would communicate once clear of the riverside villages.

The door panel opened as she approached and she slipped into the pilot module, relieved to have returned safely to the craft that would take her back to Kauri Haven. The return to her homeland longed for and dreamed of for many months had done little to dispel homesickness. Once Kaire had departed for Vina's house, she'd experienced intense fear, a blunt reminder of the reality of life in Australia for non-Whites. The starkness of desert sands and wind blowing incessantly had also unnerved her as she drove towards the Sky-ship, prompting memories of a childhood mantra often heard in the schoolyard following prolonged drought.

'Desert desert go away,' the little girls had chanted as they swung their skipping ropes, 'let us live another day.'

Pia flopped into the pilot's seat, avoiding a glance at the rounded lines of sand dunes visible from the curved window.

Sometime later, the communication panel flashed and buzzed, waking her from a dream of lush vegetation. 'SkyZ59.323,' she answered, hoping Kaire hadn't been waiting long for her response.

'Kiwa AZ2,' a faint voice replied.

'Thank the moon you're okay. Where are you?'

'AZ1 Trooper detention cell. I managed to conceal my communicator. Please hurry, they're moving me tonight.'

'To a prison?'

'I don't know, I don't know.'

'Try to stay calm.'

'I can't, I can't, it's so …' Yuki's voice trailed off but not before Pia had registered another sound, a sound that should not have been audible within the thick walls of a detention cell. It was the irregular pulse of a static communicator, the kind embedded in the work-modules found behind the reception counter in a trooper dome.

Staring at the blank panel, Pia finally acknowledged what she had suspected ever since that first conversation in the Sky-ship, something about Yuki that had triggered unease, a warning she had foolishly ignored and pushed to the back of her mind. Pia had yet to discover whether she had inherited Sannah's uncanny ability to sense imminent danger, but she knew her mother would not have ignored that first flicker of fear. She pressed the panel and entered Kaire's code.

'Unable to communicate,' came the automated reply. 'Device disconnected.'

'Disconnected?' she queried as though the equipment could sense her incredulity. A red dot continued to flash on the console, prompting a swift prod with her finger to blank the screen. Sitting back in the seat, she concentrated on her breathing in an attempt to calm jangled nerves. With a deep inhale and steady slow exhale, stillness returned. She decided to wait another hour before trying to communicate again.

Conscious of hunger pangs, she reached into a storage compartment for the supplies she'd brought, much to Kaire's amusement, a tube of Sustenance tablets being all he'd packed. Munching a crisp carrot, she thought of Kauri Haven's bountiful produce, a welcome change from the poor quality produce available in her former home.

Alone in the detention cell beneath Asian Village 2 trooper station, Kaire lay on a narrow bed, his feet sticking out over the end, the wafer-thin mattress providing scant comfort for his slender body. Apart from flimsy undershorts, Trooper Orag, the hefty individual who had felled him by the river, had confiscated all his clothing and backpack. Kaire remained confident he would be released once his ID disc had been checked, it being a copy of that held by an Education Department official who, if all had gone according to the Women's Line plan, at present lay comatose in a Brown Zone village on the opposite side of the river. The real Kapor would remember little of his unexpected sojourn and put the loss of forty-eight hours down to the delights he had experienced in a village woman's bed.

Unlike Vina, Kaire had regained consciousness after a few moments. He now believed her collapse had been a ploy to detain him until Trooper Orag arrived, for as he was led away from the river towards the house, he'd caught a glimpse of an oval face framed by curtains of straight black hair at an upstairs window.

Stretching cramped limbs, he sat up, bored from hours spent staring at blank walls reliving the events of the previous day and trying to think of a way to get a message to Pia. Apart from wanting to reassure her he would soon be freed, he was anxious about the Sky-ship, the likelihood of its discovery increasing the longer it remained in one place. Originally he had intended to spend a few days looking for Yuki, and if there was no trace of her, he'd return to the Sky-ship and relocate it before continuing the search. Imprisonment had changed his mind. He planned to leave Australia immediately after his release and conduct further inquiries from the safety of Kauri Haven.

Trooper Orag's arrival put an end to forward planning. 'Get up you idiot,' he ordered, advancing into the room. 'Some security officer you are, no sign of a mission-tag among your belongings.'

Kaire blanched; there had been no mention of a mission-tag at his briefing. 'I er …' he began.

'Save your excuses, I know where it is.' The trooper laughed, a deep rumbling that resonated around the tiny cell. 'It's over the border in a girl's sleeping chamber. Lucky for you she left a message on your communicator. "Call me, urgently," she said, so I did.' He frowned. 'Strange name, Sky Zed, where did she get that?'

Kaire shrugged.

'Like a bit of Brown-skin, do you?'

Kaire nodded, thankful Pia had responded perceptively to an unexpected question.

'Asian too I reckon, though I must admit I thought you'd broken in when I saw you slipping out of Vina's back door.'

'Bad luck for me you were patrolling nearby,' Kaire muttered, touching the bruise on the back of his head.

'Sorry about that, mate.' The trooper's lips parted in a boyish grin. 'Get going then, I want to go home. Collect your belongings from the reception counter.'

Darkness was falling when Kaire left the trooper station but he still headed towards the border, aware Trooper Orag would become suspicious if he failed to register his passage from one zone to another at an official crossing.

After an hour walking along a path running parallel with the river, he deemed it safe to communicate with Pia. Her suspicions about Yuki confirmed his conviction they must return home without delay, so he arranged to meet her at midnight where the Border River birthed in a range of hills west of Brown Zone Village 1.

Fields bordered the river path until Kaire had passed the last village, its cluster of white buildings clearly visible in the light of a full moon. Beyond the village, dry grassland dotted with stunted trees stretched as far as he could see. Tree roots snaked across the unkempt path, forcing a slower pace to prevent a fall. When lights eventually appeared in the distance on both sides of the river, he felt enormous relief he would soon be crossing the bridge.

As Kaire approached the border station, a young trooper holding the regulation stun gun stepped from the shadows into the circle of light that illuminated the entrance. The station was little more than a hut built at one end of a narrow concrete bridge spanning the river. A pedestrian-only bridge, it had been designed primarily for field work-ers from nearby Brown Zone villages to cross when a good harvest required extra labour on the other side. Government officials also used the bridge on occasion if their work entailed visiting border villages on both sides of the river.

'Officer Kapor, education audit,' Kaire announced, extracting a tiny disc from his money-belt and offering it to the trooper.

'Enter the station and place the disc in the machine directly in front of the gates,' the trooper said mechanically, without glancing at the disc.

'Certainly, goodnight to you.'

'There's nothing good about a posting in this dull backwater.'

Kaire offered a sympathetic smile. 'It must be better than patrolling a northern village.'

'Guess so.' The trooper twisted around and pressed his palm against the metal door.

After much creaking and groaning, the rusty panel began to open.

'Hang in there, mate,' Kaire advised as the trooper stepped aside and ushered him through the narrow opening.

Inside, the space was bare except for a low bench positioned against one wall and the ID machine, its red eye blinking ominously in stark artificial light. No windows looked out over the river and the only sound was the slap of Kaire's sandals on the metal grid leading to the machine. Bending over, he inserted the disc in a slot below the red light and waited for the equipment to scan. The light soon flashed green and metal gates behind the machine opened outwards. Quickly retrieving his disc, Kaire stepped onto the bridge

Water slapped against the supports as he walked at a normal pace towards a low white dome at the other end of the bridge. Light strips embedded in the railings guided his steps and a stiff breeze ruffled his short hair. Halfway over, he glanced at the river, saw the full moon reflected in dark water, its soft light easy on the eyes. Before long he drew close to a matching set of gates on the northern bank and as expected, they began to open. Then, without warning, they shuddered and stopped, leaving only a small gap barely wide enough to admit a young child.

'Gate malfunction,' announced an unseen trooper. 'Please wait while I adjust manually.'

Kaire wanted to appear relaxed, so rested his arms on the rail and stared at the river. Minutes passed, the gates creaking intermittently, the trooper swearing. Concentrating on the smooth dark water, Kaire failed to notice three troopers slip between the gates and creep towards him. They had surrounded him before he had a chance to climb the railing and dive into the river.

'Best come quietly,' advised the more senior of the three. 'I have orders not to shoot. A prize like you is too valuable to risk injury or death.' A stun gun poked into Kaire's lower back below his pack.

Kaire raised his hands in the manner he'd seen on old Earth movies in the Sky media cell.

'Turn around,' ordered the trooper, retracting the gun.

Slowly Kaire turned to face the men and remained silent as electronic wrist-bands were clicked into place.

'Proceed towards the southern gates. You are Asian Zone property.'

'Why have I been arrested?' Kaire asked as he retraced his steps. 'My ID was quite acceptable on the other side.'

# CHAPTER 8

Pia sank to the ground beside a small spring issuing from a crack in the rocky hillside, exhausted from the longer than anticipated walk from the patch of low scrub where she'd concealed the transporter to the agreed meeting point. After a long refreshing drink, she refilled her flask and stretched out on the soft ribbon of grass growing either side of the water. According to her communicator, Kaire should reach the hills in about an hour, giving them ample time to retrieve the transporter and be well on the way to the Sky-ship before dawn.

Lying on her back gazing up at silver stars and a full moon floating free in the black tropic night, she thought of those toiling in fields far to the north, adolescents denied the comfort of family for three long years. Tilling the soil, planting and tending crops, harvesting produce to be sent south for greedy White mouths. She had been released early from working party duties, sent home to learn the art of storytelling from her mother on condition she monitored a trooper and provided evidence to convict. That was life in the Brown Zone, a constant diet of lies and deceit, looking over one's shoulder, thinking before speaking, never trusting those outside the favoured circle.

Close by, dry grass rustled and her muscles tightened as she waited for something or someone to emerge from the dark hillside. When no further sound punctured the still air, she sat up slowly and peered into blackness. Seeing nothing except thin stalks, she looked down at the infant Border River trickling over the ground and almost laughed out loud. A small bush rat stood on the opposite side of the water drinking its fill. It froze when she moved again, then turned and scurried to safety. Pia smiled, delighted to have seen a wild creature and know the dry lands beyond the coastal fringe could still nurture wildlife.

Vibration caught her unawares and she almost dropped the communicator in her haste to answer. As expected, Kaire's call code appeared on the screen but when she pressed the panel, an unknown voice said curtly, 'I don't know who you are, Brown-skin, but if you have any sense you'll delete this code and never make contact again. We have your lover in custody and I'm certain you don't want to join him. On the other hand, if you have information about him that would be useful to us, don't hesitate to contact Asian Zone trooper headquarters. As I'm sure you know, there are rewards for those who cooperate.'

Pia resisted the temptation to reply and quickly noted the location coordinates before closing the connection.

She ran swiftly over smooth rock to the grassy plateau that stretched along the spine of the hills, the communicator's navigation programme giving directions. An hour later she collapsed in a heap behind a cluster of boulders, too exhausted to pick her way around the rocks and bushes that dotted the steep downward slope ahead. At the bottom of the slope, the land fanned out into a broad grass-covered plain that led to the small area of low scrub where she'd concealed the transporter. Soon she had recovered sufficiently to pull herself to a sitting position, unclip her flask and drink deeply. Flight had concentrated her mind on directions and the ground beneath her sandalled feet, but fear returned as she tried to figure out what to do.

Driving the transporter back to the Sky-ship presented no problem, but what then? Although certain the Women's Line would assist her to free Kaire, she was reluctant to contact anyone in case communications were being monitored, a distinct possibility given the recent arrests. How far the Line had been compromised was anyone's guess; Yuki and Vina could be part of a group determined to terminate its operations.

After rechecking the route, she set off again, taking care not to slip on the smooth pebbles littering the slope. The descent seemed to take forever, a freshening wind whipping up dry soil that stung her exposed skin and left a layer of grit clinging to limbs already sticky with sweat.

At last she reached the plain below and stopped to drink and rest her aching muscles. Before continuing, she scanned the grassland with the light beam, turning it in a slow arc. Wind whistled through brown grasses bending towards the earth, but as far as she could tell there were no bare patches where a trooper car or booted feet had recently trampled the ground. Her stride increased as she crossed the plain and soon she could see a stand of shaggy trees framed in the light of the moon.

The transporter remained where she'd left it, tucked beneath over-hanging branches, the rear of its silver body covered with dead foliage discovered nearby. Tossing camouflage aside, she pressed her back to smooth metal and slid sideways until she reached the driver's bubble. A living branch, which had bent as she'd manoeuvred the vehicle into place, lay on top of the bubble but didn't appear to have caused any damage. Loath to break it, she opened the bubble just wide enough to slip inside feet first, easing her legs down into the small space beneath the console while the rest of her body slid into the seat. At first, the thrusters failed to start and she wondered if dry leaves or soil had blown through the front vent and blocked the air intake. The thought of wriggling out again didn't appeal but fortunately a second attempt proved successful, the initial burst from the thrusters sending a shower of leaves over the bubble and temporarily blocking her view. Relieved, she engaged thrust-drive and the transporter began to reverse out of its hiding place.

The return journey to the Sky-ship went smoothly and Pia arrived well before dawn. Once the transporter had been safety stowed, she acti-vated the console communicator and input Mac's code. He answered quickly, his friendly face filling the small screen above the console.

Pia explained briefly what had happened and asked for advice.

'I'll ask Dona to convene a KAL meeting at once.'

'Thanks.'

'In the meantime, communicate with Neene and see if she can find out where Kaire's being held.'

'She's back in contact then?'

'Yes, it was a technical problem, her daughter fixed it.'

'That's a relief.'

'Sure is.'

'I'll be okay,' she said, anticipating his next question. 'There's plenty of food and water, Sustenance tablets too if I get desperate.' She forced a smile.

'Good. I'll get back to you as soon as I have some information.'

'Likewise.' Pia blinked back tears. 'I miss you all.'

'We miss you too.'

'Skyz59.323 disconnecting.'

After much discussion on who to recruit for the mission to free Kaire, KAL members decided to contact Tiki, a White medic based at a large medical centre in the south of the White Zone. Apart from being a known 'sympathiser' Tiki possessed specialist skills that often required her to provide assistance to less experienced doctors in other zones. During a recent conversation with Kela, Mac had learned that Tiki received her medical training at the same institution and the two had been close friends for years, so he concluded contact from a 'missing' friend would encourage her participation in the mission.

When Mac called Kela to his office for an urgent meeting, she couldn't imagine what he wanted to talk about and felt great relief on learning her part in the mission wouldn't involve visiting Australia. The punishment for deserting one's position was a minimum ten years in prison, and given she had been a prominent medical researcher, probably even longer. Mac reassured Kela that if the situation became hazardous, Tiki would be pulled out immediately.

'Could she be brought over here when the mission's completed?' Kela asked, eager for a friend to join her. Kauri Haven's medical centre had two competent doctors but neither possessed Tiki's surgical expertise. Patients requiring surgery had to be taken to the nearest town some ninety kilometres south, a costly exercise given the dearth of reliable transport along the Kauri Coast.

'Only if she wanted to come,' Mac answered. 'Leaving family and friends can be a painful experience.'

Kela nodded. 'I know. Don't think I'm ungrateful and of course I was delighted to be reunited with Sami, but sometimes I long to communicate with my parents and sister.'

Mac leaned forward and said gently, 'I feel the same about my son. We pay a price for freedom.'

'Perhaps one day, we'll be able to return,' she said wistfully.

Mac gave a melancholic smile. 'Who knows what the future will bring.'

Doctor Tiki found it difficult to contain her delight when a professor contacted the medical centre and she recognised the voice of her missing friend. There seemed to be something wrong with the visual link at Kela's end so Tiki was unable to see her, but brief answers to personal questions confirmed safety and good health. Staring at the blank screen, Tiki pondered her friend's whereabouts and the circumstances that had led Kela to leave job, family and friends without explanation or warning. The medical problem appeared simple and she was on the point of refusing the task, knowing full well most competent medics could deal with it, when Kela used the words 'White Prisoner' and 'severe complications' in the same sentence.

'I do understand complications must be dealt with quickly,' Tiki said in a suitably compassionate tone, 'but I'm sure you appreciate I have a busy workload. Give me a few hours to think about it. The train north doesn't leave until evening anyway.'

'I'll call back,' Kela said before Tiki could ask for her communication code. 'Thank you for your time and your consideration of an issue I'm doing my utmost to resolve.'

# CHAPTER 9

The trooper station at Asian Zone Village 2 had never known such an uncooperative and clearly unrepentant prisoner. Despite the fact that the authentic 'Kapor' had visited the station, the man listed as Prisoner X had refused to divulge his real name, occupation or village. He was obviously a full-blooded White but appeared to know little of Asian or White Zone life and professed complete ignorance of government policies. Privately, Trooper-in-Charge Hick considered the man mentally deranged, though how such a person could have obtained false ID and for what purpose he couldn't imagine. Standard interrogation practices having failed to elicit any useful information, Hick was duty bound to call in a security officer whose methods would be far less humane. This troubled him, for despite the gun discovered in the prisoner's backpack and the false ID, Hick believed the man represented no threat to national security and hated the thought of the handsome face being bloodied and bruised. But after procrastinating for several hours, Hick chose to disregard both conscience and personal feelings and called in the Security Department.

Night had fallen by the time Security Officer Medite arrived at the trooper station. A young officer, eager to climb the promotions ladder, he had few scruples and simply wanted results, so dismissed Hick's proposal to be present at the interrogation. He also refused the offer of refreshments and insisted a trooper escort him to the detention cell immediately.

Kaire woke with a start as the cell door opened. Blinking, he found it difficult to focus when lights he hadn't known existed blazed from the low ceiling and an officer he hadn't seen before strode into the room.

'Security Officer Medite,' the man announced, marching over to the bed and yanking Kaire to his feet. 'I want no more nonsense from you, Prisoner No Name. Silence and truculence won't wash with me.' He flung Kaire to the floor and sat down on the bed. 'Back against the wall, eyes straight ahead.'

Kaire complied at once, too stunned to consider resistance.

Medite quickly unclipped a message-board from his belt and pressed a panel to engage audio software. 'Right, I'll start with the basics. Name, home village, occupation.'

'Breta,' Kaire answered, 'that's B R E T A.'

'Now that wasn't difficult, was it, so why didn't you give your name before?'

Kaire remained silent.

'Lost your tongue again?' He sighed. 'Right, let's try home village.'

'Skyz59.'

'That's a code not a village. Shall we try again?'

'Skyz59.'

Displaying no sign of irritation, Medite carefully placed his message-board on the bed and rose slowly. In three steps he had crossed the cell and was standing over Kaire, one hand fingering a thin black cylinder tucked into his belt. 'I'll ask you once more. What is your home village?'

'It's a community, not a village, and it has always been known as Skyz59.'

The electric charge hit Kaire's right shoulder, sending him sprawling. The acrid smell of burnt flesh filled the cell.

'That was for insolence,' said Medite, his tone bland. 'I don't care what you call this Skyz59, which by the way I have never heard of.' He tucked the charger back into his belt. 'So Prisoner Breta, in which zone would I find this place?'

'No zone.'

Medite pursed his lips and looked thoughtful. 'Interesting, Prisoner Breta, are you trying to tell me you're from over ocean?'

'No, not in the precise meaning of the phrase.'

Half-blinded by the lights, Kaire didn't see the raised fist, felt only searing pain in his abdomen. Clutching his stomach, he fell to one side.

Medite laughed. 'I get it, you fell out of the sky!' A boot made contact with Kaire's backside. 'Get up, you pathetic fool.'

Kaire struggled to a sitting position and said quietly, 'I didn't fall, sir. I landed, taking due care not to damage my ship.'

'Ah, now we're getting somewhere.' Medite smiled. 'And where did you land?'

'An Asian Zone backwater near the Border River.'

'Excellent, excellent.' A second kick landed on Kaire's right thigh. 'Why did you come to Australia, Prisoner Breta?'

'I had business with an Asian woman.'

'What business?'

'I had to save her.'

'From whom?'

'Herself.'

This time Kaire didn't even see the flash that jolted through his body and left him shaking uncontrollably.

'Where did you depart from?' Medite demanded, holding the charger directly in front of Kaire's face.

'Aotearoa,' said Kaire, his voice barely audible.

'Louder, Prisoner Breta.'

'Aotearoa, the land of the long white cloud.'

A self-satisfied smile coated the officer's lips as he moved across the cell. Lifting his message-board from the bed, he said curtly, 'Interview terminated.'


A fallen branch across the tracks delayed the train taking Tiki north and it was already light when she arrived at the Asian Zone train terminus a short distance from the Border River. Apart from the unexpected delay, it had been a long night, the train journey through two zones always slow once over the border on account of numerous stops to offload materials requiring assembly in Asian village factories. Fortunately, she managed to secure a lift in a trooper car that was returning to Village 2 immediately, so was spared a lengthy walk. The young driver seemed friendly, inviting her to sit in front beside him rather than in the back seat hemmed in by the parcels he'd collected from the train. Tiki could have shown him her ID and travel tag but preferred they speak as equals. Conversation covered a variety of topics from recent heavy rains and unusually high temperatures to his previous stint as a border guard, a task he'd obviously found tedious. He also showed interest in her journey from the south, but she was careful not to supply the exact location of her home village and was suitably vague about her reason for visiting Village 2 even though she knew he would find out before long.

On arrival at the trooper station, Tiki thanked the trooper for the lift and instead of following him inside, made her way to the local inn. She felt in need of a meal and some strong coffee before tackling the trooper-in-charge. The inn seemed deserted and she was about to leave when a short, stocky man bustled in from a back room and greeted her warmly.

'Greetings to you too, innkeeper,' she replied. 'I realise it's early but could I have some food? I've been travelling all night and train fare is appalling.'

'No trouble at all, my wife's just made our breakfast. Why don't you join us?' He gestured towards the open door. 'Better than sitting out here on your own.'

'Thank you, much appreciated.'

She followed him into a combined kitchen-living room that looked out over a vegetable garden. 'You have a pleasant outlook, innkeeper, and how sensible to grow your own produce.'

'It's better than relying on the market, but my wife must take the credit.'

The petite woman standing quietly by the stove turned and smiled. 'Greetings, what can I get you?'

'Whatever you and your husband are having would be fine.'

'Fried eggs and mushrooms with freshly baked bread, followed by coffee.'

'That sounds delicious.'

'Do sit down,' said the innkeeper, indicating the recycled plastic chairs arranged around a small table.

Tiki smiled. 'Thank you.' She moved the few steps to the table and deliberately chose the only chair with a cushion, as befitted her White status.

The food was indeed delicious, the coffee strong, sweet and black just as Tiki liked it. But it wasn't just the meal that made the detour to the inn worthwhile; the snippets of conversation exchanged between mouthfuls by husband and wife provided interesting information. Tiki learned she wasn't the first White visitor to Village 2 that week. A security officer had spent several hours resting at the inn before being taken by trooper car to the train terminus.

'I suppose he was in transit,' Tiki remarked, 'and like me, couldn't face train fare.'

'Oh no,' answered the innkeeper, 'he went first to the trooper station according to the driver. He had to interview a prisoner.'

'It turns out that Whitefella the troopers caught on the border bridge was an illegal,' said the innkeeper's wife in a low voice.

'An illegal,' Tiki repeated. 'Are you sure you heard right? We haven't had illegals for centuries. Australia is hardly a favoured destination.'

The innkeeper shrugged. 'That's what the young trooper said. Anyhow, whatever the prisoner was, they've already moved him to a more secure facility.'

Tiki disguised her unease by looking down at her coffee cup.

'They took him just on dawn,' the innkeeper continued. 'I woke early, heard a bit of a ruckus coming from the trooper station so I went out in the garden to have a look. Good view from there, right into the entrance, we're a bit higher up here, see.'

Tiki looked up and nodded.

'Struggled a bit he did, shouted too, till they shoved something in his mouth.'

'Did you hear what he said?' Tiki asked, raising her head.

'Didn't make any sense, something about sky and ship and desert. I reckon he was raving.'

'Weird,' Tiki agreed. 'Perhaps he'd been drugged?'

'On drugs more like,' said the innkeeper's wife.

Her husband nodded in agreement.

Sensing she would learn nothing more, Tiki pushed her plate to the centre of the table. 'Thank you so much for the meal, what do I owe you?'

The innkeeper waved his hand. 'Nothing, I enjoyed your company.'

'I'm glad.' Tiki stood up. 'Sorry to leave so soon but I'm expected at the medical station.'

Both husband and wife smiled.

'End of the street, turn right, then first left,' said the innkeeper. 'Nothing wrong I hope?'

Tiki shook her head. 'I'm a surgeon,' she murmured and, picking up her bag, walked out of the room.

Outside the street was deserted but Tiki couldn't risk meeting anyone, so she headed away from the trooper station, slipping down side streets and between buildings until she reached the western edge of the village. Fields and the Border River lay to her right, while to her left a patch of wasteland led to what looked like a factory. She walked steadily towards the building, intending to mention a machine accident if she were approached. Much to her relief, the large metal doors remained closed as she drew nearer, so she presumed the dayshift had yet to begin. Skirting around the building, she made her way over stony ground to a collection of old sheds she'd noticed lining the rail tracks on her journey from the train terminus. An overhanging roof afforded a little shade, so she stopped to catch her breath. After checking that no one was in the vicinity, she decided to see if any of the sheds were unlocked. If they were just for storage, it would make sense to remain out of sight until just before the next southern train departed. The second door yielded to a prod, revealing a jumble of rusted track and piles of crumbling concrete sleepers that looked as though they had been there for years. Slipping inside, Tiki closed the door behind her and, taking care not to disturb anything, sat down in a narrow gap between piles.

Tiki woke to total darkness, a quick check of her timepiece revealing she'd slept for an unbelievable twelve hours! By now the train would be hundreds of kilometres south. She dismissed thoughts of a sleeping draught slipped into her breakfast, all three portions had been served from the same pan and the coffee poured from the same pot. Her exhaustion was the result of a sleepless night worrying about the impending mission. Soon after Kela's second communication, a stranger, her image also blocked, had advised the prisoner's exact location, increasing Tiki's trepidation.

News of her visit was bound to circulate around the village, so Tiki picked her way to the door, guided by her communicator light beam. Several tugs on the rusting handle (no cybernetic door panel here) and she was outside, enveloped by a night sky thick with cloud. She decided to take advantage of darkness by walking to the next station down the line. Her medic's ID should see her pass through the station checkpoint without undue scrutiny and if asked for her travel tag, she could easily recount a story about being sent initially to the wrong village. No Asian station worker would query a White doctor's explanation.

According to her navigation aid, the next village was twenty kilometres due south, an easy walk for a woman like Tiki, used to walking fairly long distances. Although entitled to use the car attached to the medical centre where she worked, Tiki preferred to walk unless the weather was inclement or the matter urgent. Walking cleared her mind and gave her a short space of time away from a climate-controlled environment, even though the outside atmosphere could hardly be termed 'fresh' when night temperatures rarely dropped below thirty degrees Celsius. The coastal strip of the southern White Zone had been a semi-arid region for more than a hundred years, prone to dust storms from the encroaching desert and gales that whipped up the sea separating the mainland from the Isle of Tasman. Tiki had visited the island, home to all politicians and senior bureaucrats, once during childhood; her family had been invited to the opening of a new high-tech medical centre on account of her father's status as Surgeon-General. The journey had been her first by sea, an adventure for a girl who seldom ventured far from home. Few Australians travelled any distance even in their own country unless work required it, and none of Tiki's contemporaries had ever been over ocean.

Lights in the distance prompted another glance at her timepiece and Tiki realised the sun would soon be rising. Several kilometres back, she had swallowed the last mouthful of water in her small travelling flask, so looked forward to buying a drink from the station vending machine. Thick cloud cover had kept the temperature high all night and the breeze, although warm, had dropped entirely around midnight. Drenched in perspiration, she longed for a shower but that would have to wait until she boarded the train. Unlike White Zone stations, where full facilities were provided in gleaming bathrooms, Asian Zone stations offered a single toilet and washbasin, usually cracked and invariably dirty. A rumbling stomach reminded Tiki she was also hungry but she would have to make do with dry crackers and a substance resembling cheese until she got home, dining modules considered unnecessary luxuries on chiefly produce-carrying trains. At least the single passenger module would be comfortable with large reclining seats, plenty of legroom and a variety of entertainment available on decent-sized individual screens.

A small brick building built close to the rail tracks came into view, so before moving into the light, she stopped to wipe away perspiration and dust, using hand-gel and a wound dressing from her bag. Then she raked a comb through her thick curly hair, applied lip-colour and wiped over her shoes with the remainder of the gel. Inside the station office, the lone worker appeared to be asleep, eyes closed and arms hanging limply by his side. Tapping on the grimy window several times failed to rouse him, so she resorted to banging her fist on a nearby door, which seemed closer to the worker's chair. Arms stretched and yawns spilled from a wide-open mouth, the man was clearly in no hurry to respond. After peering in the direction of the window for some time, he struggled to his feet, ambled over and pressed a panel on his work-module to raise the glass a fraction.

'You're a bit early for the six-fifteen,' he muttered. 'Let's have your ID then.'

Tiki pushed the plastic card through the opening.

'Sorry, Doctor, didn't mean to be rude.' He smiled and returned the card.

'No problem. I expect, like me, you've had a long night.' She opened her bag and began to rummage around as though searching for her travel tag.

'Sure have, I'm looking forward to breakfast and a long sleep.' He released the barrier.

There were no other passengers waiting on either of the chipped concrete benches positioned in front of the station building. Thankful she wouldn't have to make small talk, Tiki wandered over to the bench furthest from the station office and sat down. Her legs ached from the long walk over sodden grass and bare ground littered with puddles and slippery stones. She longed to kick off her shoes but worried in case her feet swelled. No White doctor would board a train barefoot. An hour remained until the train's arrival twenty kilometres from where she was supposed to be. Tiki wondered if the prisoner—Kela hadn't supplied a name—had known an attempt would be made to free him and what would happen now that he'd been moved to a high-security prison. She imagined he must be a high-ranking individual to warrant such intervention and dreaded telling Kela the mission had failed.

The third communication from Kela, once more audio only, came as Tiki sank into a chair in her small apartment, weary from the long journey. A lengthy silence followed Tiki's brief report.

'Are you still there?' Tiki asked, concerned she had let her friend down.

'Yes, sorry it was the shock.'

'What happens next?'

'Out of my hands, I'm afraid.'

'I'll assist if you need me.'

'Thanks, I …' Kela hesitated, unsure whether to mention the idea she'd been mulling over for days. 'Would you ever consider a new position?'

'It would depend what and where.'

'Less status and remuneration but a delightful setting and interesting colleagues.'

'Sounds intriguing.'

'Think about it, could be a life-changing experience. Communication terminated.'

# CHAPTER 10

The Sky-ship felt like a prison chamber, albeit more comfortable but nevertheless claustrophobic. Boredom had set in almost immediately, Pia accustomed to working long hours. There was a limit to the number of monitor games she could play or exercises she could do in the cramped space between seats and storage module wall. Now, after seven days with few communications from Kauri Haven and those offering little hope for a quick departure, fear had replaced boredom. She knew why the mission had failed, but so far there had been no mention of another rescue attempt. While she appreciated this was for security reasons, Pia felt frustrated at her inability to help Kaire, especially considering how much he'd assisted the Women's Line, and all for a people and a land to which he owed no loyalty. She couldn't imagine how he would be feeling now, confined in a prison chamber with no possibility of a fair trial. What if the authorities uncovered his real identity and learned he was the man wanted in connection with assisting political prisoners to flee the country? There would be no leniency then on account of his white skin, the death penalty a foregone conclusion.

Disheartened by negative speculation, Pia turned away from the console and peered out at the now familiar desert. Once more a fiery sun was sinking over the dune, turning the cloudless sky deepening shades of yellow and red. *A sunset splendid when viewed from the comfort of a climate-controlled environment,* she thought, *but a treacherous reminder of loss for those forced to live according to the Nocturnal Life Project.* She envisaged her friends in the Brown Zone, burrowing underground like animals to sleep during daylight hours, emerging only when shadow cloaked the sky.

The sky had faded to gloomy grey when Pia heard voices outside—at least four men shouting to one another, astonished by their find. Alarmed, she quickly moved away from the window and crawled into the space behind the seats. Words became indistinct; she heard raucous laughter, the thud of boots kicking metal, the scrape of knives seeking a way in. The sound of her breathing seemed to fill the capsule; surely the men would realise the craft was occupied? In an attempt to stifle sound, she held her mouth close to the pilot seat's thick fabric and listened intently for the clatter of invasion. None came and from the expletives erupting with singular regularity, she realised the men had failed to penetrate the Sky-ship's smooth exterior. Both pilot and storage module doors were difficult to see from the ground, a thin line around the panels the only sign entry could be gained at these points. By now the Sky-ship would be covered in a layer of windblown sand, the tell-tale outlines obscured. On several occasions during the past week, sand had battered the curved window as windstorms swept across the desert, shifting the shape of dunes and carrying clouds of red dust all the way to the coast.

Voices faded and Pia deemed it safe to risk a glance out the window to determine whether the men were troopers or travellers out for a jaunt in the desert. As she'd feared, a silver trooper car, clearly visible in the bright moonlight, was parked a short distance from the front of the Sky-ship. Through its open door panels, she could see two men sitting in the rear, a third in the driver's seat and a fourth about to step inside. Retreating behind the seats, she waited a few minutes before chancing another move forward, where a quick look showed a plume of sand spewing from behind the car as it sped east. She slipped into the pilot's seat and pressed the communication panel.

'Go ahead Skyz59.323,' said Mac.

Pia managed to speak slowly and calmly but he could see the fear reflected in her brown eyes as she stared at the screen.

'What should I do?' she asked finally. 'They're bound to return.'

'I agree. You must leave at once. Take the transporter and head north, following the edge of the desert.'

'How far north?'

Mac frowned. 'How far can the transporter travel before it needs recharging?'

'Not sure but I believe it's at least two thousand kilometres.'

'Right, if that's the case, head for Line Leader Zira's village. Do you know her?'

'We've spoken many times and I've seen her on screen but we've never met.' Pia shuddered, recalling the communication from Zira that had led to the current situation.

'Something wrong?'

'No, it's just a bit cold in here.'

Mac smiled. 'Sending coordinates now.'

Figures flashed into the top corner of the screen. 'Received.'

'Good. Don't worry about ID, I'll contact Zira.'

Pia nodded and saw Mac turn his head as though someone had entered his office. 'Just one more question, Mac: what's the situation with K?'

'Seeking location.'

'Get him out Mac, I beg you.'

'We're confident of a positive outcome. Connection terminating.'

Mac's shrewd response and prompt disconnection convinced Pia he knew far more but was reluctant to discuss the situation. Perhaps a rescue mission was already in hand, a team heading for the prison with plans to cause a distraction, such as the fire that had enabled Kaire to spirit her away from a smoke-filled community dome and fly her to safety in Aotearoa. She concentrated on preparations for the journey north, refusing to dwell on the negative outcomes of that mission, two fire-related deaths and the failure to rescue her mother.

Only a few provisions, mostly dried fruit and nuts, remained in the capsule locker but there was the tube of Sustenance, which Pia figured should last until she reached the fertile coastal strip where crops grew in abundance. Zira's village, remote and rarely visited, would be a safe place to wait for the ship Pia had no doubt would be sent to take her back to Aotearoa. Apart from growing tropical fruit, rice and sugar cane, the village served as the first in a line of spotter stations that monitored a wide area of ocean for the ships from neighbouring

Indonesia that frequently commandeered Australian cargo vessels or ships suspected of carrying fugitives from prisons.

Pia knew the transporter would have to be hidden some distance from the village, if possible beyond the range of a trooper car. Somehow she would also have to acquire a suitable robe before entering the village; the baggy pants and loose over-shirt worn for visiting the Asian Zone was bound to attract attention in the far north. At least she had a head-cloth for protection from the sun and sturdy sandals that should stand up to a lengthy walk across rough terrain. Quickly packing provisions and personal communicator into her small backpack, she headed for the cargo module, hoping the transporter thrusters would engage at the first attempt.

The journey north proved uneventful. She kept away from paths and super-paths, driving instead close to the outer edge of the desert across sun-baked plains roamed long ago by White pastoralists' sheep and cattle. Patches of dry grass clung on in sallow depressions but otherwise the ground was bare, dried out from lack of moisture, a maze of cracks littering the surface. Pia deliberately restricted travel to daylight hours because the transporter's climate control system worked more efficiently at a speed she wouldn't risk in the dark. At night she tried to find something to hide behind, a rocky outcrop or a dried-up riverbed with high banks, even though it was unlikely troopers would be scanning the region. The light beams capable of long-range scanning required huge amounts of energy so were never used indiscriminately.

After three days travelling north, Pia deemed it safe to turn east and after negotiating several deep depressions littered with rocks, decided to risk sliding down a sandy bank onto a dry riverbed that stretched, according to the navigation system, for a hundred kilometres. The moderately smooth surface with few potholes or loose pebbles enabled the transporter to travel at high speed for some time, but she was forced to slow down when the wheels began to slip. In the distance she could see the shimmer of water, so guided the vehicle onto what appeared to be firmer ground running parallel to a chain of shallow pools hugging the right-hand bank.

The pools became larger, finally merging into a ribbon of water that meandered from bank to bank following the contours of the riverbed.

As far as possible, Pia kept to dry ground, conscious of coming darkness and the need to find cover. Total camouflage would be impossible in this landscape but she could at least cover the two bubbles to prevent sunlight striking the glass and igniting nearby dry grasses. A fire, even some distance from a village or fields, would be certain to attract attention. After rounding a bend, she noticed what appeared to be a breach in the left-hand bank a short distance ahead and slowed to investigate. When the transporter's wheels entered the water, the splash was slight and a sideways glance showed the creek had split into two, the main branch continuing to flow due east while the tributary, a thin strip of barely moving water, appeared to be heading north. She turned with care and entered a narrow channel bounded by steep sandstone banks topped with sparse foliage. In less than a hundred metres, the water disappeared beneath a shelf of smooth rock that stretched as far as Pia could see in the fading light. Disinclined to venture much further, she pulled into the left-hand bank and disengaged the thrusters.

She woke to torrential rain striking glass and metal, the noise overwhelming, the sense of entrapment acute. With shaking fingers, she switched on the front light beam and gasped at the volume of water flooding down the gorge. The transporter would be engulfed within minutes and she had no idea if it could float! Reaching into the rear seat, she grabbed the bag containing provisions and water flask, clipped her communicator into a side pocket and extinguished the light beam. The bubble seal appeared to be stuck and it took her several attempts to lift the bubble high enough to wriggle through. Holding the bag above her head, she slipped down the transporter's convex side into the water. For a few moments there was rock beneath her feet, but it disappeared once she stepped forward and she thrashed around trying to regain her footing and keep the bag dry. Perched once more on the rock platform, water up her waist, she peered into darkness, straining to see if the transporter had moved. Rain and a new moon shrouded in cloud had reduced visibility; she could barely make out the transporter, let alone the riverbank. She was toying between trying to grab the protruding edge of a bubble or wading towards the bank where rocky outcrops might supply a foothold, when the current dragged her into the middle of the creek. Water swirled around her chest and her arms ached from holding the bag above her head. Aware she couldn't remain upright much longer, Pia threw the bag with all the strength she could muster towards the opposite bank, hoping it would lodge on a rocky ledge high above the raging torrent or come to rest on the top. After gulping mouthfuls of air, she struck out for the bank, her limbs fighting against the current.

When her bare feet finally touched bottom, her sandals having worked loose and disappeared, Pia inched her way forward, expecting to soon touch the bank and was astounded to find it no longer existed; she was walking over drowned foliage. Keen to avoid injury from broken sticks or sharp stones, she took small steps until her feet sank into thick mud and the water level dropped rapidly. A few more steps and she stood on sodden grass, a strong breeze blowing drops of water from her hair. The rain had stopped but she dared not sit down to rest, so she struggled forward blindly until a shadow loomed ahead. Feeling her way with her hands, she crawled onto a smooth rock. A small depression on one side had filled with rain but Pia scarcely noticed as she lowered her backside into the water.

Morning light revealed an altered topography. Water dominated the scene, the two creeks having merged to become a lake. Before scrambling down from the rock, Pia surveyed the new landscape, trying to determine where the creeks had been. To the north she could see a chain of rocks protruding from the lake and concluded they could be the highest part of the gorge's eastern flank. Behind these rocks, the lake extended for several metres before petering out, but there was no sign of the transporter or her bag. Her priority was to find shelter, the sun at this early hour already burning the top of her head, but first she must drink. Kneeling at the lake edge, she scooped water into her mouth, hoping that being recent rain, it wouldn't be contaminated by the residue from old mines that still polluted Brown Zone creeks. Thirst quenched, she veered away from the lake and, keeping to the right of the rocks, headed northeast towards a low ridge rising from the plain a short distance away. With luck she would find a rock crevice or bushes up there to shelter from the sun until late afternoon when she would try to retrace her steps. She knew from experience that lakes and pools created by storm run-off soon soaked into the bone-dry ground, leaving behind a mess of tangled vegetation littered with small stones gouged from riverbed and banks.

No bushes or boulders large enough to provide shade were visible as Pia climbed and she began to think her walk, much longer than expected, had been a pointless exercise. From the summit, she saw a grassy plateau and was tempted to descend, take a gamble she would find vegetation or at least a wide crevice on the other side. Halfway down, rock gave way to sandy soil still damp from the night's deluge and covered in places with dry flattened grass. A dark shape to her right promised shade and soon she encountered a rocky ledge with a hollow space beneath. Crawling inside, she welcomed the feel of cool earth on hands and feet. There was only just room to sit with her back hard against a bank of soil and her head bent, but fortunately the spoon-shaped hollow was long enough to lay stretched out.

From her vantage point, Pia took note of a range of hills in the east, beyond which she hoped would be a village, or at the very least a creek where she could bathe and drink. Haze over the hills disguised their height but she had learned sufficient geography in the school dome to know the land in this region of the Brown Zone did not rise to any great elevation. Down on the plain, she could see a gash in the earth suggesting a river had once flowed west of the range and figured if the storm had been extensive, pools of water would remain there for at least a few days.

The day seemed interminable, hours of sitting interspersed with lying on her back staring at the myriad flaws in the rock shelf above her head. Periodically she considered venturing outside to stretch limbs and torso but rejected the idea, aware her white clothing would be visible down on the plain. By late afternoon dark clouds had gathered, promising another storm, so she left her refuge and hurried back down the hillside, anxious to be well away from swollen creeks before another deluge descended. Her mouth felt dry and gritty as though she'd swallowed mouthfuls of soil; she must drink soon or risk dehydration. Food was essential too, if she were to embark on another trek of indeterminate length; without her communicator, she could only guess the distance to the coast.

Walking back to the swollen creeks, Pia thought of Australia's first people, not the White explorers from Europe she'd been led to believe were the original inhabitants, but the long departed Aboriginal tribes Kaire had told her once lived in every part of the continent. Hunters and gatherers, they had lived in harmony with the land for sixty thousand years, taking only what was needed to sustain life, leaving the rest for other creatures to enjoy or for people that followed in their footsteps. They had no need of trains or ships to transport mass-produced goods from place to place, or herds of cloven-hoofed animals that pounded the fragile topsoil until it blew away in the wind. Australia, the golden land to those that came seeking freedom from poverty or oppression, degraded now beyond repair by the greed of humankind.

Head bowed against the wind, Pia plodded the final few metres towards life-giving water, clinging to a last vestige of hope that the bag had surfaced and her Skyman's Sustenance tablets, encased in plastic tubes, would be undamaged.

# CHAPTER 11

In the administration block of an Asian Zone prison far from the Border River, Security Officer Medite and Trooper-in-Charge Eben were discussing a report the latter had received the previous day concerning their new arrival, Prisoner Breta. During a routine patrol of land bordering the desert, four troopers had lost their bearings and discovered a cone-shaped metal vehicle with wings, reminiscent of the aircraft possessed by affluent countries. Further examination by a second group had secured entry to a cockpit furnished with two seats and a highly sophisticated console. A trooper experienced in IT had been swiftly despatched to the site and after several hours had managed to activate part of the console. Subsequent manipulation had retrieved a personnel profile document, which revealed the pilot to be Skyz59.323, responsible to a Commander Breta. Unfortunately, there was no accompanying image or DNA record, and despite a thorough search of the surrounding area no sign of the pilot had been found. It was presumed he or she remained at large somewhere in the Asian Zone or had succumbed to desert heat and dehydration.

Medite asserted that the aircraft must have been engaged in surveillance when forced for some reason to land in the desert. As far as the troopers could tell, the craft was undamaged, so the pilot had obviously had sufficient time to execute an emergency landing. Conversely, Trooper Eben believed the aircraft transporting Commander Breta had simply veered off course and, running low on fuel, the pilot had decided to land in the desert and remain there until another craft arrived to replenish the tanks.

After hearing Eben's explanation, Medite leaned forward in his chair and, looking into the trooper's world-weary face, said curtly, 'Twenty-fifth century aircraft do not veer off course. They are equipped with sophisticated navigation systems that ensure adherence to a scheduled route. Besides, there was no need to be flying anywhere near Australia. We have no air bases and are not on any trade routes.'

Eben scratched his chin. 'Sure, but whatever the reason they landed in the desert, the fact remains there's no sign of the pilot and no incriminating evidence has been found either on the aircraft console or on my prisoner's personal communicator. We should tread carefully. Imprisoning this commander could cause a serious diplomatic incident. The pilot would no doubt have relayed exact location coordinates to his base, wherever it is.'

Medite nodded in agreement, then added in an authoritative tone, 'And now I require immediate access to the prisoner.'

'He will be sleeping now. You can see him in the morning.'

'I said immediate, and if you refuse again I shall contact my superior who will swiftly override your authority.'

'Very well, but I insist, as is my right, on being present.'

'Of course, it's standard practice for two officers to interview a high-ranking prisoner. What do you take me for?'

Eben wanted to answer 'an arrogant little shit' but restrained himself and slowly rose from his chair. 'The cells are below ground,' he advised, flashing a wry smile. 'It's standard practice in these parts, it prevents escape.'

Seconds before the cell lights blazed, the protracted creak of a rusting door panel roused Kaire from a light sleep. He tensed on recognising Medite, fearing a second bout of torture but relaxed a little when the trooper-in-charge entered the cell.

'My apologies for disturbing your rest, Commander,' said Eben, striding over to the narrow bed where Kaire sat hunched against the wall hugging his knees.

'No need to apologise, sir.' Kaire wondered why he had suddenly acquired the status of commander.

'Sit on the floor, Prisoner Breta,' ordered Medite. 'I wish to sit in relative comfort.'

Kaire moved quickly without straightening the rumpled bedclothes and sat cross-legged against the opposite wall, hands clasped over his still bruised abdomen. Eben continued to stand, his right boot tapping the concrete floor as though he were already bored with proceedings.

'Do sit down, Eben,' said Medite, clearly agitated, 'there's plenty of room for two.'

The older man ambled forward and, easing his large frame onto the bed, spread his legs deliberately so that his short tunic rose up and his right thigh, hairy and creased with rolls of fat, rubbed against Medite's skinny left.

'Prisoner Breta, we have discovered your aircraft,' Medite began, pulling out his message-board and laying it on his knees.

Kaire blanched. Did they have Pia in custody too?

'An impressive vehicle,' Medite continued, grimacing as he felt the heat of Eben's thick thigh. 'Capable of long-range flights, I imagine.'

Kaire nodded.

'In that case perhaps you could explain why you told me earlier that you had travelled from Aotearoa, a mere hop across the Tasman.'

'My sh … I mean craft, is employed for long or short-range flights.'

Medite looked down, slim fingers moving over the message-board screen as he formulated the next question. 'And it's programmed for surveillance?'

'A scanner is used to survey and map landscape, if that's what you mean.'

Medite leapt to his feet, sending the message-board flying. It landed close to Kaire's feet. 'You know very well what I mean. You were sent to spy on us.'

'Whatever for?' Kaire answered, keeping his eyes lowered in mock-humility as he scrutinised the message-board at his feet. 'There is nothing in this country that would interest my superiors.'

'Not even political prisoners?'

'My orders are not to intervene in the affairs of this nation,' Kaire answered, grateful the colour rising in his cheeks remained obscured.

Exasperated, Medite began to pace the cell while Eben laughed inwardly at the sight of a security officer about to lose his cool but prevented by protocol from striking a high-ranking prisoner.

'So, Commander Breta,' Eben said calmly, 'perhaps you could inform us why it was necessary to adopt a different identity when crossing from one zone to another and how you travelled from the desert to an Asian Zone village.'

As Medite paced away from him, Kaire looked up and deliberately caught Eben's eye while pressing the disengage panel on the message-board at his feet. 'My mission was to enter this country surreptitiously, which is why I landed in the desert. A woman in my department who excels at forgery supplied me with false ID. Actually she was once a prisoner herself.'

'I don't fucking care what she was,' Medite yelled, turning on his heel and marching towards Kaire. 'Get on with the fucking explanation, I haven't got all night.'

'My apologies, sir.' Once more Kaire bent his head. 'I travelled to Village 2 in my equivalent of what you call a car, for the sole purpose of apprehending one of our most troublesome prisoners who absconded some time ago. The false ID was necessary to enable me to enter the house where we believed she had been given refuge. Unfortunately, when I arrived it appeared the ever-resourceful escapee had drugged her protector and left the premises.'

'The name of this woman?'

'Kiwa.'

'And her crime?'

'Betraying government secrets.'

Medite stooped and picked up the message-board, passing it from one hand to the other as he absorbed unexpected information. Kaire sat silent and still, trusting his half-truths would be accepted, unaware Medite had no way of checking their authenticity. The Aotearoan government had severed diplomatic ties with its neighbour several centuries earlier due to Australia's poor treatment of environmental refugees.

'So we are in the same business,' said Medite, looking down at Kaire with an almost benign expression. 'However, although I appreciate you were dealing with a sensitive situation, it would have been courteous to advise my department of your intentions. Supposing we ...'

'Impossible,' Kaire interjected, rising to his feet. 'You know relations between our two countries are cool to say the least.'

Medite looked towards Eben for support but the trooper remained silent, relishing the other's discomfort.

'As I was saying,' Medite continued, 'supposing we had destroyed your aircraft in the belief it represented a threat to this country?'

Kaire laughed, confidence returning as he towered over the young officer. 'That would have been extremely foolish considering your country lacks aircraft of any kind.'

Eben stood up. 'Interview terminated. Nothing will be gained by you two sniping at one another.' He walked over to Medite. 'Commander Breta has explained his business here so I suggest we adjourn to my office to organise his return to Aotearoa. In the absence of his pilot, arrangements will have to be made to retrieve the aircraft at a later date.'

'Absence? What have you done with her?' Kaire demanded, taking a step towards Medite.

'Nothing, Commander,' Eben replied, quickly stepping between them. 'There was no trace of her in your aircraft and no unknown car has been sighted either in the vicinity of Village 2 or near the aircraft.'

Kaire paled. 'I must contact her immediately, she could have had an accident, she could be lying injured in the desert.'

Medite smirked. 'Fond of her, are you?'

'Yes, as matter of fact, but that's beside the point. More important is to determine whether she took my transporter when she left the aircraft. It's a valuable vehicle and I have no wish to return home without it. Did your troopers' report mention a vehicle in the rear compartment?'

Eden shook his head. 'According to the report, they were unable to gain entry to the rear of your aircraft.'

'That's something to be thankful for,' Kaire muttered. 'At least they won't have caused any damage.'

Eben gestured towards the opening door panel. 'You may communicate with your pilot from my office.' He turned to Medite. 'Go and fetch Commander Breta's belongings and after that organise some refreshments.'

Medite opened his mouth to protest this, in his opinion, unwarranted command, then changed his mind and hurriedly left the cell.

Back in the administration block, Trooper-in-Charge Eben made a quick call to Security Department headquarters while Kaire dressed in the adjoining office. Once connected to an officer in the Personnel database section, he asked if a Commander Breta was listed. The reply came swiftly.

'Alien operative, sir. Home base unknown.'

'Any other details?'

'I'll just check.'

'Mentioned during the 2400 treason case of Sannah the Storyteller, Village 10, Brown Zone but never authenticated.'

'Right, thank you.'

Eben had just finished noting the case details on his message-board when Kaire, dressed in clean clothing and carrying his backpack, entered the room. 'Take a seat, Commander,' Eben said brightly. 'Refreshments are on the way.'

'Thank you.' Kaire walked over to the chair in front of the work-module and sat down.

'Any luck with your pilot?' Eben asked.

'There's no response from my transporter, which is a concern. However, I was able to leave a message on her personal communicator. Hopefully she will get in touch shortly.'

'Yes, it would be most unfortunate if she'd had an accident in the desert.'

Kaire nodded. 'On reflection I think that is unlikely. When I didn't turn up at the rendezvous and she couldn't contact me, she would have returned to the aircraft as we had arranged. But as your troopers didn't find her there and I can't raise the transporter communicator, I imagine the vehicle broke down en route and she has continued on foot.'

'Surely she wouldn't risk walking in the desert?' Eben queried, astonished that anyone would be so foolish.

'She is very fit and may have been within a reasonable distance of the aircraft.'

Eben was about to ask in that case why hadn't she answered her communicator, when Medite arrived carrying a tray laden with plates of food, a bottle of wine and three tumblers.

'Ah, there you are, Medite,' Eben said pleasantly. 'Just put it on my work-module. That will make it easier for you to pass the refreshments around.'

Despite his irritation at being ordered about by someone of inferior rank, Medite complied, making sure he served the commander first.

'You're very young to be a commander,' Eben observed after taking several gulps of wine. 'In this country few reach such a high rank before middle-age.'

Immediately, Medite shifted his attention from tasty sandwich to youthful commander. 'Yes, I must congratulate you on such a swift rise through the ranks.'

'It's not such a high rank in our service,' Kaire answered, gripping both plate and tumbler to steady his shaking hands. 'It simply means I'm in command of a particular mission.'

'How odd,' Eben remarked, a frown creasing his forehead.

'It's just a question of language,' Kaire said confidently, his nerves now under control. 'I find trooper rather an old-fashioned term to use for a law and order officer.'

'Touché,' Medite muttered.

They continued eating and drinking in silence, all three eager to bring the enforced acquaintance to an end as soon as possible.

# CHAPTER 12

Night had fallen by the time Pia arrived back at the rapidly receding lake, her final steps guided by moonlight. After drinking slowly to avoid bloating or nausea, she returned to the rock where she'd rested after the storm, curled into the shallow depression and fell asleep instantly, her head resting on her arms. Sleep was deep and dreamless, a falling into welcome oblivion. Exhausted from lack of food and the trek from her daylight refuge in the hills, she slept undisturbed for many hours, the second storm having bypassed the area, dark clouds retreating seaward without releasing a drop of rain.

Now fully awake, she became increasingly aware of the hunger pangs twisting her stomach into knots and berated herself for driving into a narrow channel lined with rock. The transporter had most likely been swept downstream and, even if recovered, would probably be extensively damaged and unable to be driven. Hundreds of kilometres lay between her current location and the Sky-ship; her stupidity had cost the only means she and Kaire had to return to the Sky-ship and make their escape from this blighted land.

Faint light in the east drew Pia's attention away from past misdeeds to her present desperate situation. She had perhaps two or three days to live if she failed to find the backpack or at the very least something in which to carry water. Death was a certainty if she remained by the river—no one would come looking for her here and it was unlikely anyone ever travelled this way. Most Australians feared the ever-encroaching desert and kept to coastal paths or train lines on the rare occasions they travelled far from their home villages. She wondered how far it was to the main South-North line, and whether trains even ran this far north. Determined to think of something positive, she decided to search the riverbank for the pack and risk repeated dives to the riverbed to see if it had become entangled in debris.

Reluctant to wait a moment longer, Pia set off for the river, her bare feet squelching in warm mud as she neared the water's edge. Ahead, the rocky sides of the gorge were half-exposed now, sandstone glowing pink in dawn's pale light. A few metres downstream rock tapered to a manageable height and soon disappeared altogether, so she slipped over the side into the water. She had to wade a fair way into the creek to find clear water and drank only a small amount, uncertain how an empty stomach would respond to too much liquid. The creek still flowed fast but was contained within steep earth banks, though whether these were in the same location as before the storm, she couldn't tell. Debris carried through the gorge swirled around her, vegetation stripped from bank and rock crevice along with small branches denuded of leaves. Thick mud sucked her feet; she hoped the rock platform lay underneath. Reaching out, she grabbed a branch, figuring she could peel off the bark and make a watertight container by weaving the strands together. After throwing it onto the bank, she ducked under to cleanse dust from hair and face before wading back to shore.

Numerous dives in the vicinity of where she thought the rock platform had been failed to locate either backpack or transporter, so she concluded both had been swept far downstream. Following the left-hand bank, she made her way back to the convergence of the two creeks. Here the torrent had gouged wide arcs and a mat of rotting vegetation steaming in the sun hugged the opposite bank. With difficulty, she scrambled down and swam over but there was nothing foreign among the leaves and branches, so she took a deep breath and dived to inspect the underside. There was no sign of the backpack but she did find something to eat. A small branch clasped in her hand, she surfaced quickly and swam back to the opposite bank. The moment her feet touched mud, she picked several of the small yellow fruit and stuffed them in her mouth. Once known as Kakadu plums, (northern

Brown Zoners called them sun-plums) the fruit contained large quantities of vitamin C and were also useful in healing balms. Pia had eaten sun-plums during her time at the youth working party but hadn't realised they still grew wild in the isolated pockets of bush still remaining in the north.

Back on dry ground, she picked the branch clean, filling her pockets before tying the remaining fruit in her shirt. The sun was already hot and she was tempted to slip back into the water until the heat of the day had diminished, but dismissed that idea and set off again. Every few metres she paused to look over the bank but saw nothing except vegetation and insects taking advantage of a free ride downstream. Intermittently she stopped to eat more fruit and then slide into the water to drink and cool off, but as the sun reached its zenith she acknowledged it was time to rest in what little shade the bank afforded.

A smooth rock newly exposed by the storm provided a welcome seat. Although too small to shelter beneath, it enabled her to sit in part shade with her legs dangling in cool water and her back curled into the bank. Her head swam with fatigue and heat but she knew better than to fall asleep and risk hitting her head as she fell into deep water, so passed the time reciting stories learned from her mother.

Mid-afternoon brought extensive cloud cover, giving Pia the opportunity to continue the search. At one point she spotted a dark object up ahead and became excited, but dejection swiftly followed when she discovered it was only a pile of stones left behind by the flood. Further downstream the creek appeared to have reverted to its normal course, travelling between banks covered in places with low vegetation flattened by the recent storm water but still firmly rooted in soil. Sitting on a patch of bare earth, eating a sun-plum and idly watching the fast-flowing river, she thought of Kaire and hoped that by now he was on his way back to Aotearoa, safe aboard one of the ships she had helped build. He would be concerned about leaving the Sky-ship in the desert but she had faith he would think of a way to retrieve it. She knew Kaire had no plans to remain on Earth indefinitely and half-hoped the troopers would dismantle the Sky-ship or try to fly it and crash, anything to keep her lover in her arms. But she also realised the longer she stayed in the Brown Zone, the greater the likelihood of arrest, her name no doubt high on the wanted file for crimes against the government.

Needing to stretch, she arched her back until her hands reached the ground and cried out as something sharp dug into her left hand. She twisted into a sitting position to examine her palm and saw blood oozing from a cut near the base of her thumb.

'Shit,' she exclaimed, plucking a leaf from nearby foliage to staunch the flow. The cut wasn't deep and soon stopped bleeding, so she looked around to see what had inflicted the damage. Behind her, several broken twigs stuck out of the soil but it was a flash of sunlight on metal that caught her eye. Peering closer, she saw the pointed tip of what she soon discovered to be a knife, a small sharp knife of the type used in the Kauri Haven dining room to cut fresh fruit. Elated, she began to dig furiously with her hands, showering herself with damp earth. Before long her fingers touched something solid and she pulled out her backpack, torn and filthy but its side pockets intact.

There were two messages from Kaire on her communicator, which surprisingly functioned as normal. Although it had been secured in a watertight pocket, Pia had imagined hours submerged in swirling water would have resulted in some damage. On hearing herself addressed as Senior Pilot 323, she laughed out loud, but quickly realised from the tone that 'Commander Breta' couldn't have been in a position to speak freely. The second message, received several hours ago, was in similar vein, Kaire advising he was communicating from a trooper car, which in the absence of the transporter was taking him back to the Sky-ship. Pia quickly scrolled to communication mode.

When Kaire answered, the relief she felt on seeing his face almost made her forget she was supposed to be a senior pilot, but she soon recovered her composure and reported the consequences of the storm in a businesslike manner, giving her location coordinates and assuring him she would continue to search for the transporter.

'I should think so,' he replied, his expression grim. 'Apart from the expense of replacement, I have no desire to be marooned in the middle of a desert while you locate an alternative means of transport to the aircraft.'

'I'm certain it can't be far away, sir,' Pia replied, her tone suitably contrite. 'The flood waters are receding fast.'

'I'll communicate again once I'm back in the aircraft,' he said gruffly and terminated the connection.

After emptying the pack and laying the contents on the ground to dry, Pia turned it inside out and, using her shirt, wiped away the soil that had penetrated the main non-watertight section. As expected her provisions were ruined. She buried them before opening the tube of Sustenance tablets and, grimacing, swallowed one with water from her flask. Her spare set of clothes and the pack soon dried in the hot sun giving her ample daylight to resume her search. Every so often she stopped to swig from the flask and eat one of the remaining plums, fast becoming bruised from constant motion in her pockets.

Pia had just eaten the last of the sun-plums when she spotted something shiny protruding from the opposite bank. Leaving her pack a safe distance from the crumbling edge, she scrambled down to a ridge of hard-packed sand and swam across. A tug exposed a short length of metal tubing, which she used to scrape away surrounding earth in the hope of finding other pieces. Nothing emerged, and on closer inspection she realised the tube had probably been buried in the bank for years. Disheartened, she swam back to the other side.

When the sun dipped low, she abandoned the search and walked away from the creek. Twilight would be brief this far north, so she increased her pace, determined to put as much distance as possible from a body of water that could alter its flow and appearance within hours. The landscape began to change, becoming less arid with patches of vegetation extending a fair way onto the plain. Between grey-green bushes, tassel-topped grass fluttered in a dying breeze, shades of pink and mauve that helped soften the monotonous brown of dry earth. As the sun sank below the horizon, she made a nest among the grasses and, using her pack as a pillow, curled in a ball like the spiny-backed echidnas that once roamed the region.

The pale light of dawn woke her only moments before Kaire communicated from the Sky-ship, his beautiful smile and tender greetings easing the trepidation and despair she'd felt ever since the storm. She quickly supplied up-to-date coordinates, her relief palpable when he advised the Sky-ship would land nearby in approximately thirty minutes.

Goaded into action, she stripped off her soiled clothing and, dampening her shirt with water from the flask, attempted to wipe away dried mud and dust. She was only partially successful but at least her face felt cleaner and fresh clothing would cover the remaining dirt.

Waiting for rescue, she felt at peace for the first time since landing on Australian soil. Memories abounded, some good, some bad—but now they could be tucked away rather than remain at the forefront of her mind. The land of her first eighteen years no longer evoked a sense of belonging; the homesickness experienced at Kauri Haven had washed away like yesterday's dust. The future was all that mattered—a future she fervently hoped would be lived alongside her beautiful Sky-man.

# CHAPTER 13

The Sky-ship flew high above banks of cloud, silver wings gleaming in brilliant sunlight. *Such intensity of light,* Kaire thought, staring out at the sapphire sky. Earth fascinated him with its kaleidoscope of colour, its varied landscapes, the unknown depths of ocean separating continents. He longed to undertake further exploration, visit different countries, fly over mountain ranges and deep gorges, trace the journeys of wide rivers. Perhaps he would discover a country more suited to someone from a highly developed community where conflict was solved by non-violent means and the inhabitants were deemed equal irrespective of skin colour or position. Except, he reminded himself, Skyz59 could only sustain a finite population and each year many young men and women had to leave the ageing space station to search for another planet capable of supporting human life.

He was ruminating on Earth experiences both positive and negative, when a console panel flashed blue followed by red, indicating a high-priority communication. 'Skyz59.323,' he answered as Commander Breta's face materialised on the screen.

'Your Earth exploration is terminated, 323,' the older man said sternly. 'All craft within six month's travel of Sky must return at once.'

'Yes, sir,' Kaire replied in a small voice, the look on his face betraying utter astonishment.

'Skyz59 has become unstable,' Breta continued, his expression grave. 'Recent repairs have confirmed our worst fears: the station is likely to disintegrate in the foreseeable future.'

Shock rendered Kaire speechless.

'Are you still there, 323?'

Kaire took a deep breath before answering, 'Yes, sir.'

'As we lack an alternative home, Earth will be our destination. From your reports I realise Australia is not an option, but I would appreciate your opinion regarding the suitability of Aotearoa for our people.'

'Aotearoa would be most suitable, sir. People of any colour are welcome here. It's a small country, not highly developed, but as far as I can ascertain it possesses a sound technological base. The land is reasonably productive and livestock known as sheep are farmed in the southern island.'

Breta nodded. 'Naturally I'll have to seek permission from the government both for landing and permanent residency. Would anyone on the Kauri Haven council have dealings with government officials?'

'I don't know, sir, but I can find out. The Kauri Coast Administrator would need to be contacted first. How many Sky People are likely to be coming?'

'It will depend on how many ships can return in time. At present we have approximately four hundred children and two hundred adults on Sky.'

A quick calculation confirmed Kaire's fears. Sky-ships were built for exploration not mass transportation and even if the entire fleet were available, many would have to be left behind.

'I know what you're thinking, 323, and believe me, I'll do my best, but as the station's viability is limited, I will have to make difficult decisions.'

'I realise that, sir.'

'Communicate with the council, then get back to me.'

'Yes, sir.' Kaire hesitated, unsure whether he should reveal his whereabouts. 'It may take a few hours as I would prefer to discuss such an important issue face to face. I'm not at Kauri Haven at present.'

Commander Breta looked surprised. 'Exploring the other islands, 323?'

'Not exactly, sir, I'll explain later.'

'Very well, communicate as soon as you can. Communication terminating.'

As the commander's face faded, Kaire glanced at the route display and realised with a jolt that the descent must begin immediately, otherwise he would overshoot the rendezvous and lose precious time backtracking. Console instruments responded quickly to his touch and soon the Sky-ship emerged from thick cloud and was flying over a desolate plain dissected by a wide river.

A few kilometres from the river, Pia sat waiting patiently. Dressed in a crumpled shirt and baggy pants, her feet bare and the pack held above her head as a sun-shield, she appeared out of place in a landscape devoid of other human activity. Days and nights struggling to survive in the desert had taken their toll; she looked gaunt, huge brown eyes staring out of a sunburnt face, limbs bruised and scratched from contact with submerged foliage and rocks. In spite of sun-plums, Sustenance tablets and water, she felt empty, her stomach aching and her mouth dry. There were no more normal provisions in the Sky-ship, so she would have to wait until they reached Kauri Haven before eating a decent meal. How Sky People could survive on Sustenance and water alone she couldn't imagine, and at last understood why Kaire exhibited such a childlike delight when presented with any item of food. Fixated on her next meal, she envisaged intestines and stomach shrivelling up after generations of tablet nutrition and wondered whether Kaire's lack of a navel was the result of evolution. He had told her Sky foetuses were gestated in artificial wombs, so maybe there was no longer a need for umbilical cords. Brown Zoners were denied access to this process, so she had no experience of such matters. She recalled the first time they'd made love, stroking his pale skin, delighting in its silky texture and the unexpected absence of body hair. At first, his smooth abdomen had perturbed, evoking images of computer generated androids, but his explanation that this was the norm on Sky had reassured her. Since then she had grown accustomed to his anomaly.

The sound of thrusters rapidly decelerating banished all thoughts of anatomical difference. Grabbing the backpack, Pia jumped to her feet and waved it above her head. In a few seconds the Sky-ship had materialised, shards of sunlight striking its gleaming surface. Wheels touched down, sending a cloud of red dust billowing skyward. Still waving, she yelled his name over and over, even though she knew he couldn't hear her. The Sky-ship glided over the ground and drew to a halt close by, the force of its final deceleration almost knocking her to the ground. The pilot's door opened and a set of steps slowly descended. Rushing forward, Pia grabbed the handrail and had just started to climb when Kaire appeared in the doorway. They met half-way, arms reaching out for one another, steps swaying from the force of their embrace.

Safely installed in the small seat beside Kaire, Pia listened with growing unease as he recounted the information received from Commander Breta. Initially her response was limited to a few words of sympathy but once the Sky-ship had risen above the clouds and Kaire had set course for Aotearoa, she asked why he would risk a return to Sky when his people were leaving.

'It's imperative I return,' he replied curtly, annoyed she should question his decision to obey an order.

'But surely one small ship won't make any difference?'

'I owe it to Breta. He gave permission for me to visit Earth when my immediate superiors had already refused my request. He was the first person to really listen to me, to comprehend my desire to retrace our ancestor's steps. I cannot let him down.'

Pia reached out to touch his arm and said quietly, 'I understand.'

Kaire patted the hand resting on his wrist. 'I knew you would.'

For the remainder of the short journey their conversation was sporadic, limited to discussion about the storm and the transporter's disappearance. Kaire did not rebuke Pia for taking an easier route and thus losing the vehicle, he had more important matters on his mind. Besides, he wouldn't need a transporter for at least a year, during which time he was certain Sami and Judd could build something similar in the engineering workshop. Aotearoans might have abandoned personal ownership of cars centuries earlier in favour of a 'short-term lease as required' system, but in Kaire's opinion a land vehicle would be essential if he were to resume rescue missions in Australia.

How he had yearned to feel soil and grass beneath his feet, breathe fresh air, touch leaves and flowers, lift his pallid Sky-bred face to the warmth of a sun. But the stark reality of ravaged Earth had sent shockwaves through his body, turning dream into nightmare and reducing the much-anticipated pilgrimage to a fight for survival. Only friend-ship and desire to assist an oppressed people had prevented him from scurrying back to the Sky-ship during those first few months on Earth. *Love too,* he mused, recalling the brief period spent with Sannah. She and her friends had shown him that individuals could make a differ-ence, turn a seemingly desperate situation into one where faith, hope and a determination to effect change lifted the sagging spirits of an entire people.

'My journey may only make a difference to a few,' he said, turning to his new love, 'but the gift of life is precious.'

Pia leaned over and kissed his smooth cheek. 'I know. You've saved mine twice.'

# CHAPTER 14

On arrival at Kauri Haven, Kaire decided it would be preferable to alert Mac to the situation on Sky before bringing Commander Breta's request to the full council. Pia agreed but advised her immediate plans involved food. 'Ravenous' was the word she used as they crossed the grassy area between perimeter fence and makeshift runway, followed by a diatribe on the shortcomings of Sustenance tablets. He laughed and reminded her tablets, not animal products and vegetables, had nurtured *him* and he didn't recall her having any objections to his body. Subsequent banter made him long for official business to be over and the two of them safe in the privacy of their bedroom, door locked and curtains drawn. Outside the administrative building, they quickly parted company. Pia sprinted towards the dining room, determined not to miss another meal. Unlike Kaire, she had remembered the three-hour time difference between Australia and Aotearoa; the short lunch break was almost over.

There was no response to Kaire's knock on the open office door. Peering inside, he saw Mac sprawled in the comfortable chair kept for visitors, eyes closed and mouth open, an empty plate and mug on the floor by his feet. 'May I come in?' he asked tentatively.

Mac stirred, stretched arms and legs before answering sleepily, 'Of course, just dozing. I hadn't realised you were back. Pia with you?'

Kaire stepped inside, closing the door behind him. 'No, she's gone to the dining room.'

'Trip went well?'

'Can we discuss it later? I need to speak to you urgently, Chairman.'

'Thought I was Mac to you, Kaire.'

'You are, but this is official business.'

'Sorry, mate, not at my best when I'm woken.' He yawned. 'Pull up a chair.'

Kaire grabbed the nearest chair and swivelled it around to face Mac.

'Spit it out then. The council meeting's due in just over an hour.'

'Good timing then. My orders are to proceed with haste.'

'Orders from your commander?'

Kaire quickly outlined the space station's precarious situation and Commander Breta's request for sanctuary in Aotearoa.

'I empathise with your people's situation,' Mac replied, his face etched with concern, 'but I'm sure you realise the council isn't in a position to grant permission for numerous spacecraft to land on Aotearoan soil. However, I'd be happy to discuss this matter with the other councillors before passing the request to the Kauri Coast Administrator, Kiri, if you think that would help.'

'It might if they respond positively to the idea.'

'I imagine they would. As you know, most of us here arrived as refugees.'

Kaire nodded. 'So what authority does Administrator Kiri have regarding immigration?'

'She doesn't have the final say, of course, but her position enables her to speak directly to senior government officials.'

'How long would it take the government to make a decision?'

'That's anyone's guess but parliament is sitting at the moment— that's one advantage.'

'Permission to land is the more urgent request. Permanent residency can be discussed at a later date.'

'I agree.' Mac rose from his seat. 'I'll do my best, Kaire, but before I broach the subject at the council meeting, I have a request to make of you.'

Kaire looked up and met Mac's gaze. 'I'll do anything in my power to assist you.'

'Be careful what you promise.' He placed a fatherly hand on Kaire's shoulder. 'All I'm asking is for further clarification of the situation direct from your commander.' He raised both hands as Kaire opened his mouth to speak. 'It's not that I don't believe or trust you, simply that I feel the council would respond more favourably if I've discussed the matter with the person in charge of Sky.'

'You're right, I am only the messenger.'

'I'll organise a link now.' Mac walked over to his desk and peered down at the monitor. 'What's the code?'

'I would prefer to communicate from the Sky-ship. A link from this system could fail.'

Mac looked up, a frown creasing his forehead. 'Despite the recent upgrade?'

'Yes, communicating with a distant space station requires more sophisticated equipment than we have here. There's also the question of security. Communication between my ship and Sky is highly unlikely to be intercepted by hostile governments.'

'Good point.'

'I'll go ahead and make contact with Commander Breta.'

Mac nodded. 'See you in a few minutes. I'm just going to let Dona know where I am in case I don't make it to the start of the meeting.'

Kaire raised a hand and slipped out of the door, relieved the slight delay would give him the opportunity to speak to Commander Breta alone.

Although Kaire felt fairly confident the government would at the very least grant permission for the Sky fleet to land, he was concerned how ordinary Aotearoans would react to people with a very different social structure. On a small space station there was no real privacy, no room to establish traditional family units. Babies and young children occupied dormitories where they were nursed, schooled and generally looked after for by a team of carers. 'Mother' and 'father' were unknown concepts, 'family' a term used to describe the whole community. He strode towards the perimeter fence, recalling with fondness the period following childhood, years of relative liberty when no one knew who would be chosen to train as pilots and co-pilots and who would remain on Sky to fill the few remaining positions of carers, instructors, engineers and general maintenance personnel. Innocent years before the onset of responsibility, when life seemed full of promise and its end was never contemplated.

As Kaire stood beside the Sky-ship waiting for the ladder to descend, he was suddenly conscious of his own mortality. Eighteen months had passed since he'd landed in the Australian desert; he was twenty-seven now. In Sky pilot terms five and a half years remained before he would reprogram his ship to return to base and take an end-capsule. He accepted this practice without question. The human body deteriorated fast in space; even those who remained on Sky rarely had more than a four-decade life. How selfish he had been to request a sojourn on Earth before embarking on his primary voyage, to leave friends and colleagues behind to get on with the job. What had he hoped to achieve, confirmation that his ancestors had made the right decision to abandon their blighted planet? Now it seemed to him that they had taken the easy option, departed when the going got tough, left it to others to clean up the mess. How arrogant to imagine they could wreck one planet and then move on to another without a backward glance.

Before entering the pilot capsule, he turned his head and looked back at buildings and fields familiar now as the corridors and hubs of Sky. Down there his fellow settlers were doing their utmost to live a sustainable life, yet still found time to help those at risk in Australia. He wanted to shout out his admiration, tell them never to give up the struggle, but, ever conscious of his own responsibilities, he stepped inside and made his way to the console.

Apart from a brief comment on bureaucratic ineptitude, Commander Breta showed little emotion when Kaire informed him it could take some time for the Aotearoan government to make a decision. However, he seemed somewhat excited by the prospect of speaking to Mac and remarked it would be fascinating to learn about his role as council chairman.

'I think you've misunderstood the reason for this communication, sir,' Kaire replied, attempting to disguise his irritation. 'Mac wants information from *you*, not the other way around.'

'Does he doubt the seriousness of our situation?'

'No, sir, he thinks confirmation from you will carry weight with his colleagues.'

'Out to impress them, is he? I thought he was in charge.'

'Not exactly, sir. He calls himself "the servant of the settlement".'

Breta raised his eyebrows. 'Odd terminology.'

'Yes, sir, Earth-life has many idiosyncrasies.'

The commander responded with a nod of the head, then added impatiently, 'Where is this Mac? I have important work to do.'

Kaire glanced out of the window and saw Mac heading for the gate in the perimeter fence.

'On his way, sir.'

After closing the gate, Mac crossed the mown grass without once raising his eyes to the sleek silver Sky-ship. After six months he was used to seeing it docked in the cleared field just outside the boundary, but he found it hard to imagine a multitude of Sky-ships landing on the Kauri Coast. If the refugees from Sky were to be housed at Kauri Haven, a massive task in itself as numerous dwellings would have to be built, the runway would also have to be extended to accommodate the extra craft.

At the base of the ladder, Mac hesitated for a few moments, contemplating his forthcoming dialogue with a man who had never lived on Earth, never breathed fresh air or felt soil beneath his feet. Even if the government granted permission for Commander Breta and his people to settle permanently, it would be a difficult transition in many ways. Apart from having to adjust to a totally alien environment and culture, some Aotearoans might regard them as extra-terrestrials. Acceptance would be a long time coming. One step at a time, Mac decided as he began to climb.

# CHAPTER 15

Sitting in her pleasant office overlooking the ocean, Kiri tried to envisage life in space confined to an aged structure designed in the era of space exploration when humankind had had hopes of finding another planet capable of sustaining life. She knew from schoolroom studies that the repercussions of climate change and overpopulation had put paid to extra-terrestrial missions, governments more concerned with the scarcity of food, water and fuel. Millions had died from starvation, disease and the wars that erupted as nations fought for control of dwindling supplies. Turning away from the window, Kiri thought of her own town, once a thriving city of more than three million people. Over the centuries, sea-level rises had reduced Auckland to a series of tiny islands connected to one another by bridges, where despite massive flood mitigation schemes, king tides still inundated the lowest-lying islands where a handful of farmers struggled to grow crops in degraded soil.

Her thoughts travelled further up the west coast to the isolated community of Kauri Haven where refugees from Australia had found sanctuary for over fifty years. The communication from the new council chairman, Mac, a personal friend, had thrown her completely off-balance and she questioned her ability to decide whether to recommend acceptance of another group of refugees to her colleagues in the central government, or reject the proposal outright. In a practical sense, she knew it would be imprudent to accept up to a thousand new settlers when the country struggled at times to feed its existing population, but her conscience dictated otherwise. A decision had to be made quickly, Mac having stressed there was no time for lengthy procrastination as the space station could disintegrate at any moment.

Kiri was reaching for the desktop communicator when her assistant Bella whispered into the audio-box. 'May I see you for a moment, Administrator?'

Kiri frowned, pondering what could be bothering her normally unruffled assistant. 'Of course, come right in.'

Bella entered the room at once and closed the door behind her. 'A delegation from Kauri Haven has arrived and their chairman insists on seeing you immediately.'

Kiri looked puzzled. Mac hadn't indicated a visit during their recent communication. 'Did he say what they wish to discuss?'

'Only that a problem has arisen and it can't be discussed via communicator.'

Kiri nodded. 'Send them in. It must be important if the chairman's here.'

Bella glanced at the two visitors' chairs. 'The conference room might be more suitable. There are four of them.'

Kiri raised her eyebrows. 'Four! Yes, definitely put them in the conference room.'

Bella smiled and left the room.

The delegation comprised Mac, Meras, Dona and a young man Kiri had never met before. Mac introduced him as Senior Pilot Kaire, a former resident of the ailing space station, who had initially alerted Kauri Haven council to the dire situation facing his people.

'We apologise for arriving unannounced, Administrator,' said Mac formally, 'but we felt it imperative to pass on disturbing information received this morning from the space station commander.'

Kiri frowned. 'Has further deterioration occurred?'

'No, this information concerns a rather delicate matter.' Mac coughed and reached for a glass of water, a thick band of tension squeezing his chest as he searched for the appropriate words to raise a subject considered abhorrent.

On the opposite side of the table, Kaire noted Mac's discomfort and realised he was the only one present who could speak dispassionately.

'If I may clarify the situation, Administrator?'

'Proceed, Senior Pilot Kaire,' Kiri replied, puzzled by Mac's atypical stalling.

Kaire gave an overview of the Sky community past and present, explaining that human cloning had been adopted many generations earlier due to the low life expectancy in space, the high level of infertility, and the need for a considerable number of explorers to search for a new planet suitable for human habitation.

For a few moments Kiri sat stony-faced, mulling over the consequences of this unexpected revelation. Human cloning had been outlawed for centuries in every nation on Earth and was still regarded as an abomination, a scientific experiment that should never have been allowed to proceed.

'The proposal to bring Sky refugees to this country must now be amended,' she said gravely. 'There can be no exceptions to the global law banning human cloning.'

Kaire swallowed hard. 'I understand, Administrator.'

Kiri nodded. 'How many clones are there on Skyz59?'

'I don't have exact figures but I would say approximately three hundred children and one hundred and fifty adults. That doesn't of course include those explorers currently on their way back to Sky to rescue the inhabitants.'

'Are all the explorers clones?' Mac asked, recalling that Kaire had once said he was visiting Earth prior to exploring a far-flung galaxy.

'No, some naturals volunteer to become explorers. It's an opportunity for adventure and an escape from a restricted environment.'

Mac glanced at Kaire. 'Life at Kauri Haven must seem rather tame by comparison.'

'On the contrary, it's a welcome relief after twelve months in the volatile Brown Zone.'

Kiri, who had observed with interest Mac's rather pointed attempt to discover to which category Kaire belonged, said firmly, 'Let us return to the matter in hand. It is of no consequence whether Senior Pilot Kaire enjoys life at Kauri Haven.'

Meras raised his hand. 'If I may speak?'

'Proceed, Meras.'

The old man leaned towards Kiri. 'By my calculations, excluding clones, would leave one hundred children and fifty adults. Far less of a problem for the government, I should imagine?'

*Numbers—is that all they are to you?* Kaire thought, struggling to retain his composure. *You've just condemned four hundred and fifty people to death!*

'My thoughts entirely, Meras,' said Kiri. 'I don't foresee any difficulty in obtaining permission for such small numbers to settle. There would of course have to be a significant period of quarantine—we cannot risk the introduction of new diseases.' She turned to Mac. 'Which prompts me to ask if Senior Pilot Kaire has been cleared by our medical authorities?'

'The usual procedures were followed and he was given a clean bill of health,' Mac lied, his expression bland.

'I'm relieved to hear it.' Kiri picked up the desktop communicator and pressed a panel. 'Bella, the meeting will conclude shortly. Please organise a meeting with the head of the Immigration Department.'

'Thank you, Administrator.' Mac rose from his seat.

Kiri smiled warmly at her old friend. 'I'll keep you informed of developments. Meanwhile please let me know if the situation on Sky alters in any way.'

'I will.' Mac helped Meras to his feet and escorted him to the door.

A grim-faced Kaire followed them.

The return journey passed in complete silence, all four passengers brooding on the appalling consequences of the unspoken verdict made during the meeting. For Kaire, the deliberate killing of hundreds of his people was almost too horrific to contemplate. He envisaged the children's trusting faces as they were given a 'treat' that would end their lives, the adults that cared for them knowing their turn would come before long. Euthanasia was rarely carried out on Sky and only at an individual's request, generally because of prolonged illness or diagnosis of a terminal disease. Capital punishment had never been sanctioned, serious crime being virtually non-existent in the small self-contained community. The necessities of life were shared equally and personal disputes solved through mediation.

As Kauri Haven came into view, a sliver of optimism broke through the thick band of hopelessness encircling Kaire's mind. Commander Breta might be mistaken and Sky could take far longer than a year or two to totally disintegrate. The clones could be left to live out their lives until the station's inevitable demise; at least then they would be prepared for death. His thoughts turned to the pilot clones already on their way back to Sky, their mission to rescue as many as possible and transport them to safety. Would the pilots be eradicated on arrival in Aotearoa, or would they be permitted to return to the vast expanse of space and continue their voyages into the unknown?

Mac broke the prolonged silence as they drove into the main entrance and were proceeding slowly up the gravel drive. 'Driver, please pull up alongside the main building.'

'Where I collected you this morning, sir?'

'Yes, park on the left, please.'

'Yes, sir. Will you need the vehicle again soon?' he asked, hoping the answer would be in the affirmative. New to the region and the job, he was curious about this remote village. Earlier in the day, his passengers had been in such a hurry to depart, he'd felt reluctant to use the excuse of needing the bathroom to have a look round.

'I think it unlikely,' Mac answered, 'but you're welcome to have some refreshments in our dining room before you return to the leasing centre. Meras or Dona will escort you.'

'Thanks, I'll do that.'

'What was that, Mac?' Meras asked, stifling a yawn.

Mac twisted around. 'Please take the driver to the dining room. I'm sure you and Dona could do with a meal as well. Kaire and I would have liked to join you but we have business to attend to.'

Kaire gripped the edge of the seat. He had no desire for further discussion with Mac or anyone else and had intended to go straight to the Sky-ship to inform Commander Breta of the administrator's decision. He opened his mouth to speak but Mac had already turned away and it seemed inappropriate to argue with the back of his head.

# CHAPTER 16

Mac ushered Kaire into his office and closed the door panel, making certain to engage the rarely used security lock. Council members and other colleagues were accustomed to seeing his door at least partially open; they usually spoke into the audio-box and without waiting for a response, entered the office. Accessibility was important to Mac, a way to demonstrate he was a servant of the community not the other way round. Settlers were encouraged to participate in all important decision making, the council's role seen as one of discernment rather than enforcement. It took time to reach consensus and Mac had to admit he sometimes wished majority rule prevailed, but the community had been run this way since its foundation and so far the system had proved successful.

Mac indicated the easy chair, waiting until Kaire was seated before wheeling his office chair away from the desk. 'This won't take long.' He sat down and leaned towards Kaire. 'There's a question I need to ask and I trust you to give a truthful answer.'

Kaire remained tight-lipped, his eyes focused on a point above Mac's head.

'During the meeting this morning, you gave approximate numbers of the non-naturals in your community.'

'The term is clone,' Kaire answered curtly.

Embarrassed by his foolish evasion, Mac nodded in Kaire's direction and coughed before continuing. 'If the government grants permission for Sky-ships to land, while I trust your commander will accept the government's conditions of entry and not send clones, there will have to be checks made on arrival.'

He paused, expecting some response, not least a retort that of course Commander Breta would abide by the rules, but Kaire remained silent. 'As I understand it, the term "cloning" refers to the creation of a genetically identical organism, so tell me, how will our medical personnel determine the difference between clones and those you call naturals?'

Green eyes flickered and re-focused. 'Sky clones are created with one physical difference,' Kaire said quietly. 'They have no navel.'

Mac looked confused. 'But neither do those gestated in artificial wombs. At least, not a navel in the true sense of the word, rather a thin scar line where the artificial umbilical cord was detached at birth. I've seen it myself.'

'That used to apply on Sky, I believe, but some time ago our medics developed a system whereby clone embryos could be gestated without an artificial umbilicus.'

Mac scratched his head. 'I'm puzzled, Kaire, as to why your people find it necessary to distinguish between clones and naturals? Didn't you say it was an egalitarian community?'

'It is in most respects, but to answer your first question, cloning on Sky is strictly controlled. You are probably unaware that cloning reduces genetic diversity, which lowers disease resistance. One of the problems we have on Sky is a limited gene pool that must be protected. Consequently, clones cannot be allowed to breed with naturals under any circumstances, so they are created without the ability to reproduce.'

Mac nodded. 'I appreciate your honesty, and that of your commander. I was brought up in a society that concealed not revealed.'

'Until I came to Earth, lies were not part of my experience,' Kaire remarked sadly. 'Australia was a rude awakening.'

His words cut into Mac's mind, sharp blades digging deep into memory. How many lies had he listened to during his years in the White Zone? As a privileged White child, he had never queried why the Asian servants who toiled in his parents' home and those of their friends spent their nights in a walled compound on the edge of town. A compound he and two mates, curious to know what went on behind those walls, had once glimpsed in the early hours of a moonlit night.

Hiding in shadow to one side of tall gates, the boys had watched a trooper herd at least fifty Asians into the compound. Once the gates had closed, the three boys had tried to scale the wall by climbing on one another's shoulders and gripping the small crevices between blocks where pieces of concrete had fallen out over the years. Unfortunately, this activity had triggered an alarm that sent them scurrying back to the safety of home. It was only when Mac reached adulthood that he'd learned the truth of Australia's apartheid system and begun to question his people's brutal control of non-Whites.

'May I leave now? Kaire asked, shifting uncomfortably in his seat.

Mac pushed memories aside. 'Of course, I understand your need to return to Sky. I too would want to help save my people if our home were threatened.'

Kaire rose quickly and headed for the door, Mac following to disengage the security lock.

Standing in the doorway, Mac watched Kaire stride along the corridor and thought of his son and grandchildren living across the water in the White Zone. So near and yet so far, they might as well be clones living on a doomed space station for all the contact he would ever have with his family.

Once outside, Kaire changed his mind about going to the Sky-ship and headed for the school where Pia conducted her classes for those planning to return to Australia as part of the Truth Network. School had just finished for the day and children were spilling out of classrooms, so he took the path leading to the rear of the building. The door to Pia's classroom was ajar but a glance through an adjacent window showed him her class was still in progress. He waited for the young girl standing next to Pia to finish speaking and return to her chair before knocking.

'Come in,' Pia called as the students turned to see who had interrupted their class.

Kaire pushed the door open and stepped into the room. 'My apologies for disturbing you, Pia, but I need to talk to you urgently.'

Students exchanged knowing glances.

Concern flooded her face. 'I'll be finished in a couple of minutes, can it wait till then?'

'Yes,' he answered, regretting his tone. He hadn't meant to scare her; it was of no consequence whether he left for Sky today or tomorrow. Embarrassed, he retreated to the doorway.

Pia turned back to her students. 'We'll continue our discussion of this territory next week. Enjoy your days off.'

Chairs scraped on the polished concrete floor as students bent to retrieve the bags at their feet. 'He probably just can't wait to take her to bed,' Garna whispered to her neighbour.

'Lucky her,' replied the older girl. 'I wouldn't say no to a session or two with him.' The two girls giggled as they left the classroom.

Kaire said little on the short walk from school to house, his mind preoccupied with their forthcoming conversation. If only he had been honest with Pia instead of skirting around the truth. He dreaded her reaction, the abhorrence she would be unable to hide, the rejection of a last farewell embrace. Inexplicably, given his upbringing, he cursed his commander's morality. The Aotearoan authorities would have been none the wiser if Breta hadn't told Mac that more than half the Sky community comprised clones. What had prompted this unwarranted disclosure: a query from Mac, or a slip of the tongue? Anger abated as memory surfaced. An unexpected question, a revelation followed by an unforeseen response. He recalled the shrug of Sannah's shoulders, her comment that it made no difference to their relationship. Perhaps Pia would be similarly unconcerned and accept that he'd had no choice in the matter. Perhaps she would simply wish him well.

The moment they entered the house Pia embraced him, her arms tight around his waist, her lips crushing his. Reluctantly, he peeled away her arms and led her over to the sofa. Misinterpreting, she began to unfasten her shirt and he had to explain quickly that they must talk first. Puzzled and a little annoyed, she sat back on the sofa, arms folded, the curve of her breasts peeping from the half-opened shirt. She listened without comment as he recounted the meeting with the Kauri Coast Administrator, her brown eyes fixed on his, her expression grave but lacking the anticipated revulsion.

'I understand how you must feel about the deaths of so many of your people,' she said when he had finished speaking. 'I believe involuntary euthanasia is wrong under any circumstances.'

'Even for clones?'

She hesitated and he wondered whether she already knew his status. 'Yes,' she answered in a firm voice, 'they have the right to choose the manner of their death. In my opinion they should be allowed to remain on Sky.'

A long silence ensued.

'Well, do you agree or not?' she asked impatiently.

He nodded.

'Good, then put yourself in the clones' place and suggest this solution to Commander Breta.'

In need of space, Kaire shifted to the corner of the sofa and stared at the wall opposite. Time and again he rejected well-thought out explanations as too detached or too emotional. In the end, he repeated part of his conversation with Mac then dispensed with further words by unbuttoning his shirt and displaying his smooth abdomen. Pia immediately burst into tears and flung her arms around his neck. All attempts to prise her away failed, his assurance that no one at Kauri Haven would ever know she had been sleeping with a clone because he would be leaving the following day and never be heard of again, apparently unheard. Kaire had already decided he would refuse to transport naturals to Aotearoa whatever the cost of such disobedience.

Her head slumped on his shoulder and he realised the sobbing had ceased. Gently removing her hands from his neck, he wiped her sodden cheeks with the hem of his shirt before laying her down on the sofa. 'Rest,' he murmured, 'while I fetch you a drink.'

She opened her mouth to speak but appeared to change her mind and turned her face away.

In the kitchen, Kaire clasped the edge of the small counter as he tried to still his trembling body and erase the sound of her anguish from his mind. It took several minutes to regain control of his emotions. He longed for this last day to be over; life would be so much simpler tomorrow when he sat at the controls of the Sky-ship, his main concerns the performance of thrusters and avoidance of space debris.

He reached into the cooler for the bottle of wine made from the strange egg-shaped fruit that grew on woody vines along the perimeter fence. Despite his first taste of what the settlers called kiwifruit—he had picked one of the furry-skinned fruit, taken a bite and immediately spat it out onto the grass—Kaire rather enjoyed a glass of the sweet wine. He filled two glasses and carried them into the living room.

Much to his surprise, Pia smiled when he set the glasses down on the low table adjacent to the sofa and gestured for him to sit next to her. She appeared calm, heightened colour in her cheeks and slightly swollen skin around her eyes the only evidence of recent distress. They both reached for the wine at the same time, prompting another smile from Pia. 'Let's drink to the future,' she said softly, touching her glass to his.

'To the future,' Kaire repeated automatically.

They drank in unison, sip, swallow, sip, swallow; small sounds comforting in their familiarity. Neither spoke until the glasses were empty and placed once more on the table. Pia broke the silence, her voice smooth and sweet as the pale green wine.

'No problem is insurmountable,' she said, placing a warm hand on his knee. 'I can't bear the thought of losing another loved one, so I've decided to accompany you to Sky.'

As Kaire began to protest, she clamped her other hand over his mouth. 'Please let me finish.'

He nodded and she quickly withdrew her hand.

'Six months to reach Sky, six months with my Skyman, time enough to live and love, at least for me. After that, I don't care what happens. For the return trip, my seat will of course be filled by one of your people, I won't jeopardise another's chance of survival. Then, if you're permitted to leave Aotearoa, you can return to Sky, pick me up and we can explore the galaxy for whatever time we have left.' She sighed and slumped against the back of the sofa, emotionally drained from giving the most difficult speech of her nineteen years.

Kaire sat staring at the floor, a void in his mind where emotive words had gathered only minutes earlier. That Pia would give her life for him seemed not only reckless but also extraordinary. In his experience, love of any kind was always short-lived, beautiful while it lasted but destined to fade or die suddenly as circumstances dictated. On Sky, his life had been divided into manageable segments: childhood, basic education and specific career training. Relationships formed and ended with increasing regularity, for apart from childhood dormitories and education hubs, the sectors did not overlap, so there was little point in mourning the absence of a carer or a childhood friend's departure to another hub. One moved on, never contemplating a future other than that preordained by one's superiors. Yet he alone of the trainee and graduating pilots had chosen to flout the rules, had the nerve to approach Commander Breta and request a short visit to Earth before beginning his primary journey. And once in Australia, his emotions in super-drive due to unanticipated and traumatic experiences, hadn't he conveniently forgotten the command not to interfere with Earth-life in any way? Pia was at liberty because of *his* actions, *his* meddling in other people's affairs. The least he could do was accept the decision she had made.

'If you're certain that's what you want,' he said quietly, turning to face her, 'I would be delighted to have company on my long journey.'

# CHAPTER 17

At liberty to make her own decisions, Pia did not consult anyone before leaving the following morning. She felt beholden to no one except Kaire; her students no longer needed her, having almost completed their Truth Network training. The smartest student, Garna, who displayed maturity well beyond her seventeen years and had previous experience of taking part in subversive activities, could easily supply the remaining information before they departed for the Brown Zone. Out of courtesy, Pia keyed a parting message to Mac but only sent it when the Sky-ship had risen high into the clear blue sky. Land and ocean receded soon after and all she could see of her old world was a blue and white planet spinning in the blackness of space. *A globe of swirling colour, easy on the eye,* she thought, *a false image belying the misery, hatred and cruelty that existed on its surface, the devastation caused by a rapacious species.*

Although Pia still believed that organisations like the Women's Line, KAL and the Truth Network could effect change in time, the recent visit to her homeland had eroded considerable personal hope and engendered instead a desire for flight. 'A new life dawning in darkness,' she remarked to Kaire, still hunched over the console.

'That's an oxymoron,' he answered, lifting his hands from console panels. He stretched stiff fingers before leaning back in his seat. 'How about, "you can only see the light when you are standing in darkness".'

'Good one, Skyman.' She tapped his wrist and smiled up at him.

'Now tell me, did you make that up, read it on a screen or hear it from someone else?'

'I can't remember,' he answered honestly, 'but does it matter?'

She shook her head. 'Nothing matters except you and me.'

'And keeping this machine you call a silver bird on course,' he added, unable to prevent practicalities from entering his mind.

'Right as usual,' she murmured, noticing winking lights on the console. 'What do those lights mean? Nothing wrong, I trust.'

'Far from it.' He leaned over and dropped a kiss on the tip of her nose. 'They indicate automatic pilot has been set for the next few hours. It's our time now, my love.' And with an exaggerated gesture, he reached over and pressed a tiny panel embedded in his headrest. Curious, Pia twisted around, her smile widening as a fully made bed emerged from the wall, filling the space between their seats and the door to the storage module.

Sacrifice—the word echoed in Mac's mind as he read Pia's message for the third time. An unnecessary sacrifice in his opinion, made in haste because a nineteen-year-old girl believed love was more important than life. A girl with so much promise, so much to live for, risking everything for a few months alone with her lover in the empty blackness of space. Had she even considered what would happen once they reached Sky and Kaire was ordered to load his craft with refugees? Mac could imagine Commander Breta's annoyance on discovering a passenger had been brought along for the ride, a girl who would take up valuable space on the return journey. The commander could use his authority to detain her on Sky until another craft arrived or, and here Mac envisaged the worst scenario, the station disintegrated. Why hadn't he anticipated Pia's departure or taken more notice of the way she behaved around Kaire? Gossip abounded in the community dining room; he'd heard she had moved into Kaire's house recently, yet it hadn't occurred to him the love affair could be serious. Young members of the community typically had numerous relationships before settling down, most being thirty-plus before they requested a partnership ceremony.

In his own case, Mac had never found anyone to take the place of Aranie, his partner of many years who had died at the hands of brutal prison guards during one of his own periods of incarceration for anti-government behaviour. Since arriving in Aotearoa, there had been several love affairs, including one with the Kauri Coast Administrator, Kiri, but none had lasted more than a few months. These days, overseeing the community plus working with KAL occupied the bulk of Mac's time and energy. A few deep friendships, particularly the one he still maintained with Kiri, provided all he needed in terms of affection and somehow sexual gratification no longer seemed important.

Pia's message, along with all the others he had received that day, disappeared as Mac closed files before shutting down his computer. Outside the light was rapidly fading; he had remained in his office far longer than intended and would have to rustle up a meal from the few items in his cooler, the dining room having closed for the night.

As he walked to his small house situated behind the administration block, Mac pondered the future not only for Pia but also for all the younger generation facing the prospect of seemingly insurmountable problems. Climate change had wrought such devastation, particularly loss of arable land due to rising sea levels, that food and water shortages continued to plague most countries. The Super Powers—Europe, America and China—controlled dwindling mineral resources, the Northern Hemisphere always taking priority, while a small isolated country like Aotearoa was left to her own devices. *Perhaps that's just as well,* he thought, considering the refugees that would soon make these islands their home. Earlier that morning, Kiri had communicated to advise the government had now ratified Commander Breta's request for sanctuary, albeit with the proviso that the situation be reviewed after six months' residency. Kiri's recommendation, listing superior technology and an instant fleet of spacecraft that could easily be converted into aircraft as distinct advantages, had swayed even those politicians wary of admitting so-called aliens.

Unable to sleep following his late meal and feeling in need of exercise, Mac set off for a brisk walk around the slumbering settlement. Approaching the northern perimeter gate for the third time, he decided to venture further, unlocked it and picked his way over uneven grass to the twin strips of concrete laid as a temporary runway for the Sky-ship. The sliver of a crescent moon and a thin yellow beam from his communicator were the only light visible at this hour of the night. *It was rather a crude attempt at a runway but at least it served its purpose,* he thought, as the beam illuminated hastily-poured cement already crumbling at the edges. He doubted the runway would ever be used again; immigration officials would be unlikely to permit large numbers of Sky-ships to land at Kauri Haven even if there were sufficient space. The Sky refugees would need to be kept in quarantine for some time before they could be released into the community. Three centuries of isolation in space did not necessarily result in a disease-free population. In recent years, several diseases previously thought to have been eradicated centuries before, and with the potential to cause pandemics, had re-emerged in countries to the north, including Australia. Aotearoans had been informed that only their medics' diligence when screening new arrivals had prevented the diseases spreading south. In reality 'diligence' meant implementing the 'turn back the contaminated' policy that rejected any refugee found to be infected with or carrying the gene for a whole range of contagious diseases and returned them to their homelands.

Clouds had enveloped the moon when Mac lifted his head and looked over at the dark shapes of a dozen Kauri trees, brooding guardians of a long dead forest. Like many settlers, Mac was very attached to these trees, having come from southern Australia where forests had disappeared and 'bush' referred to the few stunted eucalypts that grew in hollows where intermittent rainfall gathered.

A gust of cool wind stirred the branches, sending shivers down Mac's body and reminding him it was time to return home if he were to accomplish anything useful in the morning. He would have to speak to Pia's class about their teacher's absence and find out when she had planned to send them to Australia.

# CHAPTER 18

Black clouds obscured late afternoon sun as a lightweight canoe beached on an island shore a short distance from the northern tip of Brown Zone Australia. The canoe's occupants, a teenage boy and girl, quickly disembarked and dragged the canoe up the beach beyond the high water line. After stowing the paddle, the boy indicated a sandy path winding through windswept foliage up to a line of small dwellings, set high on a ridge overlooking the beach. Heavy rain began to fall as the pair set off up the path, pitting the sand and sending streams of water sliding down leaves, hair and skin. Lightning split the sky and the teens began to run but were still saturated by the time they reached the first house. Sheltering under the overhanging verandah, they laughed and shook themselves like dogs. The girl, Garna, a former escapee from a youth working party, wore a floral sarong with matching head-cloth and carried a small backpack containing a change of clothes, sandals and a communicator of uncertain vintage. The boy, Toby, being familiar with local weather patterns, wore only a traditional loincloth.

One of the ships Pia had helped build for KAL had brought Garna and three other Truth Network students across the Tasman to the Brown Zone. Garna was the last to disembark, the islands in the Torres Strait the ship's final Australian destination. A communication the previous week from Line Leader Zira had advised Toby's mother, Millie, to expect a visitor who would require a few days' accommodation on the island before embarking for the mainland. Ten years before,

Millie's long-term friendship with Zira, conducted mostly by communicator, had led to her becoming a member of the Women's Line. Since then, Millie had recruited other women on neighbouring islands, and with assistance from husbands and sons also eager to undermine a government that denied them basic human rights, their small group continued to serve the Women's Line faithfully.

Earlier in the afternoon, Millie had observed a ship's arrival from her verandah. Using her telescope, she had watched it anchor in deep water well beyond the reef before alerting Toby. Her son was a fine canoeist, best on the island in Millie's opinion, so she'd felt no trepidation watching him manoeuvre his canoe through heavy surf breaking over the bleached coral reef fringing the lagoon. Once she saw the canoe had reached the ship, Millie had gone inside to prepare a meal for three.

She returned to the verandah as the canoe was recrossing the lagoon and trained her telescope on the girl huddled in the stern. The girl's dark skin surprised; Millie had expected a Brown Zoner (Zira had been quite clear on that point) not someone resembling her own daughter! Heavy rain prevented further observation, sending Millie scurrying indoors, the precious telescope wrapped in the folds of her sarong.

The ship had weighed anchor the moment Toby collected his passenger and was disappearing over the horizon by the time the storm struck. Even in this remote location far from the nearest mainland settlement and spotter station, the captain had no desire to linger any longer than necessary in Australian territorial waters. Coast security vessels patrolled the area intermittently, searching for illegal fishing boats from Asia, and could quickly become suspicious of an ocean-going vessel travelling close to shore. The islands were not on any trade route, the government considering it uneconomic to ship the few items the inhabitants produced to the mainland.

Although officially Brown Zoners, these descendants of Torres Strait islanders preferred a traditional way of life, fishing and cultivating their gardens. Considered simple people, they were left alone to pursue what government officials termed 'a primitive lifestyle choice' and were exempt from youth working party regulations as well as living according to the Nocturnal Life Project. Rising sea levels over several centuries had seen many islands in the area disappear beneath the waves or become uninhabitable due to soil salinity and lack of fresh water. Privately the government believed that the remaining islanders would soon die out, given they were denied all but basic healthcare and had to subsist on meagre rations when drought or flood wiped out their crops.

But the islanders were far from simple people and made good use of contemporary technology to communicate not only between islands but also with northern Brown Zone villagers. Given their proximity to the mainland, the islands proved useful to the Women's Line, and over the years numerous political prisoners on the run had used them as stepping-stones to liberty. Canoes could easily make landfall on isolated beaches, pick up a passenger or two deposited earlier by small craft posing as local fishing boats, and return home within a few hours.

Millie was stirring a pot of vegetable stew when Toby bounded up the stairs, the soles of his bare feet slapping the wet treads like freshly caught fish thrown in the bottom of a canoe.

'I'm home, Mum,' he called, flinging open the screen door leading into the living area.

Millie looked up, a smile on her face. 'Where's the girl?'

'Waiting on the back verandah while I fetch a towel. We got soaked coming up from the beach.' Toby shook himself before racing across the room.

'Right, well don't just stand there dripping on my clean floor,' she scolded as he skidded to a halt and peered into the pot bubbling on the stove.

'Sorry, Mum.' He tossed her a grin before rushing to the linen cupboard to retrieve a clean towel.

Millie shook her head and was about to lift the pot off the stove when she noticed the girl standing in the doorway. 'Come in please, I'm Millie, Toby's mum. He won't be a moment with the towel.'

'Thanks, I'm Garna.'

'Welcome to my home, Garna.'

The girl stepped inside and closed the screen door behind her. 'I don't want to mess up your floor.'

'No problem, Toby's done that already.' Millie moved the pot to the bench before glancing into the corridor. 'Hurry up, Toby.'

'Coming.' He poked his head around the doorframe, towel-dried black curls shaking as he struggled into dry shorts.

*No doubt he's thrown the wet loincloth onto his bedroom floor,* Millie thought, grabbing the folded towel held under one skinny arm. 'You can dry yourself in the bathroom,' she advised Garna.

'Thank you, Millie.' Garna stepped forward to take the towel. 'I'll go and change into my spare clothes.'

Several minutes elapsed before she reappeared dressed in a crumpled red sarong and carrying her wet clothes. 'Where can I hang these to dry?'

'The laundry's downstairs,' said Millie. 'Just leave them on the bench here for now. I'll wash them for you later.'

The girl smiled and placed her neat bundle on the bench furthest away from the stove.

From his seat at the table, Toby scrutinised their guest, noting with pleasure her long legs and shapely figure. Damp black curls danced on her bare shoulders as she walked towards the dining area, breasts bounced and hips swayed. Toby almost licked his lips but wisely turned his attention to the fresh loaf of bread his mother had just placed on the table.

They ate steadily, conversation confined to polite requests to pass the bread or praise for the food from both Garna and Toby. During the long silences, Garna pondered how much, if anything, her hosts knew about the mission and if they were aware of the Truth Network. Prior to leaving Kauri Haven, she had been called into Mac's office for a final briefing. After assuring her Millie was trustworthy, Mac had relayed Line Leader Zira's procedure for entry to mainland Australia. A canoe would take Garna across the strait, where close to shore a small boat, ostensibly engaged in fishing, would be waiting to transport her to an isolated village on the east coast. Once on board, she would be supplied with an islander identity disc, giving her relationship to the village family that had requested her visit.

There had been no problem for Zira in selecting villagers to pose as Garna's relatives; partnerships between far northern Brown Zoners and islanders were fairly common despite the law forbidding mixed race unions. Troopers in this remote region tended to ignore these relationships; they were up north under duress, usually the result of misdemeanours during previous postings, and had no desire to draw attention to the village under their control. Likewise, they often sanctioned visits by islanders related to mainland villagers, having quickly learned that a little benevolence reaped extensive benefits. There was always fresh produce brought as gifts, lavish family celebrations to which the village trooper was always invited and, periodically, time with an island beauty in exchange for overlooking the fact her identity disc had been left behind.

Garna had always known islander blood ran in her veins, even though neither she nor her twin brother had ever met their maternal relatives, for the story of their parents' meeting had become part of village lore. Long ago, a storm had sent a small island fishing boat way off-course; it had eventually washed up on a northern Brown Zone beach. From a distance the boat had appeared unoccupied, so the young man wandering along the shore searching for driftwood had had quite a shock when he'd peered over the side and seen a girl wedged in the prow, her hair matted with blood from a gash on her forehead. Later he'd learned the girl's father had drowned during the storm in an attempt to retrieve a piece of the rudder, broken off by heavy seas. Despite repeated offers to take her home, the girl had refused, fearing the young man would be punished by the troopers when he returned to the village, should he leave without permission. Attraction had soon replaced fear and the young woman had decided to stay permanently. Arrangements had been made with her remaining island relative, an elderly aunt, and a partnership ceremony held.

Garna wiped her bowl with the remains of her bread before looking across the table at Millie. 'How long will I be staying on the island?'

'It depends on the weather.' Millie reached over to take the empty bowl. 'The strait is subject to storms at this time of year, so you may have to stay for a week or so.'

'Not a problem, I could help in your garden, if you like? I've had experience growing vegetables.'

'Any experience in fishing?' Toby asked hopefully before his mother could answer.

He was rewarded with a brilliant smile and was about to suggest they go out in the canoe the next day when Garna shook her head. His own smile quickly faded.

'Your help would be much appreciated,' Millie replied. 'My daughter's visiting a neighbouring island and Toby shows no interest in gardening.'

'I'd do it if you asked,' he protested, stabbing a piece of fruit with his knife.

Millie ignored him, reached for the fruit platter and passed it to Garna.

'Coconut!' she exclaimed, taking a large piece. 'I haven't had any since I got out of …' Embarrassed by her mistake, she quickly pretended to be studying the coconut clutched in her hand. Both Pia and Mac had stressed the importance of anonymity; she should not have mentioned her past life. Her hosts were simply a conduit to the mainland. There was no need to mention the numerous Brown Zoners currently engaged in the Truth Network. Apart from the group Pia had trained at the Settlement, Garna herself had no knowledge of those currently disseminating the true history of Australia in villages throughout the zone.

Careful not to react to Garna's outburst, Millie turned to her son. 'The storm has passed, Toby, so you'd better get down to the beach. There are bound to be loads of coconuts scattered on the sand after that wind and we don't want to miss out.' She smiled at Garna. 'Why don't you go too and meet some of Toby's friends?'

Garna looked up. 'Sure, I'd like to.'

Toby's chair scraped on the timber floor and the table rocked violently, sending the half-empty fruit platter skidding towards the edge. After rescuing the platter, Millie noticed Garna stowing her chair neatly and wondered when her son would learn to move at a slower pace.

There was already a crowd on the beach when Toby and Garna stepped from the path onto hard-packed sand. Most were young people from nearby homes also sent by parents to retrieve the fallen fruit. Some had gathered the coconuts in bowls or buckets, while others were throwing them to one another in an impromptu game. In his haste to leave the house, Toby had forgotten to bring a container, so tucked several coconuts in the pockets of his baggy shorts.

'Shall I fetch a bucket?' asked Garna.

'Thanks. Mum keeps them in the laundry.'

'Right, I'll bring a couple.' Garna set off up the path to the house.

'Under the sink,' Toby called after her.

Garna was about to open the laundry door when she heard Millie speaking into what could only be a communicator.

'SI3 receiving you LLZ. Go ahead.'

Garna pressed her ear against the thin door.

'Understood,' said Millie. 'I'll try to make alternative arrangements.'

A brief silence followed, then Millie terminated the communication and Garna heard the sound of running water. Opening the door, she said brightly, 'Can I have a bucket, please? Toby forgot to take one.'

Millie looked up from the sink where she was rinsing Garna's sarong and head-cloth. 'Trust him, that boy's always in too much of a hurry. Buckets are in the corner.'

'Thanks.' Garna quickly retrieved a couple. 'See you later,' she called from the doorway and sprinted away down the path.

When Garna was out of sight, Millie extracted the communicator from between her breasts and returned it to its permanent hiding place, a plastic crate stored under a bench at the rear of the room. The crate contained bars of laundry soap and household cleaning cloths, mostly squares of old towelling, so the communicator, snug in a cover made of the same material, lay unnoticed at the bottom. It was sheer luck that Millie had been in the laundry when the familiar signal sounded from the crate. Generally, communications were prearranged, Zira contacting Millie at the local health centre, the site of the island's only official communicator. If another nurse answered, Zira posed as Millie's second cousin and would ask for a message to be passed on if she could not be disturbed. The messages always concerned family events, which included dates and were therefore easily interpreted. A birthday indicated Millie should communicate during the date mentioned, a partnership ceremony within a few hours and a death in the family, immediately. In the decade Millie had been the leader of Southern Island 3 branch of the Women's Line, she had only received one death notification, so thought it odd that Zira had taken the risk of direct communication. If Millie hadn't answered quickly, a neighbour could have heard the signal and gone to investigate. Island houses were sited close together, walls were thin and nobody locked doors.

As she hung Garna's sarong and head-cloth on the line strung between the verandah posts, Millie pondered the implications of Zira's message. The Women's Line had received information that previously sanctioned visits by islanders to relatives residing in northern mainland villages had been suspended, following a young man's flight with a so-called uncle the previous week. The pair had not been located, and northern spotter stations had been charged with searching for the small fishing boat that authorities now suspected had come from further afield than the islands, the uncle's identity disc having been found to be false.

*Garna could be staying for some time now*, Millie thought, disappointed the Line's well thought-out plan had been disrupted. Not that she minded having a guest, although she would have to make sure Toby didn't hassle the girl; his attraction had been blatantly obvious. Her thoughts turned to alternative methods for entering mainland villages, but the only legitimate means she could think of would be if Garna had a life-threatening illness. As a nurse, Millie knew some illnesses could be faked with the use of island herbal concoctions but it was rare for any patient to be transferred to a mainland hospital, the authorities considering the cost of transport unwarranted for islanders.

Dejected, Millie closed the laundry door and plodded back up the stairs. In the kitchen she ran water into the sink and began to wash dishes, cutlery and glasses, her hands moving mechanically through the suds, her mind still preoccupied with Garna's thwarted journey. A plate slid from her slippery hand onto the bench and landed precariously close to the edge. She quickly reached out to save it from falling to the floor. After carefully stacking the plate with other washed crockery, she glanced out of the window and noticed what looked like an outrigger canoe making its way through the gap in the reef surrounding the lagoon. Long ago Millie had often travelled with her partner Tommy to Papua and beyond during the years before twins curtailed her sea voyages. The few remaining outrigger canoes still travelled that route on occasion, trading island produce for tools or food not grown on the islands. She smiled, envisaging how proud Tommy would have been of Toby, handling a canoe with the ease of a much older man. Like many island men, Tommy had drowned at sea, his small fishing boat overturned during a severe storm no one had predicted. Nine years Millie had been on her own with the children, almost as long as her involvement with the Women's Line. During that time she'd never considered another partnership, preferring to direct her energies to assist Brown Zone women intent on undermining the White government. After all, mainland Brown Zoners were distant kin, having once been Pacific islanders, and as long as they continued to be treated as third-class citizens, Millie would be willing to engage in subversive activities whatever the risk.

But could she ask Toby to risk his young life? The question occupied her as a plan involving an outrigger canoe, island produce and her son began to form in her mind.

# CHAPTER 19

For some time, Toby had been aware that his mother and several other island women were involved in some sort of undercover group. On the first occasion, he'd burst into the house in his usual spirited manner, interrupting what was obviously not a gathering of friends. Millie never entertained old Josie, a cantankerous woman who never had a good word for anyone, or her colleague Jemma, whom she described as a pain in the neck. As for the other woman, Honey, she lived on the other side of the island and was rarely seen in the village. He might have dismissed the gathering as women's business had he not seen all four scramble to hide what looked like smaller versions of the medical centre communicator beneath their sarongs. His suspicions had been confirmed a few days later when he found a communicator in the laundry while rummaging through the crate looking for a favourite old shirt he suspected his mother had removed from his room and torn into rags. After trying and failing to operate the communicator, he'd carefully replaced it in the crate, preferring to remain ignorant of the group's purpose. Sometimes Millie asked him to pass on messages that made no sense and he wondered if she knew about his find but he never queried the request. Similarly, when Millie had told him a girl would be coming to stay for a few days, he hadn't asked where she was coming from or where she was headed.

On his return from the beach laden with coconuts, Toby became annoyed when, after lugging two full buckets up the stairs to the verandah, his mother suggested they be stored in the laundry. Then, after asking Garna to make them all a cool drink, Millie accompanied him downstairs, ostensibly to collect some washing. Once in the laundry, Toby became even more irritated when Millie closed the door behind them and he noticed that the clothes basket was empty. By the look on his mother's face, Toby imagined he was in for a lecture on treating their guest with respect, but Millie's expression softened as she beckoned him closer. In a low voice, she explained that permits to visit relatives on the mainland had been suspended for an undisclosed period and, without mentioning why, stressed how important it was that Garna visit the Brown Zone soon. Without waiting for Millie's request, Toby told her he was more than happy to transport Garna to the mainland and tossed aside pleas not to take unnecessary risks.

Later, Toby learned the crossing would involve far more than depositing Garna on the mainland and returning home immediately. The trip would involve trading with the most northerly of the east coast villages, mostly island handicrafts that were popular with northern Brown Zoners. Not only that but they would be crossing the strait in an outrigger canoe! Proud to be chosen to undertake this 'mission', as Millie referred to it, Toby's wild imagination had envisaged any number of illegal substances concealed in his cargo of woven mats, baskets and shell necklaces.

For the first part of the journey, Toby, with Garna seated behind him, paddled his own canoe to the far side of the island, beaching it in a small cove fringed with coastal palms and bush. From there it was only a short walk to the house Honey shared with her father. The screen door leading onto the verandah opened the moment they reached the bottom of the steps; Honey had obviously been looking out for them.

'Hi there,' she called, 'come on in.'

Toby bounded up the stairs and into the living room, trailing sand, while behind him, Garna wiped her feet on the woven mat.

'Thanks for the loan of your outrigger canoe,' she said to Honey. 'We promise to look after it.'

Honey smiled. 'It belongs to my father but he doesn't use it now, prefers his solar-powered fishing boat.'

'Perhaps he could sell it to Toby?' Garna suggested.

'No funds,' Toby answered, annoyed Garna had also known about the canoe. 'There's not much profit in the odd bit of fishing.'

Honey looked thoughtful. 'Dad could do with some help occasionally, if you're interested?'

Toby shrugged. 'Might be.' No way would he let these women organise his life. He turned to Garna. 'Right, we'd better get going or we'll miss the tide.'

'I've made up a food parcel and a bottle of fruit juice,' Honey said. 'They should keep you going until you reach the first village.'

'Thanks.' Toby stepped forward and lifted both items from the table. 'Have you got a container for fresh water?'

'Already stored in the canoe.'

Garna smiled. 'Thanks again, you've thought of everything.'

'Normal activity for me, I'm always packing provisions for Dad.' Honey motioned them towards the door and indicated a small jetty a short distance from the house. 'See you later,' she said casually before closing the screen door.

A small fishing boat was moored to one side of the jetty, behind it an outrigger canoe tethered to a bollard bobbed on the slight swell. Halfway down the jetty Toby could see an old man sitting cross-legged mending a net. He looked up as they stepped onto the rickety planks and then continued with his work. The canoe looked overloaded to Toby but he said nothing, confident Honey's father would know the optimum weight for their proposed journey.

'Jacka?' he asked as they approached the old man.

'Yep, who's asking?'

'Toby, nurse Millie's son.'

Jacka pushed the net aside and slowly got to his feet. 'Off to do a bit of trading, eh?'

'That's right, thanks for the loan of your canoe.'

'Too much trouble for me nowadays.'

Toby smiled.

'Know how to barter, do you?'

'What?'

'If you want to get the best price for your merchandise, you have to bargain with them Brown Zoners, you know. They're tricky customers.'

'I'll bear that in mind.'

'Don't come back empty, either.'

Toby glanced at Garna and almost asked why not; surely Jacka understood the mission's true purpose?

'I could do with some of that dark green leaf they grow on the quiet over there,' Jacka continued, tapping the side of his nose with a grubby finger. 'Know what I mean?'

'Tobacco or marihuana?' Garna asked before Toby could answer.

'Both if you can, love.'

'I'll do my best.' She glanced at Toby. 'I've seen both crops growing in case you were wondering.'

Outsmarted, Toby turned his attention to the canoe.

In spite of his experience, it took some time for him to feel at ease with the much larger two-person canoe and Garna didn't help matters by being practically useless with a paddle. Fortunately, both tide and wind were in their favour and once the canoe had skirted the island, they began to make good progress across the strait.

'I think I'm getting the hang of it,' Garna called when they had been at sea for at more than an hour.

'About time,' he retorted, secretly pleased he'd discovered something she couldn't do easily. Although a year younger, Garna exuded confidence from the tips of her toes to the top of her head and remarks made during her short stay had irritated him beyond belief. He had no intention now of trying to develop a relationship with her; a girl like that was far too hot to handle. Island girls were more his type, he decided—more pliant, less argumentative. Except his sister of course, and he laughed so much at the thought of Garna and Lindy in full flight, he almost dropped his paddle.

# CHAPTER 20

Although Pia and Kaire lived in an extremely confined space, they found no reason to argue or even exchange cross words during the six-month journey to Skyz59. Their attraction to one another, purely physical at first, had long since deepened into what both were forced to admit must be love. The possibility their relationship could end once they reached the space station was never mentioned, Pia determined to live in the moment and Kaire reluctant to voice his fears. Frequent communication with Commander Breta kept them up to date with the situation on Sky. The metal fatigue that threatened the space station's ageing infrastructure appeared to have been stabilised and total disintegration was no longer imminent. Certain areas had had to be abandoned, but this wasn't causing too much of a problem as numerous explorers had already returned from their primary voyages and were now bound for Earth with a full complement of would-be settlers. That each passenger was a natural went without saying; Kaire knew Commander Breta wouldn't contravene the ruling ordained by the Aotearoan government.

Before leaving Earth, Kaire had been determined not to convey Sky refugees to Earth, in order to make a stand against the wholesale slaughter of his fellow clones, but as weeks turned to months and the Sky-ship drew closer to its decaying base, he realised nothing would be achieved by disobeying orders. Not only would he have denied ten Sky people the opportunity to make a new life on Earth but also unnecessarily curtailed his own lifespan. However brief his next visit to Earth, the prospect of seeing another part of Aotearoa appealed. During his year of residence at Kauri Haven, Kaire had grown to love the surrounding country. He loved the forest where he often walked alone marvelling at leaf and seed and flower, the ocean that lapped and sometimes battered the curve of beach, the grey-tipped mountains in the distance shimmering in sunlight. A wealth of colour, texture and fragrance never envisaged within the smooth bland walls of his space station home, despite the myriad video files available in the data hub. Having experienced first-hand a variety of Earth environments, he had to acknowledge the files he had viewed with such delight were but a muted version of reality. Even degraded Brown Zone landscapes had seemed beautiful to Sky-reared eyes, once he became accustomed to the enormity of deserts stretching as far as the eye could see and wide rivers that promised life then snatched it away as drought gripped the land. At first, the relentless heat and humidity that sapped his strength had been overwhelming; he was used to a controlled environment, yet within months had acclimatised with no ill effects. Inexplicably for one raised in artificial light amidst the perpetual dimness of space, what he had found most difficult to bear was the time spent in windowless domes. It was as if having once experienced blue sky, clouds and sunshine, he could no longer cope with confinement in an enclosed space.

The intensity of storms and the power of ocean waves had also alarmed initially, doubtless because neither he nor anyone else on Earth could control them. Months earlier, as he taxied across a windswept plain to rescue Pia, it had occurred to him how insignificant his species were in the life of this planet. Regardless of the damage they had done, the planet would continue to evolve long after humans became extinct, space exploration having failed to discover another planet suitable for human habitation, despite the heroic endeavours of Sky People. Now that his people's long-term refuge had proven incapable of permanently sustaining life, there was little possibility of further voyaging amongst the stars.

Beside him, Pia stretched in her seat, prompting further thoughts of his return journey. If she were permitted to travel with him, they would have a further six months together, albeit in a crowded Sky-ship with no opportunity for intimacy. Kaire remained confident that Pia would be allowed to return home; Commander Breta wouldn't risk the Aotearoan government's ire by detaining her on Sky.

'Is something wrong?' Pia asked, turning to face him. 'You keep frowning.'

He shook his head. 'Just contemplating my next journey to Earth.'

'It won't be easy with so many passengers.'

'No, I'll have to impose strict discipline, roster sleeping and exercise periods.'

'How will you deal with claustrophobia?'

'That won't be a problem, Sky People are accustomed to living in a confined space. I'm more concerned about disputes.'

Pia nodded. 'As a child I was sent to the bath chamber if I misbehaved.'

'An odd place to choose.'

'Not really if you think about it. There's very little to play with down there and the floor is hard.'

He smiled and reached for her hand. 'Did you often misbehave?'

'I'm afraid so, I was headstrong from an early age. What about you?'

'Mostly I obeyed the rules. It was easier that way.'

'Easier but boring, I would have thought.'

'Sky children respond well to an ordered existence.'

As he turned his attention to the lights flashing on the console, Pia revisited the questions she had pondered ever since Kaire had confessed to being a clone. How would she react if she met his double on Sky? Or would there be numerous copies of her lover and if so how would she tell them apart? She remembered the identical twins at her youth working party, the tricks the two girls played on troopers and workers alike. For two years, Pia had shared a dormitory with the twins, yet frequently called one or other by the wrong name. She contemplated whether to ask what could be a confronting question, finally deciding to risk a rebuke or worse, silence.

'Are clones created randomly from any natural or are specific individuals chosen?'

'As far as I know there are numerous regulations. I'm not clear on the details but I am aware both physical and mental attributes are taken into account.'

Kaire appeared not in the least concerned by her query so she continued. 'Am I likely to meet others who look like you?'

'I don't know, Pia. I've never seen anyone that resembled me but that doesn't mean they don't exist.' He swallowed hard. 'Did exist, I should say. The clones may have already been eliminated by the time we reach Sky.'

'But surely Commander Breta would at least try to persuade some other country on Earth to take them?'

'I doubt it, he will obey orders as he, as we are all trained to do.'

Distraught, she began to pummel his thighs with her fists. 'Stop it, stop it!'

'Stop what?'

'Stop acting as though your emotion gene has been switched off!'

He grabbed her wrists and pinned them against his chest. 'I'm trying to face facts, Pia. There's no point in my railing against the Aotearoan government's ruling. We are not welcome there. We would not be welcome anywhere on Earth.'

'But who would know if you split up into small groups and travelled to different countries?'

He wanted to say *we* would, but kept silent, visions of an extended life with Pia burgeoning in his mind. Deception *was* possible; hadn't he adopted the role of scholar during his time in the Brown Zone in order to remain free? He envisaged false identity discs, couples or mock-family groups slipping across borders, landing small craft on remote shores, all feasible with careful planning. The only people on Earth aware of the clones' existence were the Kauri Haven council, Administrator Kiri and a few Aotearoan government officials, and they had no reason to communicate this knowledge to other nations. The agreed numbers of naturals would arrive in Aotearoa, undergo health checks and a period of quarantine and then be released into society. He assumed the initial curiosity or distrust caused by their arrival would dissipate after a few years as they proved themselves worthy citizens, and in time these new Aotearoans would forget they had once shared their lives with genetically identical others.

'You are brilliant!' he cried, kissing her with such passion that she fell sideways and they both ended up squashed between console and seats.

Once they had resumed their seats, discussion began in earnest, both determined to develop feasible strategies. Pia was excited by the prospect of assisting rejected refugees to find new homes free from prejudice. Secrets and lies had been the norm for a girl whose mother and her friends frequently risked their lives to ensure others found freedom, so Pia had no difficulty envisaging subterfuge and her enthusiasm soon erased any misgivings Kaire possessed.

After countless hours spent planning, rejecting, disagreeing and concurring, youthful enthusiasm wavered as they realised the futility of further debate. Until they reached Sky, their 'Earth Life Plan' remained an idea. Only Commander Breta possessed the authority to implement such radical action and he had given his word to the Aotearoan Immigration Department no clones would be brought to Earth. Without mentioning the idea to Pia, Kaire decided to request an audience with Breta soon after they docked, no easy task given the commander would be fully occupied with the evacuation process. And even if he were granted an audience, Kaire acknowledged there was no guarantee Breta would hear him out let alone cooperate. Most likely, he would be reprimanded for having the audacity to suggest breaking the agreement with Aotearoa and be dismissed with orders to load the Sky-ship and set off for Earth at once.

Or, and Kaire shivered at the thought, Commander Breta, the man who had sanctioned his unusual request to visit Earth, could consider Senior Pilot 323 no longer reliable and order his immediate extermination.

# CHAPTER 21

The moment Skyz59 appeared on the console screen, Kaire felt tempted to change course, bypass the space station, and head out into unknown territory where at least he would have another few years of life. Common sense and conscience soon prevailed; he could not deny Pia the rest of *her* life, and before long the ship was entering the Sky docking tunnel and locking onto the outer rim of the decontamination chamber. Seconds later a panel descended behind the ship, sealing the tunnel to allow pilot and passenger safe disembarkation. It seemed odd to be stepping onto rubberised flooring instead of soil, grass or concrete pads, and Kaire hesitated at the foot of the ship's ladder causing Pia to almost step on his head.

'Get a move on,' she shouted.

'Sorry, just recalling the last time I stood in this place,' he lied, reluctant to raise Earth issues at this critical moment.

She slipped her arms around his waist. 'I appreciate it's difficult to return under these circumstances. What happens now?'

'I imagine we go into the decontamination chamber where we'll be scanned for any disease or pollution we've brought from Earth.'

'And if any is found?'

'I don't know, Pia, this is a first for me too.'

'To have come so far,' she said, loath to complete the sentence.

He wanted to reassure her all would be well but knew better than to supply false hope. Docking procedures had never concerned him before; during pilot training the instructor had always taken over as the craft approached the space station, and under normal circumstances a Sky-ship returned to base without human cargo. On the rare occasion the decontamination chamber had been used, it was for internal problems such as a chemical spill.

'Come on,' he said, detaching her arms from his waist. 'I want to show you where I grew up.'

*You grew up in the Brown Zone,* she thought, recalling a conversation with her mother in which the words naïve and naivety had figured prominently. 'Okay, I'm ready.'

A panel slid open as they neared the tunnel's rear wall.

Except for a blue light blinking in one corner, the decontamination chamber appeared empty. Walls, floor and ceiling gleamed stark white; there was no sign of an exit. Uncertain what to do next, Kaire and Pia stood close together.

A voice, metallic monotone, startled them, prompting inaction rather than obedience. 'Remove all clothing, then stand on the designated plates to your right.'

As far as Kaire could ascertain, the sound appeared to be coming from the ceiling, although he could see no sign of the small grid found in most Sky hubs.

'Repeat, remove all clothing, then stand on the designated plates to your right.'

'We'd better do as it says.' Pia began to unfasten the silver bodysuit Kaire had insisted she wear to avoid undue scrutiny on arrival.

Quickly removing his own suit, Kaire walked over to the first of the square plates set into the rubberised floor. Oversize footprints etched into the metal indicated where he should stand. Soon Pia was standing alongside him. As they waited for the next step, Kaire pondered whether the voice would issue further commands, or the still blinking eye project a beam in their direction. Wrong on both counts, he gasped as a cloud of vapour began to fill the chamber.

'At least give me a chance to explain,' he cried, convinced the gas was poisonous.

'Remain silent, 323,' ordered a second voice, obviously human. 'Decontamination will be completed in two minutes.'

'There will be plenty of time for explanation later, Senior Pilot,' said a third voice. 'You have breached the order to return alone.'

Kaire recognised the voice: Cafel, head of pilot training and a man noted for his brusque manner and lack of tolerance. The forthcoming interview would be a challenge.

Vapour began to dissipate and a cover slid over the blinking eye. White light flooded the chamber and a door, previously unnoticed in the dimness, creaked open. Alarmed, Pia reached for Kaire's hand but he pushed it away, mindful his conduct must befit rank.

'Exit the chamber and dress in the garments provided,' ordered the first voice.

Silver bodysuits, more loose fitting than those worn on Sky-ships, hung on hooks along one wall of the tiny cubicle. Pia almost tore a suit in the rush to cover her nakedness. A stranger in a strange environment, she had felt extremely vulnerable in the decontamination chamber, exposed to unseen eyes. For a second, she regretted the decision to accompany Kaire to Sky, but a glance in his direction confirmed the rightness of her impulsive act. At this moment, he needed her. Confidence restored, she decided to challenge the unseen eyes, so pulled him to her and kissed him fervently on the lips.

They walked in single file along a narrow corridor, its smooth white walls unadorned, cushioned floor absorbing each footstep. The passage opened into a small room furnished with padded black benches arrayed against white walls and a low black plastic table that seemed to merge with the smooth untarnished floor. In Pia's opinion, this black and white cube, minimalist in its décor, seemed not only unappealing but projected an almost sinister atmosphere. Her sense of foreboding intensified when a door in the rear wall opened as she took a seat beside Kaire on the nearest bench. Before long, two men wearing identical silver bodysuits entered the room and sat down on the bench opposite without speaking.

Kaire immediately sprang to his feet and placed his left hand over his heart. 'Senior Pilot 323 reporting for transport duty,' he announced in a curt tone Pia had never heard before, even when he was communicating with Commander Breta.

'You may sit, 323,' said Cafel, the older of the two men.

Kaire returned to the bench, deliberately brushing Pia's hand with his before sitting.

For a few moments, Cafel conferred with his colleague in low tones, then rose from the bench and walked over to Pia. 'Name and rank,' he demanded, his tall frame looming over her.

Determined not to be intimidated, Pia looked up and, focusing directly on his face, said in a firm voice, 'Pia, tutor and adviser at Kauri Haven, North Island, Aotearoa.'

At the mention of Aotearoa, Cafel frowned and took a step backwards. 'Purpose in travelling to Skyz59?'

'To check that the conditions agreed by my government regarding the transport of Sky People to Aotearoa were being met,' she answered without hesitation.

'We have had no communication concerning your visit,' Cafel retorted.

'Of course not, my visit was deliberately unannounced.'

Cafel cleared his throat. 'Welcome to Skyz59, Tutor Adviser Pia.' He managed a slight smile. 'I trust you will find everything in order.'

'I would appreciate a conference with Commander Breta before I inspect the potential immigrants. I have orders to discuss what we term the Earth Life Project with him.'

'That will be arranged forthwith.' Cafel turned to his colleague. 'Communicate with the commander and organise a meeting as soon as possible.'

'Yes, sir,' he replied, already extracting his computer-strip from a side pocket.

'Not here, Landal, I have work to do.'

Landal rose quickly and headed for the door.

'Take our guest with you,' Cafel added, extending a hand and helping Pia to her feet. 'I'm sure she would appreciate some refreshment.' He smiled. 'Oh, and Landal, a tour of the data hub would also be appropriate.' Still holding Pia's hand, he escorted her to the door and handed her over to his colleague.

'Please come this way, Tutor Adviser Pia,' said Landal politely, ushering her into the adjoining room. 'I shall be delighted to show you our range of technologies.'

The door closed behind them, leaving Kaire to ponder his fate at the hands of the man who had mocked his request to visit Earth and displayed unbridled anger when a newly qualified senior pilot went over his head and secured permission from Commander Breta.

'Well now, 323, I think we should have a little talk.' Cafel crossed the room and settled himself in the place Pia had just vacated.

'Fine by me,' Kaire replied, trying to sound nonchalant. He had been astounded and delighted by Pia's audacious response to Cafel's question regarding her travel to Sky and wondered if she had made it up on the spot or had anticipated the query. Whatever the case, her fictitious explanation had secured an audience with Commander Breta.

Cafel leaned forward, hands clasped, fingers interlocked. 'Tell me,' he began, turning his head towards Kaire, 'were you aware Pia was travelling here as a representative of the Aotearoan government?'

'I had no idea, sir. I invited her along as a companion, we had become friends during my stay at Kauri Haven.'

A wry smile crept over Cafel's face. 'You expect me to believe that? Come now, a senior pilot doesn't disobey orders for companionship.'

Kaire bent his head, feigning embarrassment. 'We have been lovers for some time, I couldn't face being without her.'

Laughter filled the room, Cafel nearly overbalancing as he rocked back and forth on the narrow bench. It was some time before he could speak and when he did his voice betrayed a residue of mirth. 'To think the cool contained pilot I knew, whose only interest appeared to be Planet Earth, has been overwhelmed by a mere girl!'

Kaire raised his head. 'It's true, sir. You have no idea how enticing Earth women can be. In fact, it was her mother who seduced me first.'

'Her mother! Fancy a bit of wrinkled flesh, do you?'

'Sannah was thirty-nine,' Kaire said softly, 'a beautiful woman.'

'So why didn't you bring *her* to Sky?'

'She was killed, sir, by the brutal troopers that control her people.'

Cafel looked thoughtful. 'Nothing has changed then in the centuries since our ancestors left. Earth People remain barbarians.'

*Verbal abuse can be just as cruel,* Kaire thought, remembering past instances when Cafel had used his superior rank to intimidate and belittle many a young trainee pilot.

Beside him, Cafel stirred, stretching his legs and inhaling deeply as though waking from a long sleep. 'There's no point in detaining you further,' he said, rising to his feet. 'I'm convinced you knew nothing of Pia's mission—you always were a bit naïve.' He slapped Kaire on the shoulder. 'Go to the data hub and retrieve your orders. You'll be leaving as soon as the next group has been inspected. The engineers are servicing your ship as we speak.'

Kaire stood and, facing Cafel, placed his left hand over his heart. 'Yes, sir, thank you, sir.'

On his way to the data hub Kaire couldn't help noticing how few people were around. Most apparent was the absence of children, especially when he passed the sleeping hub reserved for younger ones. Perhaps they and their carers had been among the first to be evacuated, he thought, pleased the younger generation would have the chance of a long life, unimpeded by the limitations imposed by a space existence. He was about to enter the data hub when the truth hit him full in the face and he slumped against the corridor wall, appalled by his naivety.

# CHAPTER 22

Landal confirmed Kaire's fears, his voice betraying deep sadness. The clone children had been the first to be euthanised, followed by all clones occupying non-essential positions. Among those remaining were engineers needed to service and if necessary repair the ships recalled from primary voyages. About half the Sky fleet had returned to base during the months it had taken Kaire to travel from Earth. The rest were expected to arrive within weeks.

'I'll be sorry to see you go,' said Landal once Kaire had read the file containing his instructions. 'I would have liked to discuss your experience of life on Earth.'

Kaire smiled. 'I still have a few hours.'

'But I have work to do. All the files containing cloning data are to be deleted and it isn't a simple task. There's no special file tag to alert me, it's already taken me months.'

'Orders from the Aotearoan government?'

Landal shook his head. 'Commander Breta felt it would be prudent not to leave anything that could incriminate.'

Neither man voiced what they were thinking, that *their* very presence in Aotearoa would incriminate.

'Why not delete all the files?'

'The Aotearoan government has expressed interest in the history of Sky.'

'I see. Do you know where Pia is?' he asked, anxious to see her before he left.

'Still with the commander, I suppose. I took her to his office about ten minutes ago.'

'I'll go and wait outside for her.'

'Is that wise?'

'Meaning?'

'Her next task will be to inspect the batch of naturals you'll be taking back to Earth.'

'I'm aware of that.'

Landal frowned, leaving Kaire no option but to invent a reason for accompanying Pia. He had no desire to reveal the nature of their relationship to anyone else, even though he knew Landal would show empathy. 'I want to make sure she doesn't overstep the mark and start checking them for insignificant flaws.'

'Is that likely?'

'Oh yes, Earth people are paranoid about disease, especially dermatological and respiratory problems.' He recalled the fear displayed at the youth working party when a girl suddenly developed an unexplained rash.

'You'd better go then.'

But before he had reached the door, Landal rushed past him and turned around to embrace him warmly, much to Kaire's surprise.

'Travel well, my friend.' He looked up with tears in his eyes. 'We shall not meet again.'


No one passed by during the half-hour Kaire sat on the bench outside Commander Breta's office. The silence was unnerving, reinforcing his despair and grief, which refused to dissipate no matter how hard he tried to exorcise them with positive thoughts. The termination of his own life he could accept, but not the death of innocent children; they'd had no choice in the manner of their creation. What harm would it have done to take them to Earth? They posed no medical risk and their genes would not be passed on to a new generation. They could have lived out their lives as useful citizens even if their difference meant they were forced to live separately. He envisioned an isolated farming community on the lines of Kauri Haven, small mud-brick houses and crops waving in the breeze.

'Senior Pilot Kaire,' Commander Breta exclaimed, 'just the man I want to see!'

Startled from reverie, Kaire leapt to his feet. 'I was waiting to escort our guest to the social hub, Commander.'

'When you have delivered her, return to my office at once.'

'Yes, Commander.' *A reprimand no doubt*, Kaire thought, *for not advising that an Aotearoan government official was accompanying me to Sky.*

Behind the commander, Pia stood focusing on a point above Kaire's head, reluctant to risk catching his eye. Their Earth Life Project had been rejected, Breta at first presuming the Aotearoan government had altered their position on clones and angry he hadn't been informed earlier. When she explained the project was nothing to do with her government and was instead a plan devised with Kaire during the long months of their journey as a means to save lives, he had stared incredulously. And then it had been Pia's turn to be caught unawares, for he'd covered his face with his hands in an attempt to hide tears of remorse. But the commander had quickly regained his composure and told her in an expressionless voice that regretfully he had already carried out her government's orders, leaving Pia to rue the role she had created for herself. Now Kaire would return to Aotearoa without her and she would have to remain on Sky until the last group had been inspected.

Commander Breta moved into the corridor and gestured for Pia to step forward. 'Tutor Adviser Pia, you may proceed with your inspection.'

'Thank you, Commander.'

'Please inform me when you have completed your task, so I can authorise the next group.'

'Yes, Commander.'

'Follow me, please,' Kaire said without looking in her direction and set off down the corridor.

On the short walk to the social hub, Pia learned that a few clones remained to carry out essential duties and wondered if they could somehow be saved, although she didn't voice this hope, afraid their conversation was being monitored, as it certainly would have been in the Brown Zone. Kaire's own status divided them like an impenetrable wall, but although Pia knew he wouldn't be permitted to remain in

Aotearoa, she retained a modicum of confidence he would devise a way to escape after depositing his passengers.

They turned a corner and Pia noticed a door labelled 'Social Hub' up ahead. Her whole body stiffened as though the blood in her veins and arteries had frozen; the moment had come to say their farewells. Biting her lip, she waited for Kaire to make the first move but he had walked away and was scanning the corridor, though for what reason she couldn't imagine. Tears began to fall, silent and steady. He returned to her side, enfolded her in his arms.

'Never forget your legacy of hope,' he whispered, his lips almost touching her earlobe, 'and I promise to do everything in my power to see you again.'

When Kaire returned to Commander Breta's office, he was surprised to be greeted as though he were a close friend and they were about to have a pleasant conversation. Once the door had closed, Breta moved from behind his desk and sat on the bench placed against a wall. Without a word he signalled for Kaire to sit alongside.

'Our guest was a surprise packet in more ways than one,' Breta began, pausing to check on his wrist monitor that the security sound barrier was in place, 'and her description of the Earth Life Project set me thinking.'

'It's a bit late now,' Kaire said bitterly.

'Not for everyone.'

'What are you suggesting, sir?'

Breta leaned towards him. 'I shall of course be the last to leave. I'll pilot the old reserve craft used in the past to rescue Sky-ships experiencing thruster problems.'

'Is it still operational?'

'Yes, I checked it recently. More importantly, there's room for seven passengers.'

It took Kaire a moment to comprehend. 'Seven clones remain on board.'

Breta nodded.

'Where do you plan to take them?'

'That is no concern of yours.'

Kaire sat back on the bench.

'Sorry, I didn't mean to be brusque, but the less you know the better. I shall head for Aotearoa once I have offloaded my passengers.'

Kaire pondered his own inevitable fate and that of the other pilot clones.

'I know what you're thinking, Kaire, and believe me if I could save the other pilots I wouldn't hesitate to do so.'

'What do you mean, other?'

Breta placed a hand on Kaire's shoulder and looked directly into his eyes. 'I have another plan for you. Do you think I could destroy the only copy of my DNA?'

Cafel was both surprised and irritated when informed that Kaire had collapsed and a scan revealed a severely inflamed appendix. Commander Breta advised that as he was the only person left with any medical training, he would be performing the necessary surgery, with Pia providing nursing support. She could be spared, having completed her inspection.

The surgical creation of Kaire's navel took place in the Sky medical hub within the hour, Commander Breta resurrecting long abandoned medical skills with the help of video data files. Lacking any nursing experience, Pia followed his orders to the best of her ability.

Afterwards, Breta returned to his office leaving Pia to watch over Kaire in the tiny recovery room. She was grateful for the opportunity to unwind; assisting with a surgical procedure had been a strain and she'd struggled not to cry out when the blade cut into Kaire's abdomen, convinced he could feel pain despite the anaesthetic. Only when the wound had been sealed and the bloodied skin wiped clean had she relaxed a little and acknowledged the pain that inhabited her own body was the result of acute tension.

She was checking the machine monitoring blood pressure, pulse and heartbeat, attached to his right wrist when Kaire stirred and opened his eyes.

'Pia,' he croaked, his mouth dry, 'where am I?'

'The recovery room,' she answered as instructed, Commander Breta having decided to keep his patient in ignorance as a precaution. 'You collapsed—appendicitis. All is well now.'

Kaire's left hand touched the dressing covering part of his abdomen. 'There's no medic here now so who operated?'

'Commander Breta.'

Kaire managed a brief smile. 'Scarred for life then.' His eyes closed.

'You could say that.' Pia tucked in the sheet and went to sit in the chair by the side of the bed until he woke again.

A week later, Commander Breta conducted a post-operative examination and pronounced Kaire fit to travel. The skin graft had been successful and the donor site on the inside of his left thigh had healed, leaving only a small scar. Breta would have preferred to use synthetic skin but there had been insufficient time to prepare some in the laboratory.

After saying farewell to Pia and Breta, Kaire resumed his duties, checking sufficient supplies of Sustenance and emergency medicines had been loaded into the lockers lining the walls of the pilot capsule before the ten passengers took their places. Apart from the small washroom located directly behind the dividing wall, the storage module could not be utilised as it lacked sufficient artificial gravity for eleven persons. Personal effects including computer-strips and communicators, plus spare clothing had already been stored in the space normally occupied by a land transporter.

Calef had supervised both packing and checking. The enforced delay had continued to irritate him and he'd stomped around the docking tunnel as if his boots were made of steel instead of synthetic polymer. In his opinion, the evacuation plan should have been followed regardless of Kaire's illness and he'd found it difficult to control his temper when Commander Breta had rejected *his* offer to pilot the ship. Throughout his career, Cafel had held fast to a belief in following protocol without deviation, hence his antipathy to Kaire's request to visit Earth. Pia's arrival had also irritated him, being one more alteration to the plan, one more place to be found on the last ship leaving Sky. The presence of an Aotearoan citizen would also hinder his intention to discuss future options with Commander Breta. Whatever the other refugees decided, Cafel had no intention of remaining on a small island far from the great continents he'd observed on old video files. He wanted to live at the centre of Earth affairs where the opportunities for a man of his calibre would be commonplace. Unlike Kaire, he was no pilgrim yearning to visit the land of his ancestors. History was of no consequence. The future was all that mattered.

# CHAPTER 23

The penultimate Sky-ship departed for Earth, leaving Pia unemployed and anxious to return home. Standing outside Commander Breta's office, she hesitated before knocking, confident he would admit her but aware it wasn't her place to suggest they leave as soon as possible.

'Enter,' came the gruff reply.

The door opened and stepping inside she was surprised to find the commander staring at his monitor, hands cradling his face.

'I'm sorry to disturb you, Commander Breta, but may I speak with you for a moment?'

He nodded and gestured towards the chair in front of his desk.

'Thank you.' She moved forward and slipped into the seat.

'So the evacuation is almost complete,' he said, raising his eyes from the screen.

'Yes, Commander.'

'I have failed, Pia,' he said dejectedly.

'How can you say that? Your people will be safe in Aotearoa.'

'I failed to save the remaining clones.'

She reached forward and took his hand. 'I'm sure you did your best to persuade Cafel to leave on the last transport so you could implement your plan. It isn't your fault he's so stubborn.'

Breta squeezed her hand. 'It hasn't taken you long to figure him out. At least I was able to use my authority to override his proposal that you leave with them. I must admit I dreaded the thought of a six-month journey with Cafel as my only companion.'

Pia smiled. 'I'll try to provide a calming influence and, if necessary, act as mediator.'

'Pia, you are wise beyond your years.' He released her hand. 'Kaire is a fortunate man to have you by his side.'

She looked down and fiddled with her bodysuit fastener to hide an unwelcome blush. 'And I can't thank you enough for saving him. I couldn't bear the thought of losing another loved one.'

'Neither could I.'

Pia lifted her head, a puzzled expression on her face. 'What real difference would sparing *his* life have made to you?' She sat back in her seat. 'Sorry, Commander, I shouldn't have said that. I know you feel responsible for all Sky People.'

'No need to apologise, I prefer plain speaking. Besides you have a right to know the truth.'

'My mother was killed because she told the truth,' Pia said half to herself.

'I'm aware of that. Kaire kept me well informed of events in the Brown Zone.'

'At least you know what he had to deal with over there.'

Breta nodded and sat up straight, arms folded. 'Take a good look at me, Pia, and try to visualise a younger, slimmer, black-haired man without the lined face that responsibility and age bring.'

Pia studied him intently. 'How could I have been so blind? You're his …?' She hesitated, uncertain whether 'father' or 'brother' was the more appropriate word.

'There is no term for our relationship other than clone,' said Breta, reading her mind.

'Family member, would that do?'

Breta smiled. 'Perfect.'

'Are there others?'

He shook his head. 'And before you ask, I have no natural children. My two sons died from a rare disease years ago. Kaire is all I have.'

A long silence ensued before Pia felt able to comment on his revelations. 'Thank you for entrusting me with your history. Your secret is safe with me, always.'

Breta rose from his seat, prompting her to do the same. 'Wait a minute,' he said, and to her surprise, walked around the desk and embraced her. After a brief but warm hug, he stepped back and looking into her eyes, said in a soft voice reminiscent of the one she loved, 'Welcome to the family, Pia.'

After making certain neither the Commander nor Pia were in the vicinity, Cafel slipped into the medical hub and headed straight for the body scanner, determined to uncover the real cause of Kaire's collapse. He had been suspicious ever since his visit to check on Kaire's progress to ask when he would be fit to fly. On entering the small ward, he'd noticed that Pia was about to tip a soiled wound dressing into the sterile container on the wall opposite Kaire's bed, a dressing far larger than that required to cover an appendectomy wound. Although she must have heard his steps, Pia hadn't looked up as he approached but continued with her task before turning to greet him, which had only intensified his misgivings. If the commander had concealed a more serious issue and put an incapacitated pilot clone in charge of a Sky-ship, thus risking the lives of ten naturals, none of whom had any flying experience, Cafel was resolved to bring it to the attention of those in authority once they reached Aotearoa.

When a check of the body scanner memory file revealed no scan of Kaire's abdomen, Cafel could hardly contain his delight and danced around the room like a man possessed. Moments later, after calming himself with some deep breathing, he considered his next move. Lack of a scan didn't really prove anything; Kaire could still be suffering from a serious illness. He decided to examine the medical records and also ascertain whether Commander Breta had accessed any other files prior to commencing surgery, so walked over to the wall monitor and gave his authorisation code. Kaire's medical record revealed no health problems during childhood or adolescence apart from two episodes of vomiting as a toddler from ingesting foreign objects and an abscess on a tooth at fifteen. Disappointed, Cafel closed the file and turned his attention to recent file history.

The list revealed numerous searches on plastic surgery, especially that employed when a person was born with a deformity such as webbing of the fingers or toes. Puzzled, Cafel stared at the list for several minutes as if doing so would reveal the information he sought. His own perfectly formed index finger was about to press delete when he noticed an earlier search on cosmetic surgery at the bottom of the screen. Amused at the thought of Commander Breta seeking to reverse the signs of ageing, he quickly replicated the search. Soon a video file titled, 'Umbilicoplasty' began to play, the poor quality footage proof of its antiquity. But Cafel wasn't interested in surgical procedures; now he had evidence that could be used to destroy the reputation of one he had long resented. For years he had coveted the rank of commander and had experienced intense jealousy when his exemplary service was overlooked and the less experienced Breta had been appointed to the position.

Before leaving the medical hub, Cafel scanned both the history file list and the video file into his personal computer-strip. Then he quickly made his way back to his office adjoining the docking tunnel—more a cubicle than a room in his opinion—and began to delete any incriminating files on his communicator. Once satisfied nothing remained, he adjusted his chair to recliner mode and lay back for a well-earned rest. There would be plenty of time when he reached Earth to implement his new plan.

All that remained to be done before take-off was a final inspection of the entire complex to ensure nothing vital had been overlooked. Commander Breta divided the task into three: Cafel he directed to the western third, which included the engineering hub; Pia the centre sectors; he would check the rest. Minutes later, standing alone in the middle of his office, Breta felt an odd sense of relief that had little to do with imminent escape from a disintegrating space station. A weight had been lifted from his shoulders—for the first time in years he could look forward to an ordinary existence. On Earth he would be just one of many refugees building a new life. Turning on his heel, he left the office without once looking back and headed for the medical hub.

Everything appeared in order, pharmaceuticals neatly arranged in a glass-fronted cabinet, beds made and operating theatre immaculate as usual. He found it strange to think that within a few hours, Skyz59, home to thousands over the centuries, would become a ghost ship— silent, dark and cold, a metal cocoon destined to become another piece of space debris. A chill invaded his body as he crossed the ward, prompting a sense of doom more potent than that of mere regret, and he paused in the doorway reluctant to leave the place where he had acquired his medical training so many years before. *One last look,* he decided. His eyes flicked around the room and came to rest on a tiny green light halfway up the wall opposite the beds. He could clearly recall shutting down the wall monitor after Kaire's operation and wondered why Pia had used it. Quickly retracing his steps, he pressed his palm against the screen and was about to give the exit command when he noticed a smudge of grease on the left hand side of the monitor's white border. Automatically, he spread his hands to check palms and fingertips but they were clean as usual, an administrator's hands. A fleeting look at 'user history' confirmed his worst fears: Cafel had viewed files only an hour before.

Pia boarded first, settling herself in a small seat that folded down from the wall separating the two modules. It was going to be a difficult six months cramped in this small spaceship with two men she had quickly come to realise did not like each other. Glancing out of the window, she noticed that Commander Breta had entered the docking tunnel and was walking sluggishly, head bowed and shoulders slumped. Pia understood what he was going though; it had been tough leaving her homeland even though imprisonment would have been a certainty had she stayed. Memories swiftly evaporated as Cafel appeared in the tunnel doorway. *I must be on my guard,* she thought, *and not give the impression I prefer Breta's company.*

Breta was only a few steps from the open pilot's door, when to Pia's astonishment he swung around and grabbed Cafel by the shoulders.

'Devious bastard,' he shouted. 'Thought you could out-manoeuvre me, did you?'

Cafel tried to free himself but Breta, the much stronger man, only tightened his grip. 'Give me your computer-strip and I'll spare your life,' Breta continued. 'No one will believe your story if you haven't got the proof to back it up.'

'How do you know I haven't already forwarded the files to the Aotearoan government?'

Caught off guard, Breta loosened his grip, giving Cafel a momentary advantage. Pushing Breta to the floor, Cafel rushed past him and shimmied up the ladder only to find the door slammed in his face. As he hammered on the door in frustration, Breta grabbed his ankles and pulled him off the ladder. Then, to Pia's horror, he began to drag Cafel down the tunnel towards the exit door.

Convinced the door would unseal and both men tumble into oblivion, she flung the pilot's door open and yelled, 'Leave him or we'll all die!'

Breta responded with a kick to Cafel's stomach and a howl of pain resounded through the tunnel, drowning Pia's ongoing pleas to stop fighting. Meanwhile he took advantage of Cafel's preoccupation with pain to race along the tunnel, climb the ladder and seal the pilot's door behind him.

Thrusters roared into life, the exit door rose slowly and the Skyship began to slide down the tunnel. Breta sat hunched over the console, his face set in concentration, perspiration mingling with blood oozing from a cut where the ring Cafel wore on his right index finger had scraped his cheek as they tussled on the tunnel floor. In the co-pilot's seat, Pia stared straight ahead, clutching her knees in an attempt to quell the shaking pervading her whole body.

'Brace for take-off,' Breta instructed, without lifting his eyes from the console.

Unseen, Cafel scrambled to his feet and raced towards the emergency controls on the outside wall of the engineering hub, the noise of thrusters obliterating his shout of jubilation as he pressed a panel to close the exit door.

# CHAPTER 24

Heavy metal creaked and the door shuddered before beginning its downward slide. Suddenly, movement by the wall caught Pia's eye and she turned her head to the right. 'Cafel,' she cried, 'he's …' She hesitated, uncertain what he was doing, but Breta understood precisely. Risking damage to the roof of his craft, he accelerated to maximum speed and with seconds to spare, the last Sky-ship shot out of the docking tunnel into the vast serenity of space.

Pia had never felt such intense relief, not even when Kaire had helped her escape from her home village during the fire that engulfed the community dome. Tension quickly drained from her body but it was some time before she felt calm enough to speak. Beside her, Breta also remained silent, no longer hunched over the console although still preoccupied with flight data. At least his breathing had returned to normal, dispelling her fears a heart attack could strike him at any moment. From his appearance, she guessed Breta was close to fifty, the maximum age according to Kaire, for a natural who had spent his whole life in space. She looked forward to getting to know him during their six-month journey and hoped that once on Earth his life expectancy would be extended.

Breta broke the silence, asking if she needed medication to calm her nerves. She smiled and shook her head before thanking him for saving her life.

'I believe the saving was down to you,' he answered, lifting his left hand from the console and giving her shoulder a friendly pat. 'I simply employed my flying skills.'

'Let's just agree we both contributed.'

He nodded and removed his hand. 'Unfortunately the danger isn't over, Pia. Kaire remains at risk as long as he stays in Aotearoa.'

'Because the other …' She hesitated, loath to call them naturals; to her Kaire was as natural as anyone else, '… er, Sky People know he's a clone?'

'Some do, some don't, but that's just part of the problem.' He sighed and sat back in his seat. 'Although I doubt Cafel had sufficient time to work out how to contact the Aotearoan government before we departed, the communication code being on my computer alone, he could be doing so right now.'

Pia blanched. 'You must contact Kaire immediately and warn him!'

'Communication presents its own problems. Kaire has ten passengers, all of whom will be aware of any message I send.'

'Then send it in code.'

'What do you suggest?'

Pia looked thoughtful. 'I'll try to think of something only he and I would know. Unless you have any other ideas?'

Breta shook his head. 'The only secret we share is our DNA.'

'What about an incident from his childhood or young adulthood?'

'Apart from recent communication and an interview in my office requesting permission to visit Earth, I know very little of his life.'

*How sad,* Pia thought, recalling numerous conversations about her father with Sannah and her mother's friend, Fley. When Kaire had first described his upbringing, the lack of individual families on Sky had troubled her; she couldn't imagine growing up as one among many with a handful of carers instead of one or two parents. She recalled the shock of dormitory life on arrival at the youth working party, the insomnia experienced while adjusting to the sleep sounds of numerous other adolescents. For most of her fifteen years, Pia had shared a bed with Sannah, their tiny hillside dome having only one sleeping chamber. They had often clung to one another through the long daylight hours when Brown Zoners were forbidden to leave their domes. Shared solace, shared secrets, an intimate mother/daughter relationship that could never be reclaimed.

Breta broke the thread of memory. 'Have you come up with anything?'

'Not yet.' She turned her attention to time spent with Kaire: those final traumatic weeks in the Brown Zone, friendship and a nascent sexual relationship at Kauri Haven, six months cocooned in the Sky-ship where intimacy had blossomed and love sealed the bond between them. But how to choose something that would clearly convey the need to flee Aotearoa the moment he'd deposited his passengers?

After a few minutes a vague solution occurred to her. 'Is it possible for this craft to overtake Kaire's?' she asked.

'Unlikely, this is an old ship.'

'But he could slow down to ensure we reach Aotearoa first.'

'Yes, but what would that achieve? I will be subject to Aotearoan law.'

'True.' She leaned forward and stared out of the curved front window to hide the tears sliding down her cheeks. Stars flickered in an ebony sky, light years away from a ravished blue planet and a doomed space station. If only she could grasp their light and hold it in her hands long enough to banish the darkness to come.

'Light dawns,' Breta said suddenly, slapping his thighs with the palms of his hands. 'Mid-flight linking, transference of personnel.'

Pia frowned. 'What reason would you give?'

'Thruster problems with this craft.'

'The importance of saving your life.'

'And yours, of course.'

She shook her head. 'I refuse to leave Kaire alone.'

Breta sighed and placed a hand on her shoulder. 'It would only be for a short time. You could arrange to meet somewhere well away from Aotearoa.'

Pia remembered the plan to smuggle her student Garna into the Brown Zone via one of the remote islands dotting the Torres Strait. 'The northern tip of Australia,' she murmured.

'So you'll transfer with me?'

'Maybe.'

Fingers squeezed her shoulder. 'It's the only way to ensure Kaire survives.'

Pia knew Breta spoke truth; it would be selfish of her to insist on accompanying Kaire. His passengers would neither understand nor condone a natural risking her life for a clone. In her opinion, Kaire's so-called 'enlightened community' seemed no better than apartheid Australia. Different skin colour or identical DNA, those in charge used their authority to control the ones they considered inferior. A cloud of despair threatened to overwhelm as she pondered her future. In all likelihood there was no country on Earth where she and Kaire could live out their lives free of prejudice and fear.

'I'll transfer with you,' she said in a low voice.

Breta sighed with relief. 'A wise decision.'

'There remains the problem of Cafel,' said Pia. 'He may be stuck on Sky for as long as it lasts, but if he has contacted the Aotearoan authorities, we're both in trouble.'

'There's no need for you to worry unduly, Pia. I'll say I forced you to assist me.'

'Thanks, but I'm hardly innocent. As Kaire's lover I knew he was a clone long before the operation.'

'And you didn't have a problem with that?'

Pia shook her head. 'It made no difference to me. And you should know it was *my* decision to accompany Kaire to Sky. In fact, I had to use all my powers of persuasion to convince him it was a good idea.'

'I'm sure you did, but to return to the matter in hand, do you know anyone in Aotearoa that holds a position of authority, someone you trust?'

'I trust Mac.'

'And would he be able to find out if any files have been sent from Sky?'

'I doubt it, but Kaire said Mac seemed friendly with Kiri, the Kauri Coast administrator. She might have the authority.'

'It's worth a try.' He tapped the console with his fingers. 'What's his communication code?'

'Kauri 002.'

Kauri Haven's communication system reverted to automatic mode during the sleeping hours between midnight and six, with incoming messages categorised through voice and content analysis. Those in the non-urgent category were dealt with the following morning; urgent communications were forwarded to the council chairman's personal communicator.

Mac was deep in dream when an insistent buzz penetrated his brain and it took him a few moments to recognise Pia's voice. In the months since her departure, he had often speculated on what she and Kaire would find once they reached Skyz59, so felt relieved to learn that although unstable, the space station remained intact and evacuation had been completed. However, Pia's request for confirmation that certain Sky files had been forwarded to government data banks came as a complete surprise, and seemed incompatible with the level of efficiency Breta had demonstrated beforehand. Certain Pia wasn't telling the whole story and, puzzled as to why *she* was making the request, Mac asked to speak to either Commander Breta or Kaire. The older man's face quickly replaced hers.

'Greetings Commander,' said Mac in a friendly tone. 'I'll need details of the files for easy retrieval: name, content, whether text, audio or video.'

'They are highly sensitive files,' Breta replied, reluctant to reveal particulars. 'Medical files that should not have been transferred.'

Mac understood at once. 'Concerning banned procedures by any chance?'

'You could say that.'

'It won't be easy, I don't have access to government files, except those pertaining to Kauri Haven.'

'But it would be feasible, if a trusted colleague were shall we say co-opted?'

'Maybe'

Breta tried to think of a bargaining chip, failed, and decided on a direct approach. 'Is there anything that would make life easier at Kauri Haven?'

'Transport is always a problem, both for personnel and produce.' Mac sighed. 'But I understand my government will be taking charge of all Sky-ships.'

'That's correct, though I doubt mine would be much use being older and much smaller than the others.'

'Could it be modified to carry, say, six passengers across the Tasman?'

'What's the Tasman?'

'The ocean between Aotearoa and Australia.'

'My craft could certainly fulfil that role.'

'Then I suggest you land at Kauri Haven, Commander. There is a runway, although it's rather primitive.'

'It's okay, Kaire used it on several occasions,' Pia remarked.

'Yes, I know,' Breta answered, irritated by her interruption.

'So may I presume we have an agreement?'

'You may. File elements transferring now, text version.'

Breta pressed an icon on the left hand corner of the screen to convert speech to text. 'File category: medical, heading: umbilicoplasty, type: video. Delete if located, repeat delete if located.'

'Thank you, Commander, instructions understood.'

'One further request: please delete any accompanying text or audio files.'

'Certainly.'

'Skyz59.1 communication terminating.'

For a moment Breta stared at the blank monitor considering the response should the file be discovered. He had no doubt that whoever agreed to assist Mac would view the video prior to deletion or even download it to a personal communicator, curiosity bound to override instructions. It wouldn't take long to link umbilical surgery to the Sky clones, if one already knew of their anatomical difference.

'What have I done?' Breta cried, beating the console with his fists. 'In trying to save Kaire I have risked the lives of all my people.'

# CHAPTER 25

The settlement began to stir as morning light filtered through blinds left open to admit the sea breeze. Climate control served its purpose but most of the inhabitants preferred a natural atmosphere during cool season nights. Mac had been up for hours, sleep impossible following Commander Breta's request. The correlation between a video on umbilical surgery and Kaire's status had been apparent from the moment Mac read the file heading; he had suspected Kaire was a clone ever since the meeting with the Kauri Coast Administrator. Kaire's dispassionate responses to questions about the Sky clones had seemed contrived and when Mac had met his gaze across the table, personal sorrow was clearly perceptible.

Mac knew he couldn't ask for help in locating the files from Kiri or anyone else, so was tempted to disregard Commander Breta's request and report back that he hadn't found anything. But conscience niggled when he realised the consequences could be disastrous should incriminating files be discovered *before* the Sky-ships landed. Faced with the dilemma of how to distinguish clones from naturals, the Immigration Department would most likely refuse permission for any craft to land. One hundred and fifty people denied a safe haven due to his inaction; Mac couldn't live with that.

Whatever his personal feelings about human cloning, Mac felt great empathy for Kaire. During his short time on Earth, Kaire had risked his life on several occasions for people he had no obligation to assist, plus willingly infiltrated Australian government communication systems and databases to obtain information useful to the Women's Line. Kauri Haven had also benefitted from superior Sky technology and Mac considered whether Commander Breta knew of these deeds. Perhaps it was this knowledge that had prompted the decision to spare Kaire's life; such deception would not have been undertaken lightly.

The following evening Mac booked a car and driver from the leasing facility and set off for the small town in the far south of the North Island where parliament and government departments were located. Some time later, he alighted from the car outside a small house several kilometres from the Communications Department, having told the driver he was visiting a sick relative and, being unsure when he would return north, preferred not to book a return trip. Nobody answered his knock on the shabby front door, sparing him the trouble of concocting an excuse for the disturbance, so he turned towards the road and made a show of checking his communicator, by which time the lease car was out of sight.

The sun had dipped low in the sky and a strong sea breeze felt cold as Mac walked narrow suburban streets. It had been years since his last visit; he'd forgotten wind battered the town most days during the cool season. There were few people about and those he passed chose to ignore both his presence and his smile. Accustomed to friendly faces, he found their behaviour odd and wondered if life in the towns had become more arduous. In previous years, he'd heard rumours of food shortages, especially during the hot months of the year. Aotearoa could not afford to import high-priced food from the northern hemisphere and possessed few ships capable of reaching Asia. Most Aotearoans grew vegetables and fruit in their gardens but this could prove almost impossible in drier areas if seasonal rainfall failed. In the hot wet north, Kauri Haven didn't suffer from lack of water but some years flooding rains still wiped out crops despite an extensive network of drainage. The original settlers had found cultivation a difficult process, especially those from the White Zone unaccustomed to hard physical labour. Land left vacant following the Aotearoans' retreat south decades earlier had had to be cleared of choking weeds, and the poor soil required vast amounts of compost. It had taken some time to become totally independent of government handouts.

Before leaving home, Mac had arranged a meeting with a Communications department official, ostensibly to view the Kauri Haven archives housed in the same building. Once granted access to the archives, he hoped to implement his plan to navigate the entire communications system.

The official proved slightly more communicative than the people Mac had passed in the street, acknowledging his appointment and handing him a visitor tag before escorting him to a cubicle on the first floor furnished with a plastic chair and desk with inbuilt computer.

'The system will instruct you how to access the archives as a visitor,' she advised, standing just outside the cubicle doorway as though eager to depart. 'I finish in half an hour so if you require more time, speak to the security officer on the ground floor.'

Mac smiled. 'Thank you, I don't plan to be long. I just want to check some files I transferred recently.'

She nodded and shut the door behind her.

Mac searched the archives using firstly genuine file details and secondly the information from Commander Breta, minus the file heading. This latter search he repeated several times to provide concrete evidence of its absence should anyone check. After the third attempt he slammed both fists on the desk in case anyone was outside the cubicle, and leaping from the chair, threw open the door and stomped down the stairs to the ground floor.

'I am Council Chairman Mac and I demand to speak to the officer in charge,' he shouted at the startled security officer half asleep on a chair in the foyer.

'I'm sorry, sir, but she's gone home. I'll just check and see if her assistant is available.' He stood up and pulled a communicator from his shirt pocket. 'Security ground floor, please respond.'

Mac tapped his fingernails on the reception counter.

'Sorry, sir, there's no response. Shall I try the other officers?'

Mac advanced towards him, glaring. 'Get on with it. I've travelled a long way and I expect some answers.'

'Yes, Chairman, I'll send out an all-office directive.' The officer pressed panels with shaking fingers.

A red light soon appeared on the communicator, followed by three loud beeps. 'Officer Jenson will see you now. First floor, third office.'

Communication was clearly not the department's strong point, so Mac dispensed with a response and headed back up the stairs.

Officer Jenson proved the exception to the rule, apologising effusively that other more superior officers hadn't been available and politely offering coffee or a cold drink before Mac had even taken a seat.

'Coffee thanks, if it won't take long,' said Mac, keen to maintain his vexed demeanour. 'Black, no sugar.'

'Got it right here, Chairman. I'm a bit of an addict myself.' Jenson moved behind the desk where he pressed a panel embedded in a wall cabinet door. 'So how I can help you?'

Mac clasped the arms of the chair and leaned forward. 'I forwarded some important files earlier this month that now appear to be missing.' He gave a slight cough. 'Although archival files, they contain sensitive information that could cause the government acute embarrassment if read by unscrupulous persons.'

'I understand your concern, Chairman. I presume you received confirmation they had been received.'

'You presume correctly.'

Jenson frowned. He was about to speak when an automated voice announced coffee was ready. 'Only local brew I'm afraid. I drink too much to buy beans from up north.' He turned back to the cabinet and extracted two large mugs.

Mac accepted the coffee with a smile. 'Right, let us return to the problem of my missing files.'

'I doubt they are missing, more likely misallocated. Human error can never be totally discounted. A search of the entire database should locate them.' Placing his coffee on the desk, Jenson turned to the monitor. 'Date perimeters?'

'Within the last two weeks. File code Skyz59M.'

Slim fingers moved over the screen. 'Nothing, I'm afraid.'

Mac masked his relief by frowning. 'Could they be in some sort of holding file awaiting transfer?'

'It's possible. I'll alter the end perimeter.' A manicured nail pressed the screen. 'Ah, success, two files! One audio, one video received yesterday.'

'Yesterday?' Mac queried, willing Jenson not to open the files. 'That's not possible.'

Jenson turned the monitor to face Mac. 'Computers don't lie.'

Rising from the chair, Mac stepped towards the desk and peered at the screen. 'Twenty-six hours ago.' He looked up. 'My sincere apologies, Jenson. I wonder where on earth they've been all this time.'

Jenson shrugged. 'Floating about in the ether, I suppose. I don't pretend to understand how these errors occur.'

Mac looked back at the screen. 'The files could be corrupted so I'd better download them and investigate when I return to my cousin's place. I don't want to delay your return home any longer.' Unfastening his shirt pocket, he pulled out his communicator.

Jenson moved around the desk and stood to one side of the monitor. 'Code AO735,' he advised the machine.

The files disappeared at once. Mac lowered his eyes and watched them reappear on his communicator screen. 'On second thoughts,' he said in a sombre tone, 'I think it would be prudent to delete those parts of the files that could cause difficulties. It won't harm anyone if the historical record contains some anomalies.' He tucked the communicator in his shirt pocket.

'My sentiments entirely, Chairman.'

'I can't thank you enough for solving my, er, problem.' He reached over to shake Jenson's hand.

'I'm pleased to be of service.'

Mac made a mental note to send Jenson a packet of Kauri Haven's coffee beans, far superior to those he had just tasted. 'I'll say good evening then, there's no need to escort me to the entrance.'

'Pleasure meeting you, Chairman.'

'You too, Officer Jenson.'

Once outside the building, Mac walked at a steady pace towards the town centre, intending to stop for the night at one of the small hotels that lined the main route. There were more people about now, most walking in the opposite direction, no doubt making their way home from work. At intervals cylindrical vehicles slid past, crammed with passengers. Mac presumed they were heading for the small settlements beyond the town boundary and felt grateful for an office a few metres from his home. In his youth Mac had relished the atmosphere of a bustling town but had long preferred the slow pace of Kauri Haven. Geographical isolation suited him; surrounded by fields, grassland and stands of tall trees, he felt able to conduct his life according to his own moral code, compromise no longer necessary. Perhaps that explained why he felt ashamed of the arrogance and impatience he'd displayed in the Communication Department, even though it had been simply a means to an end.

What price a future? he asked himself as the warm lights of the Traveller's Rest beckoned him inside.

# CHAPTER 26

The mid-flight linking and transfer of personnel went smoothly, the passengers in perfect agreement with the decision Commander Breta had made and happy to suffer the added discomfort an extra person would cause in the already overcrowded capsule. Breta's report of serious thruster problems had been greeted with loud cries of anguish forcing Kaire to demand silence so he could respond, and a collective sigh of relief had arisen following his offer to pilot the malfunctioning craft back to Sky.

Seated at the smaller craft's console, Kaire imagined the animated comments pervading the other ship: Breta's munificence in granting a clone the opportunity to undertake a primary voyage should he manage to repair the ship, the promise to remain in contact. This latter thought persisted, Kaire deliberating on the point of reporting back to a commander no longer in control of anything. Once on Earth, did Breta envisage a separate community of Sky People with himself as governor? From what he had learned and observed, Kaire felt this to be highly unlikely. According to Mac, migrants were expected to assimilate quickly; alien ways discouraged even during the initial quarantine period. They were also encouraged to adopt Aotearoan dress and discard their own vernacular.

A light flashing on the message panel dismissed speculation and disturbed the sense of gratitude experienced since the transfer. After checking the thrusters, Kaire had realised Breta's sombre message had been a ploy to ensure him an extended lifespan. A voyage into the unknown, free from the usual constraints, limited only by the pilot's lifetime or the Sky-ship's malfunction. The only regret, he couldn't share the experience with Pia. Tentatively he pressed the panel.

'Message for Sky323,' the automated voice announced. 'This message will delete on completion.'

Kaire focused on the screen.

'Message created prior to transfer,' Commander Breta advised. 'No issues with craft. Discard previous instructions, companion insists she accompany. Head for Kauri Haven and await our arrival.'

Kaire laughed out loud as he envisaged the scene: Pia in her usual forthright manner announcing she would rather die than remain on Earth alone, Breta pleading with her to see sense, a protracted argument, an eventual compromise. 'Anything to shut her up,' he said aloud as Breta's face faded. A check of the on-board databank revealed message deletion had taken place.

Kaire was in the process of reprogramming the route when a brilliant red light reminiscent of the solar flares he had observed on Earth illuminated the darkness. Fingers resting on the navigation panel, he peered out of the window, marvelling at this unexpected light show. At first he thought it was a comet or asteroid but dismissed that idea when it began to diminish. After a few minutes, a faint glow was all that remained; that too soon disappeared and he was left staring at familiar blackness peppered with the light points of distant stars.

Still reflecting on the source of such intense light, he refocused on the navigation panel. 'Destination: Kauri Haven, Kauri Coast, Aotearoa, Earth. Calculate distance and duration.'

'Calculations complete,' the computer advised after a few seconds. 'Reroute arc commencing.'

Thrusters slowed and the Sky-ship executed a graceful turn. *I'm facing the future,* Kaire thought as power surged and the computer advised a return to automatic pilot. A sense of release began to flow through his veins, relaxing taut muscles and washing away the residue of self-doubt lingering in his mind. How he lived the rest of his life was his responsibility now, success or failure a matter of wise decision-making not a blind following of rules. When Pia arrived at Kauri Haven, they would make plans for the future, a life of adventure travelling the world and beyond, or settling down in one place, he didn't care so long as they were together. Breta had given him not only the gift of extended life but also the opportunity to live anywhere on Earth except Aotearoa. Apart from some of the Sky naturals, only Pia knew he was a clone and she had assured him it made no difference to their relationship.

Suddenly a flash of fear rose to the surface, ominous in its intensity. Why had he overlooked a fact so critical it could change Pia's attitude towards him and even her desire to continue their relationship? No medical procedure or medication on Earth or Sky could correct his sterility. Complete honesty was essential; he couldn't expect Pia to commit to a long-term partnership until she knew this truth.

Eager for distraction, he left his seat and lay down in the narrow space behind the seats to begin his daily exercise routine in the hope physical activity would erase or at least mitigate the thick band of tension threatening to destroy his equilibrium.

Meanwhile, in a small room at the Traveller's Rest hotel, Mac struggled with his conscience, curiosity threatening to override integrity. The moment he entered the room, he'd deleted the Sky video from his communicator without viewing it, but the audio file headed 'Skyz59.29 urgent communication to AO9300' intrigued him. AO9300 was the code for the Immigration Department director; Mac had communicated with him on numerous occasions concerning new arrivals at Kauri Haven. The Sky code also puzzled him, being different from either Commander Breta's or Kaire's, so Mac tried to convince himself the message could be important.

On the bed beside him, the communicator flashed awaiting the delete command. Ignoring it, he focused instead on a grimy patch of paintwork directly behind the low bedhead, evidence of numerous other visitors. The Traveller's Rest had definitely seen better days but fatigue had dictated his decision to enter the first hotel he'd encountered on his side of the road. At least the meal had been acceptable; he'd eaten immediately after registering, his rumbling stomach a reminder he hadn't eaten anything since leaving Kauri Haven that morning.

Minutes passed. The command panel persisted with its request, green dots striking a faded yellow wall.

'Play audio file immediately,' Mac demanded as though the machine had intentionally ignored previous commands.

The first few minutes of the message, from an engineer named Cafel, confirmed what Mac had suspected, although he was surprised to learn Commander Breta had performed the surgery to alter Kaire's status. Subsequent information stunned Mac, prompting him to replay the file to make certain he'd heard correctly. To deliberately leave someone behind on a space station that could disintegrate at any moment seemed totally callous and he found it difficult to believe Commander Breta was responsible. Briefly he considered passing on the information to the Immigration Department the following day, but then realised he would have to invent an excuse for being in possession of the file, which could prove awkward. The more appropriate action would be to communicate with Commander Breta and find out whether Cafel had in fact been intentionally left on Sky.

After setting the communicator to sleep mode, he slid off the bed, undressed and walked into the shower room. Mentally and physically exhausted, he needed to wash away the day's grime before settling down to sleep.

Back at Kauri Haven, it was late in the evening before Mac had an opportunity to communicate with the Sky-ship. Since his return at least twenty people had streamed into his office, eager to discuss what to them were important matters.

A young voice answered and it took Mac a moment to realise he was speaking to Kaire.

'What are you doing in the Commander's craft?' he asked, somewhat afraid of the answer.

Kaire explained the thruster malfunction. 'Pia's on board the other ship,' he added, much to Mac's relief.

Then it was Kaire's turn to be shocked as Mac gave a brief account of Cafel's plight, deliberately omitting reference to the video file or surgery. The ensuing silence seemed ominous.

'Could Cafel have been left behind accidently?' Mac asked after a few minutes.

'No,' Kaire replied, relieved he could give a truthful response. 'When

I departed only Pia, the Commander and Cafel were left.' He wanted to add there had also been seven clones but felt it inappropriate to raise that particular issue.

'What kind of man is this Cafel? I mean, could he be lying?'

Kaire hesitated, unwilling to reveal his true feelings. Whatever Cafel had done to him in the past, he didn't deserve to be left alone on Sky. 'Easy enough to find out,' he replied in what he hoped was a neutral tone. 'I'll contact Sky and get back to you. The communication system should still be operational.'

'Wouldn't Commander Breta have shut it down before he left?'

'If Cafel's there he will have rebooted it.'

'Yes, of course. Thank you, Kaire, I'll wait for your response.'

'It shouldn't take long. Communication terminating.'

Kaire sat staring at a point beyond the blank screen, trying to envisage what he would do if Cafel answered his communication. It would take a further five months to reach Earth; he could easily return to Sky and rescue him, an extra two months' travel of no consequence. But …  He pressed the communication panel to prevent excuses arising in his mind. 'Sky323 to Skyz59.'

There was no response, so he set the Repeat Communication Code command for one hour. It sent one RCC every minute, with space in between for the recipient's code, but there was still no answer. Lights flashed on the main Sky console followed by strident sounds reverberating through every hub after thirty minutes of non-response; an improbable scenario if Cafel had been left behind. A reprieve from the onerous task of returning to Sky and then piloting the man to Earth, where a death sentence would be carried out despite the absence of a crime; Kaire harboured no illusions that Cafel would repay his decency. *A life for a life,* Kaire thought, recalling something he had read long ago in the data hub, although he couldn't remember the context.

'Sky323 to Skyz59.001,' he said in a clear voice.

Commander Breta answered immediately, his expression sombre. 'Further issues with the thrusters?'

'No, sir, an issue with Sky.'

'I thought you might have seen the explosion.'

'Explosion? Do you mean it's …?' Kaire faltered, reality difficult to acknowledge.

'Our home is no more, Kaire. We got out just in time.'

'Not all of us.'

'I had no choice, you know that.'

'I'm not talking about clones, I'm …' Loud static swallowed the remainder of Kaire's words.

'You're breaking up,' Breta shouted. 'Send a text file.'

Kaire heard only the word 'text' and terminated the communication. The interference must have been deliberate. Eleven passengers including Pia would have heard every word he said; it seemed the commander had something to hide after all. With a heavy heart, he reported Mac's information, requested confirmation or denial, and despatched the message.

The response, swift and succinct, swept away misgivings and left Kaire feeling guilty that he'd even considered Breta could be at fault. Elation soon supplanted guilt that his second chance at life was a certainty now Cafel had forfeited his.

'A life for a life,' he said aloud, remembering the words came from an archaic eBook called the *Old Testament*. Leaning back in his seat, he pondered the ethics of retaliation and came to the conclusion that whatever the ancient wisdom had dictated he could never condone murder.

# CHAPTER 27

Sunrise bathed the Kauri Coast in gold, washing away darkness and the nightmares that sometimes haunted those experiencing a life of liberty for the first time. It seemed to Pia, sitting on the beach in front of the perimeter fence, as though every grain of sand, every wave lapping the shore gleamed, promising light and life. Space had been a challenge, enthralling at first, but without her beautiful Skyman the return journey had become tedious in the extreme. Apart from the explosion, the view from the window had been unchanged for months: ebony sky sprinkled with silver stars. When at last a grey moon could be seen orbiting a blue planet, her relief had been immense and she'd cried out in delight, prompting the other passengers to stare at her in astonishment.

A year away from Earth had also failed to convince Pia a habitable planet existed elsewhere in the universe. Unlike Kaire, she envisaged her planet as the last in a long line, a living reminder of the inevitable consequences of evolution. Birth—life—death, each had its place in the overall scheme, although she didn't believe, as some had in the past, that an all-powerful creator had designed it thus. In her opinion, deities of any persuasion would surely have exerted more control and prevented human beings from wrecking the only home they possessed.

A glance at her timepiece reminded her of the imminent meeting with Mac. Reluctantly she got to her feet, brushed sand from clothes and sandals before making her way back to the unlocked gate leading to fields of burgeoning crops. She had returned to Kauri Haven only three days earlier, having spent several weeks at an isolated quarantine centre along with Commander Breta and other Sky People. The quarantine period had passed faster than she'd imagined due to her position as the only resident who had lived on Earth. At various times, every Sky Person had sought her out, asking questions, expressing doubts and seeking confirmation about aspects of life on Earth. As she'd expected, all had eagerly embraced food, some even making a show of tipping their Sustenance tablets into a rubbish container, while others had had to be restrained from overeating, the concept of three meals a day difficult to comprehend. More confusing was the need to cook some foods while others could be eaten raw. Fortunately sleeping arrangements hadn't caused any problems, the huts being divided into dormitories similar to those Pia had observed on Sky. In some respects, she felt it would be preferable for them to form a separate community along the lines of Kauri Haven where they could adjust to Earth life in private and in their own time, but she knew they would flounder without assistance from locals. Agriculture remained the basis of life in rural communities; without it a small isolated country like Aotearoa could not exist. But Sky People had never seen crops growing and if relocated to the South Island would probably baulk at the sight of a field full of sheep.

The problems faced by new immigrants faded as she turned away from the fields towards the main building. She had a more pressing problem of her own that so far hadn't been satisfactorily addressed by either Breta or Mac. Why was she still forbidden to contact Kaire? En route from Sky, non-communication had been essential; to the other passengers she was an Aotearoan government official, her relationship with Kaire of necessity undisclosed. But during their time in quarantine, Breta could easily have taken her to a far corner of the extensive garden and allowed her a brief conversation instead of saying communication was still barred for security reasons. How could that have compromised security and whose security anyway, hers, the country's, Kaire's? Mac, on the other hand, had been simply evasive when greeting her, saying not to worry, Kaire will no doubt communicate prior to landing.

As usual, Mac's office door was open but Pia knocked lightly and called out a greeting before stepping into the room.

'Come in, come, in,' he responded, swivelling around to face her. 'I'm longing to hear about your journey and Sky.'

She smiled but once seated in the chair close to his, her demeanour altered. 'Why the secrecy surrounding Kaire?' she demanded.

Mac's expression remained benign. 'Oh, I think you know the answer to that, Pia. You did assist the surgeon.'

Pia blushed. 'How did you find out? Did Breta tell you?'

Mac shook his head. 'It's a long and complicated story and I don't intend to repeat it now. But you must realise Kaire can't reside here.'

'I know the rules but I intend to spend my life with Kaire and it doesn't matter where.'

'Even in space?'

'Anywhere in the universe so long as we're together.'

Mac reached forward and cradled her hands. 'Don't throw your life away, Pia, I beg you. Passion doesn't last forever.'

'No, but love can and it's worth remembering that the reason I'm here is because Kaire saved me from a lengthy prison sentence.'

Mac released her hands. 'Very well, I'll permit him to land and pick you up.'

'Thank you for understanding, this means so much to me.' She smiled and leaned across to squeeze his arm. 'And now I'll tell you about my space odyssey, if you still want to hear it.'

Mac grinned. 'Of course I do.'

Some time later, she rose to leave but Mac raised a hand to stop her. 'I have a proposal and I'd be pleased if you would hear me out.'

Pia perched on the edge of the chair, reluctant to stay much longer. She had messages to answer from former students at work in the Brown Zone.

'There is much work to be done in Australia, Pia,' he said as though reading her mind. 'The Women's Line is still having problems, information leaked to authorities, members arrested.'

'Which zone?'

'Asian, northern part.'

Pia blanched. 'It must be Yuki. I always suspected she wasn't as stupid as she made out.'

'You weren't the only one. The trouble is no one knows where she is or what name she's using now and all attempts to find out have failed.'

For a while Pia remained silent, trying to recall details of the brief time spent with Yuki, attitudes expressed, personal information confided when they were alone together.

'I don't believe Yuki will have travelled far from her home village,' she said at last, 'or at least she'll return there as often as possible. The bond with her son was extremely strong.'

'I didn't realise she had a son. He must be fairly young.'

'About five years, I think. He lives with his White father.'

'I see.' Mac sat back in the chair, his brow furrowed in concentration. 'You could pass as White, Pia. With false ID you could visit the region and make discreet enquiries.'

'And Kaire?'

'A travelling companion?'

'A colleague would be preferable, I believe. We'll just have to think of a plausible reason for our visit.'

'So you'll consider this mission?'

'Yes, but I can't speak for Kaire. He may have other ideas.'

Mac smiled. 'Why don't we ask him now?'

Astonished, Pia could only nod her head and smile, light radiant as sunrise transfusing her golden eyes.

Over six months had passed since Pia had seen Kaire, longer if she counted quality time together. The night before his Sky-ship was due to land, she was so excited it proved impossible to sleep or even relax and in the end she got out of bed. Padding to the window, she drew back the curtains and scanned the night sky, as though she could pick out his silver ship with the naked eye from amongst the myriad stars.

Their reunion took place on dew-soaked grass beside the gleaming Sky-ship, Kaire wrapping his arms around her waist and planting a kiss on her lips before she even had a chance to speak. When at last he released her, she felt as light as dandelion spores blowing in the wind. Grabbing his hand, she led him in a dance around the Sky-ship as a celebration of his safe return. Beneath silver wings, they indulged in a further lingering embrace before setting off across the grass towards the main building and a meeting with Mac.

Several people greeted Kaire as they walked the gravel path leading to the entrance, slowing their pace to welcome him home, but although Pia returned their smiles, she couldn't help thinking of his rightful status as 'unacceptable immigrant.' By now the abdominal scar would have faded and if he so wished, Kaire could display his torso with pride, confident he resembled every other person on Earth. *What hypocrites we are*, she thought. *Identical twins share the same DNA, yet we don't regard them as freaks.*

When they entered the corridor, Mac was standing in his office doorway, one arm resting on the doorframe. 'Welcome back,' he called, hurrying towards them, arms outstretched. After much embracing, he escorted them into his office and closed the door.

After checking that both still wished to proceed with the mission, Mac sat between them, his monitor adjusted so all three could study the maps he'd downloaded earlier. The territory covered included the northern Asian Zone and Brown Zone land adjoining the Border River. After some deliberation, they had concluded Yuki was most likely living in this region.

'Have arrangements been made for transport to and from the landing site?' Kaire asked as Mac pointed to the first village on their itinerary.

'A car will be supplied for land travel in keeping with your status as school inspectors,' Mac replied, still focused on the map, 'but you won't be crossing in the Sky-ship.'

'Why ever not?'

'KAL felt a small fishing boat would be less conspicuous.'

'Maybe, but I prefer the option of a quick retreat.'

Mac turned away from the screen. 'We cannot risk the Sky-ship being discovered a second time.'

'I appreciate that but …'

'If we locate Yuki, are we to bring her back here?' Pia interrupted, anxious to curtail what could become a lengthy argument.

'No, you must communicate with the local Line Leader *before* approaching her. The Line will deal with Yuki.'

'And what does that mean?' Kaire asked naively.

Mac sighed. 'If she *has* betrayed the Line, it's up to them to determine her punishment.'

Pia noted Kaire's grim expression, the slump of his shoulders. 'Are the ID discs ready?' she asked, turning to Mac.

'Except for a visual image, which will be added once you've both had a haircut. Kela advised short hair is the fashion for White Zoners at present.'

Pia grimaced and fingered her long tresses. It had taken her the two years since leaving Working Party 2, where heads were shaved, to grow her hair to a length she preferred.

'As for clothes,' Mac continued, oblivious to her concern, 'suitable garments have been made from items once worn by settlers from the White Zone, so you'll look the part.'

'When do we leave?' Kaire asked as Mac leaned forward to close the mission files.

'In three days. The boat will pick you up from the beach just before dawn.'

Pia frowned. 'Won't the others think it odd we've disappeared again so soon, especially as the Sky-ship will remain here?'

'I've thought of that. If you approve, my suggestion is to announce that you've both gone to assist the Sky People settle in to their new home.'

Kaire looked thoughtful. 'Has it been decided where to locate them?'

Mac shook his head. 'Several locations have been mooted, that's all I know.'

'Anywhere near here?'

'I'm not privy to that information.'

'Just one more question, if I may?'

'Of course, Kaire.'

'Would you be able to arrange for Commander Breta to visit Kauri Haven when we return from Australia? I would like to see him before I leave Earth again.'

'Are you close to him?' Mac asked, surprised by the request.

'You could say that,' Kaire replied, bowing his head to hide the colour spreading across his pale cheeks.

Images juxtaposed in Mac's mind: the son he hadn't seen for years, the grandsons he'd never seen, the face viewed on a communicator screen, a face with Kaire's unusual green eyes. 'I understand,' he said in a low voice.

Silence settled over the room, each of them recalling loved ones no longer living and those separated on account of stringent regulations. Tears threatened to spill as Pia thought of her mother's death by firing squad. Inexplicably she wanted to run from the room, fling herself on her bed and bawl like a child. Only Kaire's presence prevented flight; she could sense his grief for the friends he'd grown up with, the carers that had nurtured him, the children that would never reach adulthood.

Suddenly Mac's arms were around their waists and he was drawing them close. 'Take great care of each other,' he said softly. 'I shall be holding you both in my heart.'

# CHAPTER 28

The sun had almost set when an Aotearoan fishing boat anchored a few kilometres off the Australian coast well beyond the reach of spotter station scanning equipment. Later in the evening, the boat's tender slipped into a narrow inlet a short distance from the Asian-Brown Zone border. Moonlight alone guided the fisherman as he steered the small craft up the tidal creek to a spot where rocks and shallow water rendered further navigation impossible. After cutting the engine, he allowed the tender to drift into a bank of white sand piled high by the tide against a rock platform jutting out from the shore. Kaire, seated in the bows, quickly jumped out and held the tender steady so that Pia, burdened with their bags, could disembark easily. When she had reached the rock platform, he shoved the tender back into deep water and stood watching as night swallowed its dark shape.

Leaving the creek behind, they walked in single file along a narrow track winding between spindly trees with contorted white limbs. Ethereal remnants of a once dense forest, they punctured the cloudless night sky as though determined to spoil its clarity. Dry leaves crunched underfoot breaking the silence and reinforcing their sense of trespass. Pia tried to reduce the sound by stepping in Kaire's footsteps but it proved impossible given his lengthy stride.

They had been walking for about half an hour when Kaire stopped to adjust his bag strap, so Pia took the opportunity to step up beside him. 'When should we communicate with the Line?' she whispered.

'Might as well do it now, that way I can give my shoulder a break.'

Grimacing, he rotated his shoulder joint. 'I wish we could have taken backpacks, far more comfortable than these bags when walking any distance.'

'I agree but we have to look the part.'

He nodded and pulled his communicator out of his shirt pocket. 'Thank the stars we'll have a car soon. It seems odd not to have my transporter.'

Long forgotten guilt surfaced, forcing Pia to turn her head and pretend to be studying trackside fauna. At the time, Kaire hadn't reprimanded her for losing the transporter and she wondered what had prompted him to mention it now. Perhaps he felt insecure travelling without either Sky-ship or transporter and the superior technology they contained. She recalled his frustration when communications failed or machines broke down at Kauri Haven. *But at least we still have a home*, she reflected, *even if it is degraded*.

'LLR2, go ahead 323,' an unfamiliar voiced advised.

'We are within two kilometres of the meeting point.'

'Transport in area. Advise when within two hundred metres.'

'Will do. Communication terminating.' Kaire hoisted the bag onto his shoulder. 'Brisk pace if you can, Pia. I don't want to hang about here for too long.'

Affronted, Pia pushed past him and powered up the track.


The rendezvous went without a hitch, the egg-shaped silver car appearing only seconds after they arrived at the point where the track divided in two. The driver, a young Asian woman, slid out of her seat, gestured to Kaire and Pia and disappeared into the trees without a word.

'I hope you can drive it,' Pia whispered as Kaire slipped into the driver's seat.

He peered at the control panel. 'Don't worry, it looks like a very basic model to me.'

The car began to move smoothly down the right-hand track.

*Typical*, Pia thought, *he thinks he knows everything about our technology*. Arms folded across her chest, she sat back in the seat, staring out at stark trees illuminated by the powerful headlight. After a few kilometres, trees gave way to undulating grassland dotted with low bushes but there was no sign of cultivation or the box-like houses she had expected to see in this region. Kaire drove fast, unaware that small Australian cars lacked the suspension his transporter had possessed, and in spite of the safety restraint Pia had to grip the arms of the seat to prevent jolting. From his dour expression, Kaire was clearly determined to put as much distance between them and the meeting point as possible in a very short time, so she didn't dare ask him to slow down. Grassland soon diminished and the car rattled over a patch of gravel before climbing a low rise. From the top Pia observed a long grey road ribbon, the first super path she had ever seen. No vehicles were using the road directly below, although she could see one parked in a semi-circular area off to one side.

'The main south-north super path,' Kaire remarked, noting her interest. 'One of the few remaining in the interior, apparently.' He looked over at the stationary car. 'How about a bit of fresh air?'

'Fresh, you must be joking!'

'I need to stretch my legs.' He slid back the door panel and climbed out.

By the time she caught up to him, he had descended several metres on the other side of the hill and was sitting on a patch of bare ground hugging his knees. 'I thought you wanted to stretch your legs?' She flopped down beside him.

'I'm playing safe, Pia. We don't want to be seen and I would prefer to wait until that vehicle has recharged before descending.'

'Why do you think there's so little traffic?'

'Kela told me only high-ranking officials can afford to purchase personal transport these days and most people, even in the White Zone, use trains for lengthy journeys.'

Pia frowned. 'The situation must be dire if White Zoners are economising.'

Kaire shrugged. 'The Australian economy is of no interest to me. I'm here on a mission and once it's accomplished I shall make plans for the next stage of my life.'

Pia noted his use of personal pronouns and wondered if *she* figured in his plans. 'Well it is of interest to me,' she said curtly. 'I was thinking how difficult life must be for all my friends in the Brown Zone.'

'Sorry, that didn't occur to me.'

'No, it wouldn't, you always focus on one thing at a time.'

'That's how I was trained to operate.'

'You're not a machine,' she retorted, exasperated by his tunnel vision.

An awkward silence followed, Pia deliberately turning away.

'No, I'm not a machine,' Kaire said quietly, 'but as you know I am a clone.'

Oh, not that again.

'And that means I have what some might term a defect.'

Pia twisted around. 'I thought the operation fixed that.'

'This has nothing to do with my navel.' He cleared his throat. 'All clones are sterile.'

Her eyes widened. 'What caused that?'

'It was a deliberate adaptation to preserve the integrity of DNA.'

'Could you explain that in simple language?'

'Repeated cloning weakens immunity to disease among other things.'

'I see.' Hands clasped against her mouth, she looked down at the dry earth, considering the implications. At this stage of her life creating a family was the last thing she wanted, but what of the future? Would she regret not being able to have a child? Now she understood why Kaire had spoken of plans for *his*, not *their* future; he was afraid she would reject him.

'I understand if you want to terminate our relationship.'

Her hands flew to his. 'No, I don't want that. I want to spend the rest of my life with you.'

'But wouldn't you want a baby at some stage?'

'Perhaps, but we could always consider donor sperm.'

Kaire stared straight ahead, images of a child not of his own flesh and blood flitting through his mind. What difference would it make? Would he love the child less? No answer was forthcoming and he had to admit a reluctance to envisage future feelings.

'There is a way we could have our own child,' she said, reading his mind, 'although it would require another person's consent.'

Kaire smiled and turned to face her. 'He has the same DNA and it would extend his family.'

'Do you think he'd agree?'

'We can but ask.'

Pia nodded. 'Let's wait a while, there's no rush.'

'True, we have important work to do before we can even think of settling down.' He got to his feet and walked to the top of the hill. Shielding his eyes with one hand, he surveyed the path below. 'Clear now,' he called back to her.

The car began to move, slowly at first, its wide wheels sliding a little on hard-packed earth washed smooth by rainstorms. As Kaire began to accelerate, Pia gritted her teeth and clutched the edge of her seat until her knuckles turned white. A plume of red dust fanned out behind them, obscuring the hillside. Halfway down, patches of grey bushes appeared, forcing Kaire to adopt a zigzag route that on several occasions threatened to overturn the vehicle, or so it seemed to Pia. He decelerated when they reached the base of the hill and they crawled to the edge of the super path where he looked in both directions before speeding diagonally across and heading north.

'I could do with some tropica after that!' she exclaimed, watching numerals stabilise on the velocity panel.

'Not before our inspection, Aimi,' he answered, emphasising her fake name.

She pouted, resenting his superior tone; their IDs showed identical positions.

'We should reach the village in thirty minutes,' he continued, 'provided the surface of the secondary path isn't too badly damaged.'

'I suppose road maintenance isn't considered worthwhile if there are so few vehicles.'

'More likely it's the local authorities' lack of interest.'

'Perhaps, but I imagine extreme weather plays havoc with the pathways in this area,' she added, irritated by his condescending tone.

He glanced out of the side window. 'It's certainly arid out here, we must be some distance from the coast.'

'The desert creeps closer to the green rim every year, even this far north, you know that.' She leaned over and slapped his wrist hard.

'What was that for?'

She placed her fingers to her lips.

'Sorry, Aimi, I was going a bit fast,' he answered, his tone contrite. Thank the moon for her diligence; his careless remark could have led to others that would certainly arouse suspicion if their conversation was being monitored.

Pia sat back in her seat, her thoughts focused on Kaire's continuing naivety. Despite his months on Earth, he seemed unable to discard knowledge gained during childhood, post-industrial Earth history compiled for twenty-third century students. She felt like shaking him and shouting, 'Almost two centuries have elapsed since your ancestors left Earth. The environment has altered!'

Before long the super path veered east and the landscape began to change, grey bushes giving way to clumps of small trees. Hills clothed with brown grasses rose from the plain and pools of water were visible at the bottom of steep creek banks. Further on, they encountered the first signs of cultivation, fields of wheat and corn separated by canals covered with domed cylindrical shields to reduce evaporation. Pia sat up straight and peered into the distance, hoping to see traces of human habitation. For some reason, she felt vulnerable cocooned in a small car with no other vehicles in sight. Even an empty train line would have provided a link with the villages dotted along coast and rivers and diminished her anxiety.

'Here we go,' Kaire remarked, slowing as he prepared to leave the path. 'Ten minutes to our destination, path conditions permitting.'

'Civilisation at last!' cried Pia. 'Let's hope someone's there to meet us.'

'It was suggested we call at the trooper station first even though it's not mandatory for us to check-in on arrival in this region.'

'It makes sense to be polite, Inspector Cline.'

'Indeed it does, Inspector Aimi.'

*Aimi and Cline,* she thought. *Not quite the same ring to it as Pia and Kaire.*

'Aimi and Cline,' said Kaire wistfully, risking a further rebuke.

Pia reached over and tapped his arm. 'We are not a couple, Cline,' she said sternly.

Now it was Kaire's turn to pout.

Suppressing a laugh, she ran her fingers up and down his leg.

The first dwellings they saw appeared to rise out of the fields of waving corn like the bunkers of old built along the coast to observe the passage of enemy ships. Square blocks of concrete, flat roofs topped with semi-vertical solar panels, were strung together by covered walkways and resembled factories rather than homes, with their small, high windows placed at regular intervals. There were no signs of the inhabitants or any vehicles visible on the path ahead.

'Even windowless domes looked more inviting,' Pia remarked.

Kaire wished he could remind her she no longer lived in a Brown Zone dome and should consider Kauri Haven's mud-brick houses home, but remarked instead, 'It's of no consequence what type of structure one inhabits, Aimi. The people one shares the space with are what matters.'

'Right as usual, Cline.'

Ahead, a large vehicle emerged from a narrow track running parallel to the path, forcing Kaire to decelerate quickly. 'Hey, it pays to look when entering a path!' he shouted as though the driver could hear him.

Several heads turned to look back at their car.

'A worker carrier,' Pia remarked. 'Probably heading for the local factory.'

'Late I expect,' said Kaire, glancing at the console timepiece. 'School begins in an hour, which gives us time to check in at both the trooper station and the inn before we begin our inspection.'

Pia nodded. 'Good, I could do with a cold drink and something to eat.'

Kaire laughed. 'Always thinking of your stomach, Aimi.'

'I am not!'

He squeezed her hand. 'Just thinking of your figure, dear colleague.'

Conversation petered out after that, as both contemplated the imminent inspection, hoping they would appear authentic, ask the right questions, make the right responses. Pia felt far from confident, having read that at least five years' teaching experience was required prior to taking up the position. Apart from looking too young to be a school inspector, she felt a few months teaching at Kauri Haven was very little to draw on.

As it turned out, Pia was only required to play a minor role during their first inspection, the school's chief instructor, used to dealing with male troopers, addressing most questions to Kaire. A tiny woman with brown hair piled on top of her head, the chief instructor welcomed them in a friendly manner but appeared eager to complete the inspection, leading them through the three classrooms with undue haste. Kaire was surprised to see a smattering of White children among the rows of Asians but refrained from comment, aware he knew nothing of Asian Zone regulations regarding racial mixing. The children were dressed in what he presumed was compulsory school dress: sleeveless blue tunics reaching to the knees for the girls, shorter blue tunics with baggy shorts for the boys. Both sexes wore their hair long and tied back with a black ribbon. Footwear was not in evidence even among the White children and all seemed small for their age, their faces thin and eyes listless. It was the same in each classroom, a total absence of vitality and lack of interest once introductions by the chief instructor had prompted a polite but muted greeting. When they reached the third classroom, Kaire tried to engage an older boy in conversation, but he only replied in monosyllables to questions concerning school subjects.

Pia was shocked and dismayed to see undernourished children in an area where crops appeared to be growing in abundance and could only surmise there had been a severe drought the previous year. She also noticed the vintage of message-boards lying on the chipped and faded plastic desktops, the cracked concrete floor. *More underprivileged than Village 10 School,* she thought, pondering the obvious lack of resources. Could she risk a few questions once the tour had finished?

The initial impression gained on entering the village had been one of order and an attempt to create a less austere environment. The concrete houses set either side of the secondary path were plain but a line of rocks painted white defined each small front garden, inside which neat rows of what looked at a glance like vegetables had been planted in the red soil. At the far end of the village the trooper station, also constructed of grey concrete, was surrounded on three sides by small eucalypts, evenly spaced, some of which were flowering. A gravel path led up to the entrance, a concrete pad painted green and shielded from heat by a large blue sun-shield. On the opposite side of the path, a low concrete wall enclosed school buildings and the sun-shielded play area. Although the play area consisted of nothing but hard-packed red earth dotted with recycled plastic benches, a few grey-green shrubs had been planted directly behind the wall.

After the inspection, the chief instructor escorted Kaire and Pia to her office, where she rambled on about the school's academic achievements. Pia appeared attentive, a polite smile plastered to her lips, but she remained determined to ask about the children's health. An opportunity arose when the instructor's communicator began to hum.

'Excuse me a moment.' The chief instructor reached over and quickly silenced it.

'The children seemed rather listless,' Pia observed. 'Has there been illness in the village?'

Kaire shot her a warning glance; this was no time to play the over-zealous inspector. Their safe passage through the region's villages depended on completing inspections promptly without drawing attention to themselves.

The chief instructor hesitated, fingers nervously twisting the hem of her faded tunic. 'No more than usual, Inspector Aimi. As I'm sure you know, this region is prone to respiratory diseases.'

Kaire leaned forward. 'Yes, we are aware of that. May I suggest keeping the children indoors during dust storms or crop harvesting?'

'We already have those rules in place,' she said, her expression betraying annoyance. 'I'll remind the class instructors.'

Kaire rose from his seat. 'We must leave now.'

Reluctantly Pia got to her feet.

Outside in the street Kaire demanded to know why she had acted so recklessly. Green eyes blazed and her explanation that she'd felt compelled to express concern for the children's health failed to placate him. 'From now on you keep to the script,' he ordered, anger visible in the set of his mouth. 'White school inspectors do not raise contentious issues that have nothing to do with education.'

'I am not White,' she countered.

'Keep your voice down. Do you want to alert the troopers?'

'Sorry, sorry, I didn't think a simple question would cause a problem.' She sniffed back tears. 'I just couldn't bear to think of children going hungry. It shouldn't happen, even in this country.'

His expression softened as he looked down at her. 'I know, I know, but we're not here to query Australian government food policies.'

'Do you think the government are deliberately reducing food supplies to some areas?'

'It's possible, especially during times of drought. You told me yourself the best produce is always sent to the White Zone.'

'Yes, but we were never hungry.'

'Forget it, Pia. Asian Zone social issues are not your concern.' Turning on his heel, he began to walk towards the inn.

Left alone in the middle of the street, still upset by what she had observed and frustrated by her inability to effect change, Pia almost envied Kaire's ability to disengage emotionally from matters that were not his immediate concern. But another thought soon surfaced and she began to run after him. No one had coerced Kaire into helping her people, not now, not years before in her mother's dome high on Storyteller Hill. Kaire had chosen to disobey his commander's orders; he had not remained a dispassionate observer.

# CHAPTER 29

Subsequent inspections did little to allay Pia's fears about malnutrition but wisely she kept her thoughts to herself. Time was running out for the mission and so far they had failed to discover the whereabouts of Yuki's son, despite being provided with a file containing the names and identity number of every child enrolled as they entered each school. Further communication with Line Leader Roe confirmed the boy had been resident in Asian Village 2 until one year ago; however, his current location and that of his White father remained unknown. Given the father's years of residence in the north of the Asian Zone, it had come as no surprise to learn he was a trooper. Of Yuki there had been no sightings for some time, leading Kaire to believe she had left the area permanently, perhaps to follow her lover and son. Pia wasn't so sure, figuring Yuki would remain where she had friends that could help her evade detection. Relocating legitimately wasn't an option; Yuki would still be on the 'Escaped Prisoner File' distributed to troopers-in-charge throughout the country.

'Why don't I pay a visit to her friend Vina while we're here?' Pia suggested. 'She's never met me.'

They had walked a short distance from Village 2 inn, having decided to enjoy the relative cool of the evening. Their inspection was scheduled for the following morning.

'Too dangerous. She could become suspicious if you asked about Yuki.'

'I'd be discreet.'

Kaire frowned, remembering Pia's question during the visit to Village 8 school. 'No, it's imperative you stay in the role of school inspector.'

'I could mention Yuki's son,' Pia persisted, 'express a professional interest in how he's adjusted to a new school.'

'I doubt a school inspector would know he had relocated. None of the files we've received so far have listed anything other than current enrolments.'

'Supposing Vina has a child of her own at the school, he or she might have known Max.'

Suddenly Kaire stopped walking. 'Oh my stars, how could I have forgotten? Vina is a Chief Instructor?'

'Do you think she'd recognise you in a different context?'

'It's possible.'

'I'll make some excuse for your non-attendance.'

'To think I could have blown our cover.' He turned his attention back to the path, a narrow strip of cracked earth bordered on either side by dust-shrouded bushes.

On arrival at the school, Pia explained that her colleague was suffering from gastroenteritis and had thought it wise to remain in his room at the inn, prompting no comment from Chief Instructor Vina other than hope of a swift recovery. Unlike previous inspections, Vina escorted Pia straight to her office, where she spoke affectionately of the students, focusing on their good behaviour and willingness to learn rather than academic achievements.

In the first classroom, the children exhibited none of the listlessness observed in other schools and were eager to answer Pia's questions. The classroom had been freshly painted and the children's desks, although faded, showed no sign of chips or cracks, while their message-boards gleamed as though they had just been removed from the packaging. Plump arms and round faces were also much in evidence, malnutrition clearly not an issue here. These pronounced physical differences suggested to Pia that Vina had access to those in government departments other than education. On the surface Village 2 resembled all the other villages they'd visited, drab concrete houses positioned either side of a dusty path, a small marketplace, an inn and a trooper station. Trees planted around the trooper station and school appeared healthier as did the vegetables growing in tiny gardens, but that could be explained by the village's proximity to the river.

Movement in the front row refocused Pia's attention and she watched with interest as a small boy, darker-skinned than most, slipped out of his seat carrying what looked like a strip of bark. Stepping forward, he presented her with a bark painting depicting a river bordered by trees and several stick figures swimming.

'Thank you so much,' she said, smiling down at him. 'I shall treasure this always.'

Beside her the class instructor beamed. 'Royal is an excellent artist for his age.'

'How old are you, Royal?' Pia asked.

'Six years and one month,' he answered proudly. 'I'm the oldest in this class.'

'And that means you must set a good example, show your friends how grown up you are.' Pia smiled indulgently.

The boy gave a toothy grin, which quickly subsided. 'My best friend had to move,' he said sadly.

'That's a shame, but maybe you could visit him sometime?'

The boy shook his head. 'I don't have a boat.'

'A boat?'

'Max said he was going to an island in the middle of a big bay.'

Vina cleared her throat. 'It's time we moved on, Inspector Aimi. You may sit down, Royal.'

Back at the inn, Pia showed Kaire the bark painting but decided not to mention the boy's friend, Max. Uncertain how far Vina's influence extended, she felt it prudent not to pursue the matter until they had left the village. To her surprise, Kaire recalled having seen paintings of this type in documentaries he'd studied in the data hub and suggested the boy Royal could be descended from indigenous Australians. Unlikely, Pia told him, as those people died out long ago during an epidemic that had spread from the African continent. In truth, she was only repeating a conversation overheard months earlier; Sannah and Fley had made certain Pia knew the true history of her own people's flight from their swamped Pacific islands but had never mentioned

Australia's original inhabitants. Kaire felt it was pointless to argue about the boy's heritage when neither of them knew the truth, so left further questions unasked.

As they drove towards the last of the border villages, Pia could hardly contain her excitement. Convinced Max and his father were now living on one of the bay islands only a short sea-craft journey from her home village, she planned to communicate with Maris when they stopped to recharge the vehicle.

Line Leader Maris had just returned home from Island 1's spotter station, where she worked, when the tiny communicator she kept hidden in an inside pocket began to vibrate against her thigh. Weary from a long shift, she tried to ignore it, but the persistent vibration began to get on her nerves. 'LLM receiving you,' she said automatically, pressing the centre panel without taking note of the incoming code. 'How can I assist?'

'Sky 323 requiring information,' Pia answered.

Maris fell back against the bed but quickly recovered her composure. 'Where are you?

'Sending coordinates now.'

Numerals appeared on the screen and she gasped. Pia was less than a hundred kilometres away. 'Oral or text communication?'

'Oral, secure this end.'

'Give me time to go upstairs.'

'Okay.'

Maris hurried up the stairs to the living chamber where she opened the rear door panel and stepped into her lush garden. 'Go ahead 323.'

'A trooper from AZV2 arrived in the bay region approximately one year ago. Island unclear. His son Max, five or six years old, may be with him. We need confirmation of location and if possible a DNA sample from the son.'

'I'll look into it. The latter request could be difficult but I'll do my best.'

'Thanks.' Pia noticed Kaire had moved away from the recharging machine and was heading for the car. 'All done,' she called out to him.

He raised an arm and slid into the driver's seat.

'Someone with you?' asked Maris.

'A beautiful Skyman.'

'Lucky you. LLM terminating.'

Maris couldn't stop smiling as she walked away from the stand of palm trees planted in memory of her partner Jade, who had drowned while on a Women's Line mission. *Pia deserves some happiness,* she mused, bending down to pick a scarlet flower from a hibiscus bush. 'Keep safe,' she called to the cloudless sky.

True to her word, Maris did her best and Max was soon located on the other large island in the bay, a former rocky promontory isolated from the mainland by rising sea levels centuries before. A Women's Line member, recently transferred from a mainland village, confirmed the boy's presence. As the island's only medical worker, she had the authority to access the DNA records of all the island inhabitants should the need arise, so direct contact with the boy could be avoided. After copying Max's file, she forwarded it to Peni at Kauri Haven for her to compare his DNA with Yuki's.

Less than an hour's driving time from the meeting point where they had arranged to return the car, Kaire's personal communicator, kept in his bag on the back seat, began to hum. Kaire ignored it, preferring to wait until they had reached their destination.

'I'll get it,' Pia offered, reaching over to open the bag. Unexpectedly, the sight of Mac's friendly face brought tears to her eyes. 'Inspector Aimi here. How can I help you?' Pia answered, struggling to keep her voice steady.

'The mother-son relationship is confirmed,' Mac reported.

'Thank you for such a prompt response.'

'We now suggest a longer stay to deal with the situation.'

'What? You must be joking!'

Kaire reached over and snatched the communicator out of her hands. 'Reception poor, Chief Inspector, we will communicate later. Terminating.' He tucked the communicator in his over-shirt pocket. 'Whatever is the matter with you, Aimi? That was no way to speak to a superior.'

'I'm sorry, I can't explain my behaviour except to say I just want to go home.'

Kaire sighed and patted her hand. 'The first extended period away from home is always difficult, Aimi. Don't worry, you'll get used to life in the Asian Zone.'

'Thanks for understanding, Cline.' She sniffed. 'I'll send my apologies to the Chief right now.'

Kaire nodded his approval.

They drove on in silence, considering the implications of a longer stay. A change of plan would involve far more than rescheduling the boat, but with no path-side foliage to hide behind, they couldn't risk stopping to contact Line Leader Roe. Pia felt physically sick at the thought of remaining in the region for an extended period. It was too close to the Brown Zone; too close to the border court dome where she'd spent time as a prisoner following her arrest two years earlier. Likewise, Kaire felt it would be unwise to travel any further north, if that was what Mac had in mind and failed to see why local line leaders couldn't takeover the mission at this point.

They turned onto a narrow unmarked track, stands of palm and ti-tree replacing the patches of bush and brown grasses growing beside the secondary path. There were no villages in this low-lying area, flooding being prevalent during the wet season. Since Mac's communication, they hadn't encountered any recharging stations, so Kaire presumed the track didn't link up with other paths and would soon peter out.

'The inn at last,' Pia said brightly as the end of the track came into view.

Kaire smiled. 'I'll be pleased to get out of this vehicle, it's a little cramped.' He pulled off the track onto a patch of dried grass and disengaged drive.

Nearby palms offered a little shade, so after retrieving their bags they walked over and sat with their backs against smooth trunks to wait as instructed for the car's new driver. At the last recharging station, Kaire had sent Line Leader Roe their estimated time of arrival and in return received instructions for the rendezvous with the fishing boat. They were to make their way to an isolated beach a few kilometres' walk from the track and take cover in a cave at the southern end. As before, a small tender would materialise on dusk to return them to the boat.

After a few minutes, two figures dressed in similar clothing to their own appeared on the track, entered the car and drove away in a cloud of dust.

'We'd better get going,' Pia remarked, reaching for her bag.

Kaire raised a hand to his lips and gestured with the other to a patch of tangled grass a short distance away, where a man wearing the boots and tunic of a trooper could be seen making his way towards them. As he drew closer, it became apparent the man was much older than was usual for a trooper, and instead of a stun gun he carried a bag and what appeared to be a long pole.

Puzzled, Kaire scrambled to his feet and called out a greeting.

The trooper stopped walking and stared at them for a moment. 'Greetings to you, young man. I am Trooper Reyd. I've come to investigate what sounded like a vehicle speeding away.'

'You don't know pleased we are to see you, Trooper Reyd,' Kaire replied. 'We are the victims of a vehicle snatching.' He indicted Pia still sitting beneath the palm trees. 'My er, colleague and I came here for a little privacy, if you know what I mean, and …'

Trooper Reyd glanced at Pia and smirked.

'And just as we were making ourselves comfortable, two people emerged from the bush and stole our car.'

'You left it unsealed I suppose.'

Pia got to her feet. 'Yes, we didn't think anyone would be around here.'

'Your minds on other things,' Trooper Reyd muttered, stepping towards Kaire. 'And how do you suppose they knew the code? I presume you had the sense to disengage drive?'

Kaire nodded. 'I imagine it's possible to override the code?'

'Not too difficult for the technically minded.' He stared at Kaire's face and then lowered his gaze to the pale hands protruding from the sleeves of the over-shirt. 'Not from around here, are you?'

'No, my colleague and I are school inspectors. We've been in the area for several weeks.' Kaire reached into his trouser pocket for his ID and handed it over.

Trooper Reyd peered short-sightedly at the small plastic disc. 'Inspector Cline.'

'That's right.'

Pia stepped forward, holding out her disc. 'I'm Inspector Aimi.'

'Put them away, I can't verify them without my work communicator.'

*He's not on duty then,* Pia thought, *which explains the lack of a weapon.* She replaced the ID disc in her pocket. 'Enjoying a bit of fishing?'

'I was until I heard your vehicle.'

'Have you a vehicle nearby?' Kaire asked. 'We would really appreciate a lift to the nearest village.'

'I have a boat.'

'Anything will do. We just need to get somewhere we can hire another vehicle or board a train so we can get to our next inspection.'

The trooper grinned. 'You two will have a bit of explaining to do, eh? The nearest school is some distance away.'

Pia looked at the ground as though embarrassed.

'Don't worry, my dear, I promise not to tell. Shall we say two bottles of tropica?'

'Three will be fine,' said Kaire, 'if you can direct us to an inn.'

'There's one in my village. Come on, let's get moving, I'll communicate the vehicle theft back at the boat.'

Leaving their bags stowed in long grass behind the palms, they followed Trooper Reyd, taking care to tread where his boots had already flattened the long grass to avoid disturbing snakes. After walking for what Pia estimated was no more than five hundred metres, they reached a large sand dune. From the top they had a clear view of the ocean and a white beach stretching as far as the eye could see both north and south. The Border River estuary wasn't visible, leading Pia to believe they were further down the coast than she'd thought.

A small boat could be seen lying on the sand and she pondered whether they could risk overpowering the slightly built trooper and steal it. The boat wouldn't take them to Aotearoa but they could probably reach the narrow inlet further down the coast where they'd made landfall weeks earlier. Plans evaporated when she noticed what looked like oars sticking out of the bow; no way could they row all the way to the inlet.

'Excellent exercise,' Trooper Reyd remarked, noting her gaze.

She smiled in his direction. 'Good for you, most people would prefer power.'

'I sit on my arse all day at the station, damn trooper-in-charge won't let me out on patrol, he thinks I'm too old.'

'Surely not,' she flattered.

'Eighty-nine next month. He only keeps me on because I know the area and he's too mean to employ someone younger at a higher wage.'

'Is your village far?' Kaire asked.

Trooper Reyd pointed south. 'A half hour row on the right tide.'

Kaire shaded his eyes with his hands and looked down the coast. 'Could get rough, I imagine.'

'Yep, but I don't come up here then. Those days I fish from the shore.'

'Very wise,' said Kaire and, risking a second look, searched the ocean for signs of a fishing boat.

# CHAPTER 30

An immense sand dune covered with a tangled mat of Carpabro-tus, a succulent commonly known as 'pig face', protected Asian Village 23 from ocean storms and erosion. Several rows of concrete dwellings stretched from the dune to a small freshwater lake gleaming green in bright afternoon light. Along the shore facing the village, market stalls stood empty beneath a sun-shield while a second shield shaded the play area of the adjacent school.

Trooper Reyd's home, closest to the sand dune, appeared older and shabbier than the rest, at least from the outside. Pia stood in the shade of a wind battered ti-tree opposite the door waiting for Kaire and Reyd to appear, reluctant to enter the house even though she'd been told it wasn't locked. The men had remained behind to secure the boat to its mooring, one of numerous concrete bollards arrayed either side of a long narrow pier. When Trooper Reyd had suggested she make her way to his home and pointed out a track leading around the base of the dune, she'd presumed he wanted a word with Kaire in private, though for what reason she couldn't imagine.

There was no sign of life either in or around the nearby houses, for which Pia was grateful. No doubt Reyd would take them to the trooper station at some point but she was anxious not to share the tale of their 'rescue' with the villagers. News travelled fast and she hoped a reasonable length of time would elapse before troopers began to search for the car. She had no idea where the vehicle had originated and, apart from giving its current occupants a head start, she wanted to be well away from this village before it was located. Kaire's communicator remained tucked in his over-shirt pocket so she couldn't use the time alone to contact Line Leader Roe and alert her to their predicament.

Movement caught her eye; she saw the two men emerge from behind the palm tree marking the end of the beach track. Stepping out of the shade, she waved and called a greeting. Reyd waved back; Kaire, an oar under each arm, smiled but was too far away for Pia to notice his expression. As they approached, she searched Kaire's face for signs of trouble and seeing none she began to relax, presuming Reyd had simply wanted man-to-man conversation about their supposed detour and the car theft. She walked over to join them.

'What are you doing out here?' Reyd asked. 'You don't want to burn that lovely skin.'

Pia smiled. 'Don't worry, Trooper Reyd, I've been standing in the shade. Besides, any damage would have been done on the boat.'

Reyd studied her face. 'Yes, you are a bit pink.' He stepped onto the cracked concrete pad in front of the house, crossed to the door and pushed it open. 'Come in, come in.' He ushered Pia inside and gestured towards the chairs surrounding a low table.

In the doorway Kaire stood holding the oars. 'Just lean them against the wall,' said Reyd, anticipating Kaire's question.

Following some welcome refreshments, Trooper Reyd escorted them to the trooper station, a square concrete building set apart from the rest of the village on the far side of the lake. The trooper on duty, who looked even older than Reyd, took their ID discs and slotted them into a scanner, perched on the far edge of the counter. Much to Pia's surprise, he then proceeded to chat with Reyd instead of reading the data on the screen. Although Trooper Reyd mentioned the theft of the car in some detail, his colleague merely shrugged and said it would be long gone by now and wasn't worth pursuing. Pia suppressed a smile, relieved they had chanced upon such incompetent troopers.

'No problem here.' The trooper handed back the ID discs. Both Kaire and Pia smiled before pocketing their discs.

'In the absence of transport, we would be grateful if you could direct us to the nearest train line,' said Kaire, resting his elbows on the counter.

'No problem, I'll take you there myself in the trooper car—it's a long walk. My shift finishes in a couple of hours. In the meantime, why don't you take a look around the village? The market should be starting soon.'

'Thank you, we'll do that.' Kaire moved away from the counter.

'Don't forget my reward for rescuing you,' Reyd called.

Kaire smiled. 'I won't.'

The door opened and Kaire stood aside to let Pia pass.

When they reached the marketplace, most of the stalls had been uncovered and a throng of villagers were queuing to purchase goods. For a few moments, Kaire and Pia stood on the periphery, surveying the nearest stalls to see if anyone was selling bags. Boarding a train without a bag of any kind would look suspicious. They still had some Asian Zone tokens left, with a bit of luck sufficient to buy two bags. At the very least, they would have to travel a few stations down the line. In communication with Line Leader Roe as they walked from trooper station to marketplace, she had advised it would take several hours to organise a car to take them to a safe house near the coast. The wait for another boat to pick them up could be lengthy, as the Aotearoan vessel initially sent had departed soon after they failed to show. Roe had also confirmed the car had been returned safely and was now parked near the factory from where it had been stolen weeks earlier.

'Over there.' Pia pointed to a stall on the opposite side of the market where numerous bags hung like colourful fruit on a structure resembling a tree. They wandered over, pausing here and there to glance at other stalls.

Pia examined several bags before spotting a plain one she hoped wouldn't use up too many tokens. 'How much for the red one?' she asked the skinny young man behind the stall.

'Ten.' He plucked the bag from its branch and opened the catch. 'Plenty of pockets inside for all your bits and pieces.'

She stepped forward, feigning interest before counting her tokens. 'It's just what I need. Beautiful workmanship.'

The man smiled and took the proffered tokens. 'Should last you years.' He handed her the bag. 'New here, aren't you?'

'Visiting for the day, courtesy of Trooper Reyd.'

The man nodded. 'Enjoy the rest of your stay.'

Pia smiled and turned to suggest Kaire purchase one of the brown bags, but to her consternation he had vanished and she found herself staring down at a young woman clutching a large basket to her chest. 'Excuse me, did you see …' Pia began, then realised her question was best left unsaid. 'Did you see any good produce on the fruit stall?'

The woman shook her head. 'Sorry, I haven't been near the fruit stall.'

'Better see for myself then.' Pia slipped past the woman and walked slowly to the edge of the marketplace where she searched for Kaire's tall figure, certain to stand out amongst the much shorter villagers.

He was nowhere in sight.

Anxious now, she considered what to do. Returning to Reyd's house and making some excuse about having left her colleague at the market was an option, but she felt uncomfortable at the thought of concealing her concern and engaging in what could prove difficult conversation. Instead she decided to search the entire village, so slung the bag over her shoulder and set off towards the adjacent building, figuring no one would think it odd for a visiting school inspector to take a look at the village school.

She had reached the gate leading into the play area behind the school and was about to open it when she heard footsteps crunching on the gravel path behind her. Twisting around, she saw the stallkeeper rounding the corner of the building and heading her way. A smile plastered to her face, she hurried over. 'Did I leave something on the stall?'

'No, I forgot to give you this.' He pressed a package into her hand. 'I always give my special customers a free headscarf with the purchase of a bag.' He smiled. 'Well, aren't you going to look at it?'

Tentatively Pia untied the red ribbon and pulled the wrapping apart. 'It's beautiful,' she exclaimed. 'How kind of you.'

'Try it on then.'

Carefully she unfolded the delicate white scarf, revealing a sliver of black plastic.

'It only works over short distances,' the stallkeeper explained, 'but it should be sufficient for you to communicate with your friend.'

Speechless, Pia could only stare at the tiny communicator nestled in white fabric.

'He's safe for now, but I suggest you communicate before visiting the inn … and give the school a miss.'

Pia looked up. 'How did you know?'

'A message from LLR to my partner.'

'But why did my, er, friend leave so suddenly?'

'We have another unexpected visitor today, I noticed her in the market.'

'Who is she?'

'Chief Instructor Vina from Village 2.'

Pia gasped.

'Don't worry, my partner managed to get your friend away before Vina could approach.'

'Why the inn?'

'It's the safest place. My brother works there.'

'Won't Vina contact the troopers?'

'I doubt it, she's not here on official business so probably won't want to draw attention to her presence.'

Pia frowned. 'I'm still confused. Did Vina know we were here?'

'We don't believe so. She comes here occasionally to visit a friend, a fairly new arrival. We've been keeping an eye on both of them for a while. It's not usual for a chief instructor to befriend a carer.' He glanced over his shoulder. 'I'd best get back. I've told my brother you'll be calling in for a drink.' And without another word, he turned and began to walk back to the marketplace, leaving Pia hoping the day's bad luck had just metamorphosed into good.

# CHAPTER 31

Despite lack of proof, Chief Instructor Vina remained confident the man she'd seen standing near the leather-worker's stall was the White man she had admitted to her home more than a year earlier. That he had disappeared without a trace within minutes of her looking his way seemed more than a little suspicious, but he had not appeared to be in a hurry. At the time, there had been two other people by the stall: a White woman examining a bag whose face Vina couldn't see, and a villager patiently waiting her turn. It had taken some time for Vina to move through the crowd to the stall and by then the White woman had also vanished. Vina had approached the villager, whom she recognised as the mother of a small boy friendly with the children her friend cared for, but gained little information other than the White woman was a stranger. The stallkeeper, Teo, who worked at the inn in the evenings, had proved useless, maintaining all Whites looked the same to him, so he couldn't say whether he had seen the woman before.

As she left the marketplace, Vina thought she saw Teo rushing towards the school but when she turned and looked over at the stall, he was still there serving a customer. Puzzled as to why anyone would be in a hurry when the school was closed, she considered following the man, then dismissed speculation and headed for her friend's place instead. After the visit, she would go to the inn for supper. The White strangers were bound to be there, it being the only place in the village where meals could be purchased. She walked at an unhurried pace, stopping briefly to exchange greetings with one of the school instructors on her way to the market before turning into the third and last row of houses.

Later in the evening, Vina made her way to the inn. Her friend had been a little disappointed when she declined an invitation to supper, but the present of a bag of fruit purchased at the market soon smoothed ruffled feathers. As usual, the bar was crowded with villagers, mostly those from the nearby factory enjoying a drink at the end of a shift. Vina made her way over to the counter where the ever-charming Teo was busy serving customers. For an instant, Vina forgot her mission and wished she were younger.

'Evening Teo,' she called. 'The usual when you're free.' He answered with a brilliant smile and a wave of the hand.

Perched high on a bar stool, Vina could look over the heads of the crowd standing by the bar to the tables and chairs reserved for those eating meals. Set along one wall, close to the windows, they were to her annoyance unoccupied. She surveyed the crowd but apart from old Trooper Reyd, a perennial nuisance to her friend with his gifts of inedible fish and penchant for lengthy chatter, she could see only faces resembling her own.

'Wonderful to see you again so soon, Vina,' Teo remarked from the other side of the counter. 'You're looking splendid—that red scarf really suits you.'

'Why thank you, Teo.' She handed over a token and picked up the glass of tropica he had placed on the counter in front of her. 'Any other visitors today?' she asked casually. 'I thought I saw a couple of White faces by your stall.'

'Day visitors, long gone.'

Vina struggled to hide her disappointment. 'I'm sure I recognised one of them from an education conference I attended a couple of years ago.'

Teo frowned. 'I don't think that's likely, Vina. The woman I spoke to said she had something to do with transport.' He turned away to serve another customer.

Vina sipped her drink, wondering if the visitors could have requested some privacy and been shown into the room at the rear, generally used for village meetings. Though why Teo would lie about their presence she couldn't imagine. *Trooper Reyd will know,* she thought, draining her glass and replacing it on the counter.

She slipped off the stool and was on her way over to him when Teo called out, 'Vina you've left your scarf.'

Automatically she touched her neck before turning around. To her embarrassment, Teo was prancing around behind the bar, twirling her scarf above his head, much to the amusement of nearby patrons.

'Thank you, Teo,' she said, approaching the counter. 'No need to make a fool of yourself.'

Teo grinned and handed it over. 'Lighten up, Vina, it's the factory holiday tomorrow!'

She forced a smile and pocketed the scarf. But when she turned to retrace her steps, Trooper Reyd was nowhere to be seen.

The cellar was cold, damp and cramped but at least Teo had supplied them with warm soup and a drink before locking the door behind him. Neither Pia nor Kaire risked speaking, even though the cellar walls were thick, at least a metre of rough concrete and the floor above also concrete. Instead they communicated via text, the tiny communicator Pia had been given proving slow but adequate. Only twenty minutes remained before they were due at the trooper station and both queried how anyone could get them away from the inn without their being seen. From what they'd observed, there was only one path leading to the inn and apart from being narrow, it ended only metres from the other side of the entrance.

The minutes passed slowly. Pia began to shiver and before long was forced to bite her lips to stop her teeth chattering. On the floor beside her, Kaire hugged his knees and stared at the wall opposite. His greatest fear, but one he hadn't shared with Pia, was that Teo had deliberately hidden them and intended to hand them over to Vina. He wanted to believe it was pure coincidence she happened to be visiting the village at the same time as he and Pia, but remained unconvinced. The stall-keeper must have suspected Vina's presence meant trouble, otherwise he wouldn't have given Pia the communicator. And what of Trooper Reyd? Was he involved too?

The sound of a heavy door creaking pushed doubts and questions to the back of Kaire's mind. Pia was already on her feet and racing up the stone steps leading to the cellar door, which opened as she reached the top step. Teo stood in the doorway, a small metal barrel cradled in his arms.

'We need to leave now,' Pia said.

'Quiet,' he hissed as the door closed behind him.

Alarmed, Pia backed down the steps and almost collided with Kaire.

After descending slowly, Teo placed the barrel in the space beneath the steps and turned to face them. 'Firstly, we know your plans and have made alternative arrangements. Secondly, I'm not Teo. I'm Dyne, Teo's twin.'

Kaire stepped away from Pia. 'How did you know about our plans?

Dyne grinned. 'Trooper Reyd can never keep his mouth shut once he's had a few drinks. He was full of his rescue operation this evening. Told my brother and anyone else that would listen how you'd been the victims of a vehicle snatching. Even mentioned that Trooper Meto would be taking you to the nearest station.'

'So how did you alter the arrangements?'

'Easy, Teo told Trooper Reyd you had decided to walk.'

'And he fell for that? Surely he'd have wondered why we didn't just call into the trooper station and tell Meto ourselves?'

'He was drunk, mate.'

'And if Trooper Meto comes here in a few minutes looking for us?'

'Teo will pass on a message from Reyd. It's all pretty informal around here.'

Kaire and Pia exchanged glances. 'So where are you taking us?' Pia asked.

'We're going to a safe house in the next village on LLR's orders. You can check with her once we're out of this cellar.'

Kaire nodded. 'I'll do that.'

Dyne gestured towards the rear of the cellar. 'This way.' He led them into a narrow space between two large barrels and placed his palm over what appeared to be a rough patch of cement on the wall directly in front. Instantly a portion of the wall moved sideways and lights set into the tunnel roof illuminated the concave concrete walls.

'Follow me. Single file in the tunnel, it's narrow.' He turned to Kaire. 'You might have to stoop, the roof's low. It was built long ago for we smaller Asians.'

'For what purpose?'

'Smuggling, mate. Spirits, drugs, people.'

Progress was slow, the tunnel narrowing in places, forcing both Pia and Kaire to walk sideways, taking care not to scrape their heads against walls dotted with green slime. At intervals water dripped from the roof, sliding down faces and necks already moist from the damp atmosphere. Then, just as Pia was beginning to feel claustrophobic, Dyne halted before a door similar to the one in the cellar wall.

'I'm going to turn out the lights as a precaution before opening the door. Give me a couple of minutes to check there's no one around before you exit.'

'Thanks for warning us,' said Pia, reaching for Kaire's hand.

For a moment a thick blanket of darkness enveloped them; then the door creaked open revealing a smattering of stars and soft moonlight shining over dry grass. Dyne stepped outside and disappeared from view. Kaire squeezed Pia's hand and brushed her cheek with his lips.

'We'll be okay,' he whispered, though he felt far from certain. Hours locked in a cellar, plus the near encounter with Vina, had eroded any confidence he'd had left after their failure to leave the country. Recent months spent in a spaceship that responded to his every command had only served to accentuate his inability to control his destiny on Earth.

Dyne reappeared and signalled for them to emerge. As the door closed behind them, a mat of interwoven grasses and palm fronds slid into place, concealing the tunnel entrance. They crossed a patch of coarse springy grass without leaving footprints and began to climb the sand dune, Dyne last in line, obliterating their steps with an improvised brush made from a fallen palm frond. On the other side of the dune, the sand leading down to the ocean was hard, having been pounded by the waves on a recent high tide. Moonlight revealed a small white boat bobbing just beyond the breakers.

'You can wade out,' said Dyne, 'or swim. It's not deep—there's a sandbar a few metres out.'

'You aren't coming with us?' asked Pia.

'No need, Teo will take care of you.'

'I thought he was serving behind the bar.'

'He was an hour ago, but the inn is closed now.'

Kaire glanced at his timepiece. 'It didn't take us an hour to walk through the tunnel.'

Dyne grinned. 'Correct, but as you know my brother and I are interchangeable, very handy when it comes to subterfuge.'

'Thank the moon for identical twins,' said Pia, stepping forward to give Dyne a quick hug. She removed her sandals and tied them around her waist with the white scarf that either he or Teo had given her by the school gate. 'I suggest you sell this again.' She handed Dyne the red bag. 'The communicator's inside.'

Dyne nodded and turned to Kaire. 'Fair exchange,' he said, removing his tunic belt and passing it over. 'I can soon make a new one.'

'Thanks.' Kaire took off his sandals and attached them to the belt.

Footwear secured, they waded into the ocean. Pia swam as soon as the water reached her thighs. Kaire walked forward cautiously, determined not to lose his footing. Swimming wasn't a skill needed on Sky.

The boat took them a fair way down the coast before turning into a broad estuary. Teo steered for the left hand shore, slowing the engine as they touched bottom. 'End of the ride,' he announced. 'Good luck with the rest of your journey.'

Pia smiled. 'Thanks for rescuing us from whatever Vina had in mind.'

'Thanks,' Kaire echoed, 'and I'm relieved you and Dyne will be keeping an eye on her.'

'We'll keep you informed, through LLR.'

'Good, and don't forget we're keen to know her friend's identity.'

'Sure.' Teo stood in the stern watching Pia jump out of the boat into shallow water. Behind him, Kaire swung his legs over the side for an easier landing.

As they reached the high water line, a woman stepped from the shadows and began to walk down the beach towards them, her bare feet leaving a trail in the soft sand. After a short distance, she paused to wave at the departing boat.

'You were right, it's going to be okay,' Pia said to Kaire before skipping up the beach to greet the woman.

Her name was Edna and she had been assisting the Women's Line for over ten years. She lived in a small house set some distance from the village, close to the left bank of the estuary. During the short walk to her home, she explained the house had belonged to her late father, a fisherman who had preferred living near his boat and always dismissed other villagers' fears that a storm would inundate his home. These days she lived alone, except when her twin sons and their families came for a visit. Pia and Kaire would be staying until a boat could be despatched from Aotearoa, with luck within a week—although bad weather could cause delays, small fishing vessels at risk of capsize when crossing the Tasman during rough conditions. In the meantime, Edna said to make themselves at home and not worry about being disturbed. Apart from her sons, she had few visitors and no one could approach her house without being seen.

# CHAPTER 32

In the village Pia and Kaire had recently vacated, a couple lay awake, concerned by raised voices on the other side of the wall yet reluctant to interfere. Only a few words were clearly audible, which was irritating. Deprived of sleep, the couple would have preferred to hear the whole argument. Earlier in the evening, they had heard Salli, the carer employed by neighbour Bruno, answer the door and greet a woman they had previously discovered was Salli's friend Vina. There had been no sound from next door when they retired to bed, leading them to assume the friend would be staying the night as sometimes happened when Bruno was away from home on business. They had exchanged few words with Salli, who seemed painfully shy, although Bruno said she was good with the children. She had cared for his children of five and six years, ever since their mother's tragic accident at the village factory some months earlier.

Suddenly the couple heard Salli screaming. 'No, no, no, not the desert, I couldn't bear it.'

This was followed by a brief silence and then the older woman said loudly in an exasperated tone, 'Then give me more names.'

The couple couldn't hear the response, only the clatter of shoes crossing the room and the eventual slam of the front door. Sighing with relief, they turned on their sides and prepared for sleep.

In the adjoining house, Salli—her real name Yuki—lay on her narrow bed shaking with fear. Vina had been adamant this time.

'Give me the names of all those you know or even suspect are part of this Women's Line, or I'll hand you over to the authorities and you will be sent back to the desert.' Over and over again, the words tumbled through Yuki's head like speech from a faulty communicator. She had already supplied Vina with at least six names, three of them line leaders—surely that was enough? If Vina hadn't seen her standing in the school play area talking to Max all those months ago none of this would have happened. Interfering woman, why did she have to come out of her office? Couldn't she have sent a junior instructor to investigate? Tears began anew, coursing across Yuki's cheeks and soaking into the pillow. Exhausted, she curled into a ball and tried to sleep.

She woke before dawn, relief flooding body and mind as the significance of Vina's disclosure became apparent. If the pair Vina had seen in the marketplace really were Kaire and Pia, betraying them would guarantee life-long liberty. Yuki got out of bed and headed for the bathroom.

Last night's crusted tears were soon washed away, hair combed and clothes straightened. The face in the mirror looked calm and confident; she felt ready to embark on her mission. Taking care not to wake the children, she crept along the passage and let herself out the door leading into the small rear garden. Slivers of light guided her steps towards the gate in the back fence that opened onto the path running behind the row of houses. A glance up at the twins' bedroom window reassured her as she reached the gate; there was no light on, a common occurrence if they woke early. Opening the gate a fraction, she slipped out and turned to the left.

Bruno's house was three from the end of the block and only a few minutes walk from the marketplace and the path around the lake. Yuki headed for the inn, determined to discover if Pia and Kaire were staying there. At this hour neither Teo nor his brother would be up, so she could slip inside and check the guest file on the bar computer. On first coming to the village, Yuki had worked and lived at the inn so knew the doors were rarely locked. Once she had confirmed the guests were in residence, she would return home and resume her childcare duties. Later, when the children had been deposited at school, she would return to the inn and surprise Pia and Kaire as they ate breakfast in the room adjoining the bar. Yuki smiled to herself as she envisaged their faces when they learned the reason for her visit, their appreciation her resourcefulness had saved them from imminent arrest. After taking them back to Bruno's house, she would contact Vina and before long all three would be gone from her life.

In less than fifteen minutes Yuki was back in the house, disappointment and anger etched into her face. No guests had been booked into the inn and to make sure it wasn't an oversight on Teo or Dyne's part, she had risked being discovered and checked the two rooms. Judging by the cobwebs and dust, no one had stayed at the inn for some time. Her only option now was to try to discover the identity of the White visitors and where they were headed. She decided to bake a cake and visit old Trooper Reyd.

The chocolate cake, decorated with swirls of caramel butter icing, looked inviting and Yuki felt confident a few slices would elicit some helpful information. Mid-morning sun would melt the icing, so she covered her basket with the ice-sheet used when taking the children's lunch to school and set off at a brisk pace.

The old trooper proved most cooperative. After listening to his long-winded rescue tale, Yuki asked him to describe the two school inspectors, ostensibly because she'd recognised them in the marketplace, but they had disappeared before she could approach and thank them for helping a child she'd once cared for. The genial trooper then gave her a precise description of Pia and Kaire. He also offered to send a message from her to the Education Department for which she thanked him profusely.

Back home, Yuki pondered her next move. She still had no idea of Pia and Kaire's whereabouts even though Trooper Reyd had mentioned they planned to catch a train from the nearest station. She knew they could be back in Aotearoa by now if they had flown over in the Sky-ship. For a moment, she considered communicating with a Line leader and then thought better of it. Whoever she contacted would check where the communication had originated, blowing her cover. Yuki had been back in the Asian Zone for over a year now, moving from job to job and village to village every few months in her quest to find out where Max and his father had been relocated. So far the ID provided for her by Mac and then altered by Vina following their unanticipated meeting had been accepted, but for how long? It occurred to her that Kaire wouldn't have come over without his personal communicator and she wished she knew his code. Mac would know of course, but could she risk communicating after this length of time? By now he probably thought she was dead.

Initially she had sent him reports about her attempts to discover who had infiltrated the Line in the region, but since the initial confrontation with Vina she'd deliberately remained silent. Blackmail had altered the equation; for the past year *she* had been the one betraying the Line. Tears splashed on the kitchen bench as she struggled to banish images of women incarcerated beneath desert sands, women denied any contact with their children or partners.

'I did it for love of Max,' she cried out before crumpling to the floor, huge tears staining her tunic.

Late that afternoon, Yuki was walking her charges home from school when she suddenly remembered Pia's communication code. As the children prattled on about painting, games in the play area and story time, she tried to think up an excuse to offload them while she attempted to communicate with Pia. Her neighbours seemed friendly; perhaps one of them would look after the children.

'It's no trouble, Salli, I assure you,' said her neighbour a few minutes later. 'I'll give them a drink and a snack. You go and take a headache pill and lie down for a bit.'

'Thank you so much, Rubi. I should be okay soon.'

'No need to rush to pick them up, I'll enjoy playing with them.'

Yuki turned to the children. 'Now you two be good for Rubi.'

'Course we will,' they chorused. 'We love Rubi's biscuits.'

Rubi ushered them inside.


Holed up in Edna's tiny house for twenty-two hours a day, Pia and Kaire relished their nightly walk on the nearby beach. Although it had only been two days since their arrival, it felt like two weeks and they longed for news of a rescue date. Storms were forecast for the next few days, which would no doubt prolong their stay, and now they had the added worry of Yuki's unexpected communication. Following a host of questions, Yuki had explained her long silence was due to lengthy home detention following a factory accident, but reassured Pia her ID had not been compromised as local troopers had dealt with the matter.

On checking her exact location, Kaire had been astonished to learn she was communicating from the village they had just left! After logging the coordinates, he had told Pia that Yuki was in the region but deliberately withheld details, preferring to wait until they were alone on the beach.

Huge waves were rolling into the estuary and the strong wind made progress along the beach difficult, but Kaire and Pia continued their walk. Neither wanted to inform Line Leader Roe about Yuki, believing it too dangerous. They'd contacted Maris, a senior Line leader on Island 1 and asked her to check if a factory worker had been under house arrest recently in Asian Zone Village 23.

'Thank the moon you put a cloaking device on my communicator,' Pia remarked as they turned to retrace their steps, 'otherwise she would have known where we were.'

'And no doubt sent her friend Vina to retrieve us.'

'If they are working together. I'm still not convinced.'

'I am, and furthermore I'm certain both Vina and Yuki recognised us in the marketplace.

That would explain the communication. Yuki was probably afraid we also recognised her, so decided to invent a reason for her non-communication. I doubt she's worked out that we're over here to locate her.'

'We should contact Mac.'

'Yes, but let's move out of the wind first.' He shone his torch up the beach. 'That clump of bushes should give us a bit of shelter.'

Windblown sand and rain pitted their faces and a flash of lightning took them by surprise, but before long they were snug and dry in the middle of dense bushes.

Kaire had forgotten about Earth time zones, but in spite of the late hour Mac answered promptly. His instructions were clear: on no account must they attempt to apprehend Yuki and they should wait twenty-four hours for Maris to get back to them before communicating with Roe. Meanwhile he would try to expedite their departure.

'None of this would have happened if we'd flown over,' Kaire said curtly as he replaced the communicator in his pocket. 'Why did I agree to Mac's proposal?'

Pia touched his arm. 'Because he was right. It would have been too risky to bring the Sky-ship. Besides, we wouldn't have heard from Yuki if we hadn't ended up further down the coast. I'd call it a stroke of luck.'

'I suppose you could call it that.' He began to stroke her bare arm.

'It's a bit cramped in here. Why don't we wait until we get back to Edna's?'

'The walls are too thin. I feel inhibited.'

'Why? I'm the one who makes all the noise.'

Without a word he reached out and snapped nearby dry branches. 'Enough room now, my love?'

# CHAPTER 33

Chief Instructor Vina stepped from the train and looked around for the car that was supposed to take her to the village for the regional schools' concert and prize giving. She carried a small bag containing a change of clothes and her new wafer-thin computer pad, a gift from grateful Security Department staff. Generally, she preferred to return home after events such as this even if it meant a late night, but Yuki had persuaded her to stay, saying she had important news. The two rooms at the inn had already been booked, so Yuki had arranged accommodation at her neighbours' house, her employer Bruno having returned home.

A small car entered the station compound and drew to a halt at least ten metres from where Vina stood, even though no other vehicles were present. The driver remained in his seat and did not open the passenger door. Scowling, Vina strode towards the car.

'Chief Instructor Vina,' she announced, knocking on the tinted window with her knuckle and startling the driver who had just settled down for a nap, mistakenly believing she would be on the next train. The passenger door slid open.

'Sorry,' murmured the oldest trooper she had ever seen before reaching across and grabbing the bag held in her arms. 'I'll just put this in the back so you've got a bit more room.' Before she could warn him to be careful, he had chucked the bag onto the seat behind.

'I have a brand new computer pad in that bag. I hope you haven't damaged it.'

'Don't expect so, the seat's a bit soft.' Trooper Meto scratched his head. 'Anyhow, they have protective covers, don't they?'

'Of course,' Vina said haughtily.

'No worries then.' He tossed her a smile before engaging drive and moving out of the station compound at a speed more suited to a lame person.

When they finally reached the village, Vina asked the trooper to drop her near the marketplace, explaining she wanted to purchase a gift for her hosts.

'No problem, Chief Instructor. I need some veggies myself.'

Vina forced a smile.

He parked almost inside the first stall, leading Vina to question both his eyesight and driving ability, but she refrained from comment. Whatever her position, an Asian woman did not query a White man's competence. Retrieving her bag from the rear seat, she bid him farewell and hurried into the market.

Trading had virtually finished for the day, so there was little choice on the produce stalls. Vina decided to try a stall on the opposite side where she could see brightly coloured scarves tied to a rack blowing in the late afternoon breeze, but by the time she reached the stall, Dyne had started to pack up his stock.

'Just caught me, Vina,' he said brightly.

'Good to see you, Teo.' She smiled. 'I won't be a moment.'

'Take your time,' he answered without correcting her mistake.

She chose a blue and white scarf. 'How much, Teo?'

'Two tokens for you, Vina.'

She handed them over, waited while he rolled the scarf into a neat cylinder and secured it with a blue ribbon. 'Thanks.' She picked up the scarf. 'Are you going to the concert?'

'Wouldn't miss it.'

'See you there then.' She turned and walked away, leaving Dyne annoyed he would have to miss the concert now, as his brother would be there. Thank the moon his daughter was too young to attend school; he would have been hard-pressed to think up a valid excuse for staying at home.

After spending a short time with Yuki's neighbour Rubi, who was delighted with the scarf, Vina went next door to join her friend for an early evening meal prior to the concert. Yuki seemed more volatile than usual, chattering happily one minute and looking as though she would burst into tears the next. By comparison, her young charges appeared subdued, barely saying a word throughout the meal. Their father, Bruno, home early from the factory he managed in order to attend the concert, responded to Vina's polite questions about his children with obvious pride, telling her they were the youngest ever to receive prizes for reading.

'Well done,' said Vina, turning to face the children sitting opposite. 'I shall give you an extra smile when I hand over the prizes.'

The boy reddened and looked down at his plate but the girl smiled back and said, 'Thank you, Chief Inspector Vina.'

Both Bruno and Yuki beamed, pleased with the little girl's good manners.

After the meal, Yuki took the children to their bedroom to change into fresh clothes while Vina insisted on helping Bruno clear up. He was a handsome man, some years older than Yuki, and Vina wondered whether a sexual relationship would, or had already developed. It could be useful to have Yuki permanently within easy reach; she would do anything to ensure her continuing freedom.

As though reading her mind, Bruno began to talk about the young woman he knew as Salli, commenting on the excellent job she was doing with his children who had been so traumatised by the death of their mother. 'If I didn't know better,' he concluded, 'I'd say Salli has firsthand experience of losing a parent as a child. It's almost as though she can put herself in the children's place.'

Vina had no knowledge of Yuki's childhood so simply nodded in agreement. Most likely, Yuki's empathy was the result of losing her son. The boy was the same age as Max and must remind her of him every hour of the day.

Once the dishes were dried, Vina excused herself to freshen up and made her way to Yuki's small room at the rear of the house. Soon after, Yuki appeared and motioned Vina to sit next to her on the bed. The wealth of information that tumbled from Yuki's mouth both delighted and astounded; Vina hadn't thought her capable of making such perceptive observations, especially the one concerning a red bag, sold to a White woman and then seen for sale the following day.

'Leave the rest to me,' she advised. 'You've done well. We'll soon have that troublesome pair tucked away in the desert.'

'And then?' Yuki asked, hopeful Vina would mention the possibility of a legitimate transfer to a village close to where Max and his father were living.

'One thing at a time, my friend.' Vina smiled. 'But in the meantime, I'm sure I can arrange for Max to visit his old school on one of your days off.' Thin arms tightened around Vina's neck and kisses smudged the make-up on her cheeks. Gently she removed the clinging arms. 'Calm down now. It's time for the concert.'

After the concert and prize giving, it took Vina some time to leave the school, the local instructors keen to impress by showing her the artwork, pottery and carpentry displayed in each of the classrooms. Then, to make matters worse, they insisted on plying her with homemade cakes, tarts and iced tea laced with something Vina didn't recognise but suspected was alcoholic. She made certain not to drink more than two glasses; a clear head was essential tonight. Finally, she was able to say her goodbyes and set off down the gravel path leading from the school to the rows of identical terraced houses, pointing like grey fingers towards the towering dune.

Once clear of the school grounds, Vina stepped off the well-lit path and pulled out her communicator. After checking that no one was around, she gave the code for a Security Department officer she'd had dealings with on several occasions. Advised that Security Officer Medite wasn't available at present but could be contacted in an emergency if the correct code was given, Vina hesitated. She'd had no opportunity to substantiate Yuki's suspicions and would look a complete idiot if they proved incorrect. Cradled in her hands, the communicator grew warm and pinged as it disconnected. Glancing down at the blank screen, she decided it was definitely an emergency; for all she knew, this Pia and Kaire—both on the wanted file for crimes against the state, according to Yuki—could leave the area within hours. There was no way she could handle the two of them alone, even with the stun gun she'd concealed in a pocket of her shoulder bag. She pressed the centre of the screen and took several deep breaths before giving the emergency code.

'Security Officer Medite, please state level of emergency.'

'Code 4.'

'Details.'

'I have information regarding a White female and White male wanted for crimes against the state. They are currently working as school inspectors under the names Aimi and Cline. Their real names according to a trusted source are Pia and Kaire.'

'The names are vaguely familiar but I'll have to check. I note you are not in your home village.'

'I'm here on Education Department business.'

'Right, have you met either of these persons?'

'Yes.' Vina gave a full description of Pia, a less accurate one of Kaire.

'Have you any information regarding their current location?'

'Nothing concrete, but my friend believes they could be staying with a woman called Edna in Asian Village 24.'

'I'll check it out and get back to you in a few minutes.' The blank grey screen faded to black.

Vina pocketed her communicator, relieved to have handed over the information and hopefully the responsibility. She ambled down the path as though she were enjoying the cooler night air, turned left and made her way to the first row of houses where she debated whether to head for Rubi and her partner Gen's house or take the path to the beach.

Warm sand caressed her naked feet, reviving memories of her grandparents' home on the coast. Childlike she ran all the way up the dune and stood breathless at the top, gazing at moonlit water. Inhaling deeply, she relished the taste of salt air, the touch of ocean breeze on warm skin. The communicator buzzed as she flew down the other side, shoes in one hand, the bag slipping from her shoulder. Collapsing in a heap, she quickly retrieved it and gave her Security Department code.

'I had a bit of trouble locating the woman,' Medite advised. 'It turns out she's not White.'

'Really? She looked White to me.'

'Brown-skin—a Split, I imagine. But you were right about her name. She is Pia, Apprentice Storyteller, missing from Village 10, Brown Zone since 2400 and wanted in connection with the freeing of political prisoners. A man named Kaire also disappeared from Village 10 at the same time. Inquiries revealed his ID to be false. All we know about him is he appears to be an alien of unknown origin.'

'An alien? Do you mean from another planet?'

'That's what this Pia's mother said at her trial.'

'It must have been a lie.'

'Of course, but that's not important. Now return to your lodgings, I am on my way.'

'When will you arrive?'

'That is no concern of yours. Leave the village as planned. Communication terminating.'

Vina stared at the ocean, disappointed now that she would play no part in the forthcoming arrests. *It's a pity about Edna,* she thought. *She seemed a pleasant woman when I met her a few months ago at the village inn. Still, she should have known better than to shelter criminals on the run—especially a White man.*

As prearranged, Security Officer Medite left his car on high ground close to the northern bank of a wide river before making his way on foot to the beach below. He didn't have to wait long for the signal, a beam of red laser light followed by blue then green, visible in spite of the sea mist that had rolled into the river at dawn. Before long, the pointed bow of a sleek silver vessel, similar to those used to pursue Asian pirates or illegal fishing boats, nudged the shore and a man leapt out holding a rope, which he wrapped around a rusty bollard protruding from the sand. Medite waded into the water and, grasping the metal ladder attached to the port side, hauled himself onto the narrow deck. Edging sideways towards the stern, he had just jumped into the cockpit when he noticed a second man blocking his way to the cabin. A beam of light hit his face and a harsh voice demanded ID. Half-blinded by the light, Medite struggled to retrieve the tiny plastic disc concealed in an inside pocket of his tunic. A hand grabbed the disc and waved it over a miniaturised scanner.

'Welcome aboard, Medite. I'm Ocean Officer Itall.'

'Greetings, Officer Itall.'

'Sorry about the light, new security measures.' The door slid open as Itall gestured for Medite to follow him into the cabin.

Rough water greeted them as the vessel reached the point where river and ocean merged. Medite clutched his stomach and wished fervently he were back on dry land. Once out to sea, movement became smoother, much to his relief, and he was able to give Itall his full attention. During the short time it took to reach the wide estuary close to Village 24, Itall divulged particulars of the apprehension mission. Sea mist still clung to coast and river, allowing the vessel to slip unseen into the estuary and beach on the narrow strip of sand where days before Teo had deposited his passengers. Medite and Itall jumped out onto wet sand, leaving the crewman to secure the vessel.

'First house we come to,' Itall advised in a low voice as they walked up the beach. 'It's some distance from the rest of the village so no issues with noise.'

'Good, I doubt they'll come quietly.'

'Silence from now on,' Itall whispered as they reached the low dune that separated beach from coastal foliage.

Medite nodded and peered through the mist at stunted windswept trees interspersed by tangled bushes. They climbed in single file in order to leave one set of tracks. On the other side of the dune, Medite followed Itall along a sandy track that wove through bushes and clumps of dry grasses. They emerged in an open space, part grass part sand, beyond which a small house stood facing the ocean. No lights were visible and Medite grinned at the thought of interrupting slumber. Woken without warning, the occupants would be at their most vulnerable.

One behind the other, Medite and Itall stepped onto the cracked concrete pad in front of the door and quietly removed their boots. The beam from Itall's laser gun disabled the lock without a sound and fortunately the door slid into the wall with minimal noise. The two men entered what appeared to be a living room, and as their eyes grew accustomed to the gloom the dark shapes of furniture became clearer. A small table covered with a cloth stood beneath the single window, three upright chairs spaced around it, while a low couch sat against the opposite wall. Skirting the end of the couch, they entered a narrow hallway, light from Itall's torch revealing two closed doors on either side. The first door opened without the need for a laser beam and led into a bathroom. The door opposite was slightly ajar, so after covering the torch beam with his hand, Itall peered inside. A shaft of moonlight shining through a hole in the window shield revealed a narrow bed containing a single occupant, not their main interest. Backing away, Itall signalled for Medite to follow and they crept towards the third door, fingers wrapped around weapons set to firing mode. Once again there was no lock.

'Lovers, how sweet,' Itall roared from the doorway, waving both torch and gun in the direction of the bed. Bodies quickly untangled, tousled heads shot up from pillows.

'What the sun?' Pia cried, shielding her eyes from the torch beam with her hands.

Beside her Kaire stared in disbelief at the familiar figure following the first man into the room.

'Commander Breta,' Medite exclaimed. 'My, you do get around!'

Kaire remained silent as Medite approached the bed.

'So sorry to disturb you, Commander, but you're under arrest.'

'You too, Brown-skin.' Itall dragged Pia out of bed and flung her to the floor. Naked, she sprawled on bare concrete, shivering from fright and confusion. *Why had he addressed Kaire as Commander Breta?*

Kaire put up his hands in surrender and swung his legs over the side of the bed. 'If I could put on a garment?'

Medite nodded and stood aside while Kaire grabbed tunic and pants from the floor and quickly slipped them on. 'Get hers now.'

Kaire padded across to the single chair and picked up Pia's clothes. With his back to the security officers, he managed to slip his communicator from his tunic pocket to hers, figuring he would be the first to be stripped and interrogated.

The first bedroom was empty when they passed its open doorway and there was no sign of Edna elsewhere in the house.

'Leave it,' Medite ordered as Itall veered into the kitchen nook and began opening cupboards. 'The local troopers can deal with her, we have the main prize.'

Itall grumbled but obeyed and before long officers and prisoners were walking towards the ocean, sparkling now in bright morning sunlight.

It was cramped with four in the small cabin and Pia worried the boat's motion could trigger the laser guns pointed at the left side of their chests. Since embarkation, the men opposite hadn't spoken, and even on the walk from Edna's house had exchanged few words. Pia hoped Edna had managed to get away from the village and send a message to her sons so they could organise a rescue before the troopers discovered her hiding place. But what if Teo and Dyne were followed? Pia shuddered at the thought of a whole family's arrest and lengthy detention.

'Cold?' demanded the younger officer who had addressed Kaire as Commander Breta.

'A little, sir.'

Medite laughed. 'You'd better get used to it, girl. It's colder underground.'

Pia's eyes widened and a cold sweat broke out on her forehead. 'Are you taking us to the desert prisons?'

'That will no doubt be your final destination, Brown-skin.'

*At least I'm not going direct to the desert,* Pia thought. The hard edge of Kaire's communicator dug into the soft flesh at the top of her left thigh as she shifted slightly. Bowing her head, she focused on the wristbands binding her arms together.

Beside her Kaire stiffened. 'I trust a desert prison won't be *my* final destination? As an Aotearoan security officer I must have some rights in this country.'

Itall frowned and turned to his colleague. 'You didn't mention this, Medite.'

'Of course not. My brief was to arrest a man known as Kaire. Commander Breta was the last person I expected to find in bed with this particular Brown-skin.'

'What do you suggest we do with him?'

'Hand him over to the Department.' Medite glared at Kaire. 'Most likely he'll be deported for over-staying his visit.'

Itall nodded and lowered his weapon. 'I need some fresh air, care to join me?'

'Sure, there's no need for us to be confined in this unventilated cabin.' He rose quickly, slipping his gun into the holder attached to his belt.

Kaire held out his arms. 'I don't suppose you could remove these, Officer Medite? I find the metal irritates my skin and it's not as though I can escape, is it?'

'Later, Commander. I find your presence irritating.'

The door closed behind the two officers and a lock clicked into place.

Leaning sideways, Kaire reached into Pia's pocket and retrieved the communicator. By holding it taut in his left hand and twisting his right wrist, he managed to key a brief message to Commander Breta and Mac, which included their current position and possible destination. An immediate response from Mac advised local Line leaders would be informed and asked Kaire to forward their exact location once the boat reached land.

'That could prove problematic,' Kaire whispered in Pia's ear as she leaned over to read the message.

'We'll find a way,' she muttered through clenched teeth. 'I am *not* going to the desert.'

# CHAPTER 34

News of the dawn raid on Edna's home swept through Village 23 courtesy of Yuki's neighbours. Rubi had risen earlier than usual to prepare breakfast for their guest, leaving her partner Gen in bed asleep. She was setting the table in the living room when snippets of a one-sided conversation filtered through the thin wall from the spare bedroom. Curious, Rubi pressed her ear to the wall.

'And the woman, Edna, has she been arrested?' Vina asked.

Shocked, Rubi slapped a hand over her mouth to suppress a cry. Edna was a close friend.

'I'm pleased to hear that,' Vina remarked after a short pause. 'These troublesome women are a threat to national security.'

Rubi's eyes widened.

'No, sir, the friend I told you about has no idea of your plans for her.'

Puzzled, Rubi frowned.

'An excellent location, if I may say so, sir. Close enough for infrequent sanctioned visits to family but lacking ease of access.'

Rubi strained to hear Vina's next remark, the only audible words 'island' and 'network' intensifying the mystery.

'Yes, sir, I leave this morning.'

*Probably the ten-thirty train,* Rubi thought.

'Thank you, I appreciate the department's generosity. Communication terminating.'

Rubi recalled the brand new computer pad she'd noticed lying on the bedside cabinet.

In all her forty-one years, Rubi had never moved so fast. After less than a minute, she was standing beside the bed, shaking Gen's shoulders.

Hazel eyes half-opened. 'Morning already?' he mumbled.

Rubi nodded and bending towards him quietly repeated Vina's words.

'Leave it to me, my love.' Gen pushed back the sheet and swung his legs over the edge of the bed. 'I'll go to Edna's place now.'

'I'll have breakfast with Vina and keep her occupied until you return.'

Gen grinned. 'That shouldn't be a problem with your fondness for conversation.'

'Me! You can talk!' She slapped his wrist playfully and padded to the door.

Scorch marks in the centre of the door panel were sure signs Edna hadn't willingly admitted the arresting officers. Inside, Gen noted further evidence of rude awakening: tangled sheets in both bedrooms, cupboards open in the kitchen, Edna's sunhat still on its peg in the hall. There was no sign of her communicator or the knife she kept under her pillow in case of intruders, which led him to believe she had somehow managed to escape from the house. Standing in the hall, he pondered the identity of Edna's visitors and how Vina had known of their presence. Her visit for the school concert and prize giving had been arranged months earlier according to the local instructor, always eager to flaunt her friendship with a chief instructor. Could it really have been pure coincidence that Vina happened to be in the village when two women wanted by the authorities were secreted in Edna's home?

Gen pulled out his communicator and gave the code for the inn in his own village, hoping either Teo or Dyne would answer. Although Teo already knew about the raid, having heard from Edna minutes after she fled the house and hid in a clump of bushes near the beach, he feigned ignorance and after a cry of dismay, said he found it hard to believe his mother was involved in anti-government activities.

'So you have no idea who these women were,' Gen asked, beginning to think Edna had been tricked into sheltering them.

'No, Mother never has visitors apart from family.'

'We must try to find out where she's been taken.'

'It would help if we knew who had arrested her. Do you think …'

'No problem, mate,' Gen interrupted. 'I'll call at the trooper station, say I'm concerned because she's not at home and the place looks as though it's been turned over.'

'Thanks, mate. Either Dyne or I can come down tonight if you think it necessary.'

'It might be better if you stay away at the moment. But don't worry, I'll keep you informed.'

'What about Vina?'

'I'll sort it. See you.' Gen left the house, sliding the damaged door panel into the closed position to prevent more sand blowing into the house.

On the long walk home, Gen fingered the knife concealed in the pocket of his baggy work pants as he concocted an excuse to get Vina out of the house and down to the beach where they could have a little chat about her extra-curricular activities. He had no intention of hurting her, just wanted to wipe the supercilious expression from her face with threats of a scandal that would affect her career. Sexual misconduct perhaps—he felt certain someone could be found to accuse her of unlawful behaviour with students, or, and this was the more feasible, manipulating school accounts for her own benefit. Rubi had remarked that Vina's clothes were of a quality usually reserved for White women, and then there was the shiny new computer pad, the elegant leather shoes. No one could afford such luxury these days, when years of drought had caused food prices to soar and the average family found it difficult to afford even the basics.

It proved simple to entice Vina down to the beach. Well aware women found him desirable, Gen flirted with her when Rubi had retired to the kitchen to clear up the breakfast dishes and was soon escorting Vina down the sandy path to 'view the ocean in all its glory'.

Expensive shoes discarded, Vina chased Gen down the beach to the water's edge. Low tide had exposed rock pools where tiny fish and crabs cavorted in clear turquoise water.

'It's beautiful,' she cried, grabbing his hand and leading him from one pool to the other. When they reached the far end of the beach, she leaned against a rock shelf and flung back her head, eyes closed against harsh sunlight. Shapely thighs peeped from the slit in her skirt and her short tunic rose, revealing smooth honey-hued flesh.

Gen sighed and stepped forward. 'You're more beautiful than any rock pool,' he murmured, running his hands over her skin. Legs and eyes opened, he felt the heat of her.

'A swim first,' she asserted, sitting up and unfastening her skirt. 'I want to taste salt on your skin, lick you dry.'

'Whatever the Chief Instructor wants,' Gen concurred, swiftly discarding tunic and pants.

Cool and calm, the ocean caressed hot skin. Her long hair floated like strands of dark seaweed, wet skin glistened and premeditated threats dissolved as desire overwhelmed. Swimming alongside her, Gen lifted her floating body, held it tight against his chest, sensed her own desire as breasts pressed hard and legs entwined.

'I've always wanted to make love to a mermaid,' he said, his voice strangely hoarse. She responded by untangling her legs and pulling him into shallower water where they could both stand firm.

Afterwards, remorse struck a blow so hard, he could have sworn a seabed eruption had created a tsunami that sucked him into a vortex of sand and water, where drowning would be the only outcome. He thrashed around, searching for something solid to cling to, encountered at last a slender honey-hued log floating just beneath the foaming surface. With the last of his strength, he made a grab for the smooth timber and, wrapping his strong hands around it, pulled tight.

At the trooper station, a distraught Gen related his unsuccessful attempts to save Vina from the massive shark. 'I told her it was dangerous to swim in these waters,' he repeated for the umpteenth time, 'but she wouldn't take any notice, said she'd often swum in the ocean as a child and it was perfectly safe if you kept to the shallows.'

Trooper Meto pointed to the dried blood and lacerations on Gen's wrists and ankles. 'You'd better get off to the medical station, Gen. Don't want them getting infected.'

'I'd rather go home and let Rubi fix me up,' he replied quickly.

'Won't she be at the factory now?'

'It's her morning off.'

'Okay, but promise me you'll take care of yourself.'

Gen nodded and bit his lip as pain seared his skin. After slashing Vina's legs with a jagged stone in the hope a shark would be attracted by the blood, he had carried her body into the ocean with the aim of towing it as far out as possible, which would validate his story should the tide wash the body ashore. However, the sudden appearance of a fishing boat heading for the coast had put paid to that idea.

Trooper Meto smiled. 'And there's no need for you to go to work today. I'll communicate with the factory.'

'Thanks, I could do with some rest.' He tossed a weak smile and limped out of the building.

But rest was the last thing on Gen's mind, his immediate task being how to face Rubi. A confession of unpremeditated murder would be easy compared to admitting infidelity. With every step, pain from his legs reminded him of that fateful swim, his succumbing to desire like a hormone-charged adolescent, his frantic attempt at resuscitation when he realised what he had done.

Manic activity had followed his aborted swim, the result a shallow grave beyond the high water mark and gashes to his own limbs made in the shallows after he'd washed Vina's blood from his skin. As the knife cut into his skin, he'd made vague plans to exhume the body late at night and transport it further down the coast for burial at sea.

# CHAPTER 35

In the middle of a windswept plain near the northern tip of the South Island, a refugee camp had been erected, surrounded by strong metal fencing topped with barbed wire. Inside the compound, rows of hurriedly erected masonite huts squatted on bare earth, their corrugated iron roofs gleaming in hot midday sunlight. The occupants were nowhere to be seen, except for one middle-aged man striding across a patch of gravel to a small hut set apart from the others.

The camp had been home to Sky People ever since their release from the quarantine station weeks earlier. Immigration officials had yet to determine a suitable place for their permanent settlement, the media having atypically whipped up anti-refugee sentiment in a relentless campaign, which had been beamed into every Aotearoan home. The government, generally tolerant towards refugees but fearing defeat in forthcoming elections, felt unable to promote a different view, so had arranged for a camp to be hastily constructed in an area some distance from the nearest town.

Outside the hut that served as the manager's office, Breta shifted his weight from one foot to the other, impatient for a response to his request.

'The manager will see you now,' the audio-box announced.

Breta waited for the door to open but it remained closed.

'Please turn the door handle and push,' the audio-box advised.

*No time to install cybernetic panels, I suppose,* Breta thought as he obeyed the instructions. He stepped inside.

'Thank you for seeing me promptly, Manager Botha,' he said before venturing further into the room. 'I won't take up much of your time.'

'Have a seat.' Botha indicated the upright chair in front of his desk.

Perched on the edge of the chair, Breta leaned forward. 'Sir, I have received grave news this morning concerning my adopted daughter, Pia, who lives at Kauri Haven in the far north. She has been injured in an accident and is not expected to live.'

'I'm sorry to hear that. Is there anything I can do?'

'Yes, I seek permission to travel to Kauri Haven in order to say farewell.' Breta wiped tears from his eyes with trembling fingers.

'Granted, of course. I'll arrange for a car to take you to the port.' He glanced at his monitor. 'You should be in time for the afternoon ferry.'

'I thank you with all my heart, sir. This means so much to me.'

'I too have a child, Breta.' He turned to his monitor. 'Authorisation for your visit will be forwarded to your communicator in a few minutes once I've checked with the Kauri Haven administrator.'

Breta looked hurt.

'As a former commander, I'm sure you understand I must follow correct procedure.'

'Yes, sir.' Breta stood and, after reiterating his gratitude, left the room.


The car travelled to the coast at high speed but Breta almost missed the ferry when the driver took a wrong turn on reaching the port and began to head for the cargo dock. Fortunately, he quickly realised his mistake and deposited Breta alongside the ferry just as the passenger gangway was beginning to fold into a compartment in the vessel's side.

'Wait, please,' Breta yelled at the seaman standing on deck controlling the gangway's passage.

'Too late, mate,' the seaman yelled back. 'Catch the next one.'

'But my daughter's dying,' Breta shouted. 'I must reach her tonight.'

The gangway shuddered and was still.

'Did you say dying?'

'Yes, an accident. She's not expected to live.'

The gangway began to unfold. Mac had arranged for a car to meet the ferry at the North Island terminus, a pleasant surprise for Breta. The driver, Sami, had volunteered to undertake the journey to satisfy his curiosity and meet the man who had sanctioned his friend Kaire's visit to Earth. Without Kaire's help, Sami's life at Kauri Haven would have been very different—lonely certainly and less fulfilling. Since his partner Kela's arrival, Sami had felt complete for the first time in years, their lengthy period of enforced separation now a faded memory.

Breta proved a stimulating travelling companion, their conversation ranging from voyaging into far-flung galaxies to life in a refugee camp. From the moment greetings had been exchanged, Breta told Sami the title commander was redundant now that Skyz59 had ceased to exist. They touched briefly on the mission to free Kaire and Pia, Sami offering assistance but aware details were best left undisclosed. Breta's strong resemblance to Kaire suggested they must be close relatives but Sami felt it would be impolite to ask. Most likely the similarity was the result of the small gene pool on Sky.

They arrived at Kauri Haven in record time, Sami having pushed the car to its limits once they'd left populated areas behind. Mac was waiting for them outside the main building and greeted them both without the usual handshakes and smiles.

'Prepare the Sky-ship for take-off please, Sami,' he said, his expression grave, his eyes betraying deep melancholy. 'I'll arrange for someone else to return the car.'

'She'll be ready in thirty minutes,' Sami replied.

'Good man.'

Sami forced a brief smile before setting off at a brisk pace to collect equipment from the workshop.

The main corridor was deserted and remained so as Mac and Breta walked its length, but neither spoke, each preoccupied with the forthcoming mission.

'Any further communication from Kaire or Pia?' Breta asked as Mac opened his office door.

'No, but I have news. We'll talk in private.' He stood aside to let Breta pass.

'Good news?' Breta asked as the door panel closed.

'I've received information from a reliable source that they're being held in an Asian Zone prison some distance from the coast. This will be only temporary, of course, Kaire being White and Pia Brown.'

Breta scowled at the mention of skin colour, an issue irrelevant on Sky. 'So where are they likely to be sent?'

'Back to their zone of origin.'

'That's not applicable to Kaire.' He glared at Mac. 'Surely there's some sort of diplomatic arrangement between Aotearoa and Australia?'

'Not these days, I'm afraid,' Mac replied, beating a hasty retreat to his desk. He would feel more in control of the dialogue half-hidden behind his monitor.

Breta began to pace the floor, muttering about the utter idiocy of conflict between so-called advanced nations.

'I agree entirely but it's not in my power to alter the situation. Right now my priority is the rescue mission.'

Breta sat down heavily in the chair nearest the desk. 'My apologies, I'm allowing emotion to overrule common sense.'

'Understandable. I too have a son.'

*Is he choosing to overlook the fact that Kaire is a clone?* Breta thought. 'My only son,' he said in a soft voice, turning his head as tears threatened.

'Mine too. I also have two grandsons, unfortunately they reside in the White Zone.'

'Are you able to communicate?'

'Not for years, I'm afraid.'

'I could bring them here, if you were able to arrange a meeting place.'

'Maybe later, they are in no danger.' Mac cleared his throat. 'The prison is situated in a remote area just south of the border with the Brown Zone. The exact location has already been forwarded to the Sky-ship computer along with landing coordinates.'

'Thank you, Mac. Will I be landing close to the prison?'

'Within three hundred kilometres.'

'So how do I travel from landing place to prison?'

'You won't. Kaire and Pia will be brought to you.'

Breta frowned. 'But surely, if provided with false ID, I would stand a better chance of securing their release than, er, locals?'

'We don't believe that would the case. Your safety and that of your craft is paramount.'

'Do you intend to keep the Sky-ship here?'

'With your permission. It is your property.'

'No longer, I'm afraid. The authorities have confiscated our other craft. Payment for giving us sanctuary, they said.'

'In a refugee camp?' Mac's voice rose in indignation. 'You must realise that until your people are granted permanent residence, your situation remains precarious.'

Breta raised his hands. 'We can discuss these matters on my return. I presume someone will contact me during the flight?'

'Her name is Tiki. She's a doctor.'

'Genuine or fake?'

'Genuine. She has recently taken over as prison medical officer for the Asian Zone.'

'Does that entitle her to examine all prisoners?'

'Only White Zone political prisoners and those suspected of having come from over ocean.'

Breta rose and approached the desk. 'I can't thank you enough for all the work you and your colleagues are doing to help secure Kaire and Pia's release.' He leaned across the desk to shake Mac's hand. 'Especially as my son's welfare is not your people's responsibility.'

'Our responsibility is to all those seeking freedom from tyranny.'

Breta squeezed Mac's hand before releasing it. 'May I join you in this task when I am free to travel legitimately?'

'Of course, my friend.'

Breta looked thoughtful. 'I am grateful for your friendship, Mac.' He turned and marched to the door.

When Breta climbed into the Sky-ship, he found Sami sitting alongside the pilot's seat, safety harness in place. 'You don't have to do this, Sami.'

'I'm well aware of that but I have experience in these matters and could prove useful. Besides, I could do with a change from building and maintaining farm machinery.'

Breta settled in his seat. 'Does Mac know?'

Sami shook his head. 'And I see no reason to inform him.'

Breta reached for the controls. 'Pleased to have your company, Sami.'

The roar of thrusters drowned Sami's reply.

# CHAPTER 36

Doctor Tiki arrived at Asian Zone Prison 20 late in the evening, the beam from her car headlight illuminating a high concrete wall topped with broken glass. A camera flashed as she pulled up in front of unguarded metal gates, making her eyes water in spite of the tinted windscreen. After a few minutes, the rusting gates creaked open revealing stark concrete block buildings arranged in a square and surrounded by bare red dirt. As she proceeded up a narrow graded path towards the illuminated entrance, the searchlights mounted on each corner merged to form a wide beam that tracked her progress. Signage indicated parking places to the right, so Tiki turned slowly to avoid skidding and stopped facing the building.

After retrieving her medical bag and small backpack containing a change of clothes and toiletries, Tiki secured the vehicle and walked up a gravel path to the entrance where she could see a trooper slumped on a chair the other side of glass doors. He made no attempt to disguise his irritation at being disturbed, watching her through narrowed eyes before extending one arm unhurriedly and pressing a panel to open the door. She noted the stun gun lying across his knees, a green glow on its tip indicating active mode.

'Doctor Tiki, here to examine a prisoner,' she announced, passing him her newly issued ID disc.

Apart from a loud sigh, he made no comment and slotted the disc into a cylinder attached to the arm of the chair. 'You can't examine the prisoner until morning when a senior officer will be on duty,' he advised without raising his head.

The cylinder emitted three clicks and ejected the disc into his out-stretched hand, prompting a second sigh. 'A room has been prepared for you in the staff quarters,' he said, pointing with his free hand to a squat concrete building opposite.

'Thank you.' Tiki stepped forward. 'My disc, please.'

The trooper nodded and handed it over. Obviously he had no intention of escorting her to the room, so she pocketed her disc and left the building, pondering whether he would even bother to watch her cross the courtyard.

The staff quarters' door opened before she had a chance to speak into the sound-grill, revealing a trooper so young his chin bore no sign of shaving. Unlike his morose colleague, he smiled before greeting her formally and ushering her inside. His courtesy extended to escorting her to the room but he made no mention of refreshments and departed the moment the door panel opened. Fortunately, Tiki still had some water in her flask and a few dry biscuits leftover from lunch, but she still spent a restless night in the cell-like space furnished with only a hard narrow bed and an upright chair.

Wide-awake before dawn, Tiki considered the forthcoming mission and the unexpected communication from Kela that had led her to apply for the position of Prison Medical Officer, Asian Zone. After some consideration, Tiki had applied, figuring Kela would not have contacted her after more than a year's silence without good reason. She still had no idea of Kela's whereabouts or which medical establishment, if any, she worked for and attempts to release the blocked code had proved unsuccessful.

When informed she was the successful candidate, Tiki had speculated how Kela had managed to influence the selection committee. In fact, there had been several more suitable candidates, all male, but the committee preferred to appoint a female doctor, confident a woman could be more easily manipulated. Kela's suggestion had been nothing more than a wish to have a supportive medic in the prison system. So far, Tiki's new role had involved visiting local prisons to introduce herself to administrators and on no occasion had she been required to examine any prisoners. There had been no further communication from Kela; that is until the previous day, when her voice had betrayed extreme agitation.

The departmental order to travel north and examine a recently detained White man from over ocean had come less than an hour after Kela's communication, a coincidence Tiki wasted little time trying to comprehend. After advising her staff she would be absent for several days, she had set off in the small car that came with the job, taking the main south-north path almost to the border before swinging west onto a secondary path that terminated at the prison.

Early morning sunlight striking grey buildings and baked red earth did nothing to relieve the vision of desolation as Tiki sat on a hard plastic chair waiting for a guard to escort her to the cells. Despite the new ID disc tucked in an inside pocket of her white robe, she felt far from confident in her ability to complete the mission. Footsteps drew her attention away from the window and she saw a middle-aged man in a well-pressed tunic enter the foyer from the rear and stride towards her.

*Administrator*, she thought, offering a polite smile.

He returned the smile without slowing his pace. 'Greetings, Doctor Tiki. I trust my staff have looked after you?'

'Yes, thank you, Administrator Adem. Breakfast was delicious.' She stood and walked towards him. 'Have you any instructions before I conduct the examination?'

'I'll give you the prisoner's details as we descend to the cells.' He set off at a brisk pace down a narrow corridor to one side of the reception desk, leaving Tiki to quickly retrieve her bag from under the bench. She caught up with him outside the lifts, perspiration beading on her forehead, nerves frayed. She hadn't expected the Administrator to accompany her to the cells and fervently hoped he wouldn't be present during the medical.

The lift, nothing more than a steel cage, arrived within seconds of his command and he ushered her inside with a polite 'After you.'

Conscious of the red security eye blinking in the corner opposite, Tiki adopted a solemn expression and focused her attention on his face as he began to speak. It appeared there was some uncertainty as to the prisoner's identity and country of origin; Tiki was asked to try to uncover the truth.

'A woman's touch may help,' he alluded, his steel grey eyes travelling down her body. 'He is a handsome young man.'

She held the bag against her thighs, grateful for its bulk. 'I'll do my best, Administrator.'

As they stepped out of the lift into a dimly lit corridor, a trooper came towards them. 'Greetings, sir, Doctor. Come this way.'

Trailing after the two men, Tiki glanced at the doors placed at regular intervals on both sides of the narrow passageway. In the middle of each door, a rectangular light panel revealed a number followed by two or more letters.

'I trust there will be more light in the cell,' she remarked officiously to the Administrator's back. 'I can't examine the prisoner in virtual darkness.'

'We have a range of lighting to suit every purpose,' Administrator Adem soothed, turning to pat her arm. 'Trooper Levis will show you how to adjust it.'

'Thank you.'

Trooper Levis halted outside the last door on the left and pressed the light panel. As the door opened inwards, harsh light flooded the cell revealing a young White man lying on a narrow bed, a grey blanket covering the lower half of his body, hands shielding his eyes.

'On your feet, prisoner,' Trooper Levis shouted, stepping inside.

Kaire rose and moved to the centre of the cell, his bare feet making little sound on the unpolished concrete floor. Tiki noted his height, well above average for White men, and the pale legs protruding from a prison tunic way too short for him.

'I'll leave you to it then.' Trooper Levis retreated to the corridor.

Administrator Adem ushered Tiki into the cell. 'I'll be in my office should you need me after the examination, Doctor Tiki. Levis will escort you from the cell to the lift. Speak into the sound-grill when you're ready to leave.' He gestured towards the grid in the centre of the door.

Tiki smiled. 'It shouldn't take long. At first glance he appears to be a healthy specimen.'

'Take all the time you need, Doctor,' he added in a low voice and, turning on his heel, marched out into the corridor.

The door closed automatically, the ring of steel on steel reverberating through the cell.

Tiki walked past the prisoner and deposited her bag on the bed. 'Remove your tunic and sit on the bed. I need to take blood, saliva and hair samples,' she ordered, addressing the wall.

Kaire obeyed instantly.

'Right, blood first.' She opened her bag and extracted a syringe and a small plastic box. 'I hope you're not one of those who faint at the sight of blood.'

He shook his head, eyes focused on the syringe.

'Make a fist.' She leaned over him.

Eyes widening, Kaire watched her unscrew the syringe and shake out a minute disc, which she inserted into a slit in the side of the box.

'Press hard.' She indicated a round indentation next to the slit. 'That's it, I'll seal it in a moment.' The box lid slid open, revealing black text on a silver background.

As Tiki busied herself with a genuine syringe, swabbing the inside of his mouth and placing the blood sample inside the plastic box, Kaire concentrated on reading the brief mission instructions, noting with relief the advice that data would be deleted once read. Having no prior knowledge of the doctor's visit, he had been half-afraid she'd been sent from the Security Department with orders to drug him prior to his removal to a southern prison.

'Can I let go now?' he asked.

She glanced at the box and took it out of his hand. 'Yes.' Her thumb pressed the side of the box to eject the disc. The lid closed over a blank screen.

After returning box, syringe and samples to her bag, she sat down beside him and began to stroke his thigh. 'It's such a shame I don't know your real name,' she said, making certain to face the security camera and recording device positioned high up on the opposite wall. 'Breta or Kaire, which shall I shout out at the moment of ecstasy?'

'Neither,' he answered, pulling her close. 'My name is Cafel.'

She fondled his other thigh with her free hand. 'And where is your home, Cafel?'

'Among the pure white light of stars and moons, far from this ruined blue planet.'

She turned away from the winking camera and buried her face in his neck to smother a smile.

Later in the morning, Tiki left her room in the staff quarters and returned to the entrance foyer armed with test results and a grim expression. 'I must see Administrator Adem,' she barked at the young trooper lolling in a chair behind the foyer counter. 'The matter is urgent.'

'First on the right, Doctor,' said the startled trooper, struggling to his feet. 'Shall I'll tell him you're coming?'

'Don't bother.' She glared at him before marching through the foyer, head held high.

The trooper must have disregarded her comment or else Adem had heard her raised voice, for the door panel opened before she reached it. Striding into the office, she headed straight for the desk, slid her message-pad towards him and stood back, hands on hips.

'Ever seen anything like this before?' she asked as he studied images of egg-sized lumps on Kaire's neck and in his left armpit.

'Can't say I have. What is it?'

'It's bubonic plague.'

'Impossible! It was eradicated centuries ago.'

She stepped forward and, leaning over the desk, flicked the screen to display the test results. 'It's highly contagious, caused by fleas and rats infected with the bacteria Yersimia pestis.'

The Administrator looked up. 'There are no fleas or rats in my prison.'

'I didn't say there were.' She took a deep breath. 'But it may interest you to know that in the past it was never found in Australia, which of course implies that your prisoner came from over ocean.'

'We suspected as such, Doctor. According to Security Department data forwarded from the arresting officer, Commander Breta is an agent for the Aotearoan government, but we haven't been able to confirm that.'

'I have already checked the historical medical data. Bubonic plague was eradicated in Aotearoa in 1911. Besides, the prisoner told me his name was Cafel.'

'I know, I heard him tell you. He also said he came from outer space!' Fingers drummed on the desktop. 'After being bitten, how long does it take before these, er, lumps, appear on the body?'

'The term is "buboes" and it takes about a week.'

'So the woman could also be infected.'

'What woman?'

'The Brown-skin arrested with him. They were found in bed together.'

Tiki frowned. 'Close contact. I shall have to test her as soon as possible.' She glanced around, picked up the nearest chair and carried it over to the desk.

'So sorry, I forgot my manners entirely.'

'No problem, Adem.' She sat down, smoothing her robe to occupy her hands. 'May I call you Adem?'

He nodded and smiled. 'I'll take you to Pia's cell shortly.'

'She's here?'

'Awaiting transfer to the Brown Zone.'

Tiki nodded. 'In the meantime, both prisoners must be isolated in a sterile environment. Is there a medical station attached to this prison?'

'I'm afraid not, the nearest is fifty kilometres away at Prison 19.'

Tiki made a show of considering this fact. 'In that case I'll have to transport them there myself.' She looked down at her hands and gave a small cough. 'Under normal circumstances, person-to-person infection is rare but as I have, er, been in close contact with Cafel, Breta or whatever his name is, I shall also have to be isolated for at least a week.'

'Such is the price we pay for diligence,' the Administrator murmured.

She would have liked to add that sex with the handsome young man was worth a week in isolation but decided against making such a frivolous comment. Intimacy had been faked not only for camera and audio recorder, but also so she could inject Kaire's neck and armpit with a chemical known to cause skin eruptions. 'Shall we adjourn to the cells, Adem?'

As expected, the female prisoner displayed no sign of a buboe on either her neck or under her arms, but Tiki managed to pinch the soft skin in her groin which made Pia cry out.

'How long has that been tender?' Tiki asked, removing her hand and gesturing for Adem to step forward.

'A few days, I think,' Pia answered, glancing down at the patch of red skin.

Tiki nodded. 'About to erupt in my opinion.'

Adem stepped backwards so fast he almost fell over his feet. 'I'll go into the corridor and communicate with Prison 19 medical station.' He hurried to the door and pressed a panel.

Pia turned to Tiki. 'What is it, Doctor?'

'Bubonic plague.'

'You're joking surely?'

'No joke.' Tiki picked up her bag. 'I'm taking you and the man arrested with you to the nearest medical station where you will be placed in isolation and treated for the infection. Modern drugs should clear it up quickly.'

'And then?'

'You'll be transferred to a prison in your zone of origin, I imagine.' She slapped Pia's shoulder. 'Straighten your tunic and gather any belongings, we must be on our way.'

Pia twisted around and slid her feet into the sandals lying beside the bed. 'There's nothing else?'

Tiki faced the security camera, a puzzled look on her face. 'What were you expecting, prisoner?'

'Er, nothing.' Pia smoothed her tunic, hope of rescue swiftly fading.

Before releasing the prisoners, Trooper Levis attached electronic wristbands to Pia and Kaire's wrists, taking care not to touch their skin. Although he had no idea what the two prisoners were suffering from, he understood it must be serious otherwise the doctor would have treated them in situ. Determined to find out, Levis decided to confront Administrator Adem once he'd escorted prisoners and doctor off the premises.

Doctor Tiki led the way to her vehicle, now parked outside the staff quarters. Behind her, Pia and Kaire shuffled, sandals scuffing dry soil, heads bowed. Trooper Levis took up the rear, his stun gun raised in case of trouble. Pia remained in ignorance of their real destination, there having been no opportunity for Tiki to enlighten her. For his part, Kaire dared not even smile in Pia's direction. They made a strange procession crossing the dusty yard: the doctor with her loose white tunic and pants billowing in the desert wind, the prisoners clad in ill-fitting prison garb, the slightly-built trooper wearing an overly large uniform puffed up with his own importance.

As she drew near to the car, Tiki pressed a panel on her communicator to release the door locks before ejecting a tiny gadget designed to deactivate electronic wristbands.

'Thank you, Trooper Levis,' she said turning to face him. 'I can manage from here.'

Boots scraped the ground as he came to an abrupt halt. 'I shall remain until you have departed, Doctor.'

She flashed a brilliant smile. 'I appreciate your diligence.'

'Prisoners enter the vehicle by the rear panel,' Levis barked.

Pia and Kaire stepped forward in unison.

'One at a time, you morons!' He prodded Pia in the back with the tip of his stun gun.

'You may take your place, Doctor.'

Before sliding into the car, Tiki leaned over and pushed her medical bag onto the passenger seat. Feigning loss of balance, she clutched the back of the driver's seat to steady herself, making certain not to spread her thumb and index finger. Slowly loosening her grip, she dropped the deactivating device onto Kaire's lap. Once she had taken her seat, a glance in the mirror showed the two passengers crammed together in the small space usually reserved for luggage. It would be an uncomfortable journey; she couldn't risk stopping en route to alter seating arrangements. The car began to move, automatic navigation ensuring smooth reversing and departure. The mirror revealed Trooper Levis still standing erect as though rooted to the spot so Tiki raised her hand in farewell.

The route to Prison 19 would take them due south for twenty kilometres, then swing east for a further thirty. Tiki's instructions were to proceed to the cross-paths before executing an emergency stop on account of Kaire's arms, wristbands dangling, tightening around her neck. His actions and threats to kill her unless she vacated the car would be recorded on both the console camera and her work communicator, which for security reasons had been set in active mode for the journey. Alone and dazed on the roadside, Tiki would then wait an hour, unless another vehicle appeared, before advising Administrator Adem of her plight.

Tiki did not speak to her passengers and they in turn made no attempt to engage her in conversation, neither did they talk to one another. Silence suited all three, each pondering the outcome of the journey. There was also the possibility the car had been fitted with a recording device, although Tiki felt this unlikely given her position and her recent Security Department clearance. Behind her, Kaire envisaged the Sky-ship waiting in the desert; Breta's name on the text communication proof that everything possible was being done to ensure a swift exit. Pia, a close examination of her groin having revealed nothing lurking beneath the surface, surmised their destination was a safe house far from any prison.

As the car sped towards the cross-path, Tiki deliberated on her need to remain in Australia. Her parents had died in a car accident the previous year and she had no siblings or partner. She would miss her friends, mostly colleagues from her former workplace, and if she were honest, the freedom and luxury afforded someone in a senior government position. Yet here she was, risking everything to free two political prisoners because an old friend knew her to be in sympathy with those attempting to undermine the tyrannical government. *Kela has to be over ocean,* she thought, *in a safe location where helping to plan missions such as this one is not only possible but actively encouraged.* She glanced at the console, ten kilometres to the cross-path, seven minutes to determine the course of the rest of her life.

Pia broke the silence with an unexpected question. 'Excuse me, Doctor, but have you ever met a Professor Kela?'

'Yes, we were colleagues some time ago,' Tiki answered, careful not to mention they had been close friends. 'Why do you ask?'

*Why indeed?* Kaire thought, turning his head and frowning at Pia. 'I imagine she asked because I spoke highly of Professor Kela when we were discussing the Australian medical profession with colleagues recently. I came across her a couple of years ago in the course of my work. Pia has never met her.'

Tiki nodded. 'In a few minutes, we'll be approaching the cross-paths,' she announced in an officious tone. 'My navigation system advises the path surface is in poor condition from there to Prison 19 so I suggest you hold on to the back of the seats to avoid injury.'

'Thank you for the warning, Doctor.' Pia manoeuvred her linked wrists from lap to seat while Kaire kept his already uncoupled wrists out of sight of the console camera.

Once the cross-paths were visible, Tiki reduced speed and then, ignoring her own advice, increased speed once the car had turned. As Kaire's hands encircled her neck, the car slid sideways on loose gravel and her arms flailed in an attempt to reach the console.

'Emergency sto …' she shouted, the command trailing off as if she were fighting for breath.

'Deactivate camera and sound systems,' Kaire ordered, making a show of loosening his grip, 'or I'll strangle the life out of you.'

Shaking hands reached forward, fingers pressed console panels while Pia, wristbands now unfastened, heaved herself over into the passenger seat.

'Now open the door panel and get out of the car.' Kaire removed his hands and pushed Tiki forward. 'I said now,' he shouted.

Clutching her bruised temple, Tiki raised her head from the console and screamed as Pia pushed her sideways.

'You can't leave me out here,' Tiki cried, grabbing the edge of the open door panel to cushion her fall.

'Watch me,' said Kaire, sliding over into the driver's seat.

Tiki struggled to her feet and hurried to the other side of the path, expecting the car to speed away, but Kaire felt apprehensive, the final directive had been disobeyed. Jumping out of the car, he ran over to join her. 'What are you playing at?' he asked, grabbing her shoulders. 'You turned right at the cross-paths instead of left.'

'Did I?'

'I'm not in the mood for deception.'

She smiled. 'I am, but don't worry, your liberty hasn't been compromised.'

Kaire frowned. 'So where does deception come in?'

'A wrong turn suggests my subconscious knows what's best for me.

That, plus your following me across the path indicates my future has been decided.' She looked up at him, her eyes shining. 'I'm coming with you. And hopefully I'll soon meet up with the dear friend who asked me to take part in this mission.'

'And who might that be?' Kaire asked, releasing her shoulders.

'Wait and see,' she replied, determined not to put Kela in any danger should the escape be unsuccessful.

# CHAPTER 37

The entire community had gathered to welcome Pia and Kaire home. For safety reasons they stood behind the perimeter fence well away from the makeshift runway, small children in front, the elderly sitting on benches carried from the dining room, the remainder standing in rows according to height. As the Sky-ship landed a great cry arose from the crowd, arms waved madly and children rattled the metal fence. Thrusters disengaged, the pilot's door opened and Breta began to descend the ladder followed by Pia, Kaire and Tiki. Welcome calls faded and joyful song burst from the crowd, voices young and old melded in harmony.

Mac stepped from the crowd and hurried over to the already unlocked gate. Soon he was running across mown grass to Breta's side as though he hadn't seen him for months instead of days. The two men embraced while Kaire and Pia stood to one side waiting their turn. Tiki lingered a few steps behind, unsure of her welcome.

'Welcome back, friends,' Mac cried, moving away from Breta and spreading his arms wide. 'And who have we here?' He smiled in Tiki's direction.

'Doctor Tiki, faithful friend and magnificent medic!' shouted a voice from the crowd.

'Welcome to Kauri Haven, Doctor Tiki,' said Mac, walking towards her, arms outstretched.

The crowd parted as the group approached the gate, forming a passageway wide enough for Pia and Kaire to walk side-by-side, arms linked. Hands reached out to touch them, children waved and called out greetings. Suddenly Sami appeared behind Tiki, swept her off her feet and carried her over to Kela, waiting patiently at the end of a row. The two friends joined hands and stood gawping at one another as though they couldn't believe their eyes.

The community regrouped in front of the main building where a 'welcome home' sign painted by the children hung over the entrance. Mac turned to face the crowd and raised his right arm, the signal for silence. One after the other, right arms rose and chatter dwindled until the only sounds were the wind blowing in from the sea and the rustle of leaves on the bushes and small trees planted in haphazard fashion around the building.

'We welcome back our fellow settlers, Pia and Kaire, liberated from prison by Doctor Tiki, now the newest member of our community, and flown home by Breta, former Commander of space station Skyz59.'

Applause greeted Mac's words, forcing him to remain silent for several minutes. When he spoke again it was to thank the community for a magnificent welcome and gently remind them it was now time to return to work or school.

But before the crowd could disperse, Breta moved to Mac's side. 'If I may speak for a moment, Chairman?'

Mac nodded and gestured for Breta to step forward.

'As the council chairman told you, I once held an important role in my community.' He paused and, glancing over at Kaire, declared, 'However, what Mac didn't tell you was the role I value most, that of father to my only son Kaire.'

Murmurs of approval spread through the crowd, prompting a range of emotions as parents moved to embrace their children and others quietly remembered those who had died or remained beyond their reach across the Tasman Sea.

Pia found it difficult to descend from her emotional high and some time passed before she could sleep through the night or get through a day without bursting into tears and laughing hysterically at inopportune moments. Kaire on the other hand, spent his days in the workshop with Sami, learning how to maintain the machinery so vital to the settlement's survival. In the early evening he returned to the small house he shared with Pia. After a meal and conversation, they fell into bed and made love in the light of the moon shining through open windows, sea breezes caressing naked flesh.

True to his word, Breta returned to the refugee camp, where he reported the good news of his adopted daughter's recovery to Manager Botha and thanked him profusely for permitting the visit to Kauri Haven.

'And I wish to thank you for coming back,' the manager replied after a long pause, during which he stared at his monitor. 'To be honest, I thought you would take the opportunity to flee the country and head for a more developed nation where your skills would be utilised.'

'I have no doubt my skills will be utilised here in due course. A fleet of aircraft is of no use without pilots to fly them and I would be happy to train those interested in pursuing a career in aviation. There are several pilots and aircraft maintenance engineers among my people, who I'm sure would volunteer to join me in this enterprise.'

Manager Botha raised his hand. 'I must stop you there, Breta.' He smiled. 'Yesterday I received a communication from the Immigration Department. The government has decided to resettle Sky People in a new town being developed on the east coast a few hours' travel from here. Many personnel are required for this project, the first of its kind in almost fifty years, so your people will be gainfully employed and training provided if needed.'

Breta leapt from the chair and, leaning over the desk, pumped Botha's hand repeatedly. 'Thank the stars, now we can begin to live again.'

'Please sit down, Breta, there is more I must tell you.'

Embarrassed now, Breta hurriedly resumed his seat.

'The government is in the process of establishing an aviation taskforce and I have been instructed to ask if you would be interested in the position of director.'

Breta resisted the urge to leap from his seat. 'I can't believe I'm hearing this. It's as if they had read my mind.'

Botha nodded. 'So your answer is …?'

'Yes, I would be pleased, no, delighted to take up the offer.'

'Good. Minister Gordon will also be delighted.'

'When do I begin and where?'

'Next month at an old abandoned airfield in the middle of the North Island on the shores of a lake.'

'If I recall correctly, that's not too far from my daughter. I presume there'll be some leisure time?'

'You presume correctly.' Botha looked down at his monitor. 'Your people, minus those qualified and willing to join the Aviation Task-force, will be relocated in two weeks. Tradespeople, mostly refugees from Australia, are already in situ. At present accommodation is in demountable buildings and there's a cafeteria for meals plus a few shops selling basic items.'

'Will men and women be separated in this worker's camp as they are here?'

Botha shook his head. 'I'm assured families and couples without children will be housed in separate dwellings. Nothing luxurious, I'm afraid, and rather small, but they are comfortable.'

Breta nodded but refrained from mentioning the concept of 'family' was unknown to Sky People. It would be an interesting exercise working out who belonged to whom.

Botha leaned forward. 'Have you any questions?'

'Just one. I understand payment for labour is the norm here?'

'That's correct and of course your people will be paid according to their skills.'

'My people will find Aotearoan practices perplexing. They have no experience of a monetary system or differing rates of pay for diverse work.'

Botha frowned. 'Are you saying Skyz59 was a communist society?'

'I suppose so, but in the true meaning of the word. Everything one needed on Sky was provided equally: accommodation, food, schooling, medical care.'

Botha considered this statement for a few moments, his eyes focused on the desk. 'But that's not the whole truth, is it, Breta?'

'What are you implying?'

'You had a two-tier system on Sky,' Botha replied without looking up. 'Those born naturally and clones.'

'We call ourselves "naturals",' said Breta, his eyes betraying deep sadness. 'Both groups were treated equally on Sky.'

'Nevertheless there was an anatomical difference, I believe?'

'There are, I mean, were, two.'

Botha's head jerked upright. 'Two?'

'As well as having no navel, clones were sterile.' Breta sighed. 'And before you ask, they were created that way in order to preserve the integrity of our gene pool.'

A long silence ensued, both men considering the ramifications of this admission. Guilt cloaked Breta's mind as he recalled the men, women and children he had ordered eliminated. So many lives cut short to ensure a future in Aotearoa for those considered acceptable. Why had *he* chosen to live? Suicide would have freed him from the waves of self-reproach that so often washed over him during the hours before dawn when he would wake layered in perspiration, faces revolving through his mind like images on a screen, reminding him of that fateful moment when he had made the decision to adhere to Aotearoan immigration conditions. And what of that other face, the younger version of himself? Hadn't he broken his word by saving Kaire? A purely selfish act that he now understood would haunt him forever.

On the other side of the desk, Botha struggled to remain calm as anger rose to the surface. He had served his employer, the Immigration Department, diligently over many years, could recite word for word the regulations governing refugees and asylum seekers. Some rules, such as rejecting those carrying the gene for a serious disease, he considered harsh, yet he had never flouted or even questioned this rule, believing it his duty to remain an obedient public servant. What concerned him at this moment was the knowledge that the Sky clones had posed no threat to the health of future generations. If the government had been aware of this, why were the clones refused sanctuary? Anger subsided and sorrow took its place; fear of difference was the answer, a trait that had caused countless wars, killings and exile throughout the long evolution of humankind.

'Race, colour, creed,' he said quietly, resting his chin on clasped hands. 'Why are we so afraid of those who are different from ourselves?'

Breta looked up, his lips curved in a sad smile. 'That is a question many have asked over the centuries, I'm sure, but I doubt there has ever been a satisfactory answer.'

'You speak my mind.' Botha rose from his seat and walked around the desk to shake Breta's hand. 'Let us hope some day human beings will learn to embrace difference.'

'And eliminate discrimination.'

Botha nodded. 'I hope your new life is fulfilling.'

'I hope so too. Why don't you come and visit me sometime?'

'I might just do that.'

Side by side, the two men walked to the door, each satisfied the labels of 'refugee' and 'camp manager' had dissolved as friendship birthed.

# EPILOGUE

New Year's Eve, a time for celebrating in ages past with champagne and fireworks, had long been relegated to a change of numerals in a world preoccupied with the ravages of climate change and environmental degradation. However, one small community on the Kauri Coast of North Island Aotearoa planned to end the year 2402 with a long anticipated partnership celebration. Breta had arrived two days earlier, supposedly to assist with the arrangements and spend time with Kaire and Pia, although in truth he intended to devote far more hours to cultivating his relationship with Tiki. Several months before, during a visit to Kauri Haven, Breta had renewed his acquaintance with the doctor and they had discovered a mutual attraction. Ever since, they had communicated frequently, lengthy discussions that revealed common interests and ethics, particularly a desire to assist the oppressed people living in Brown and Asian Zone Australia.

On the first day of his brief stay, conversation with Tiki centred on plans only hinted at when using communicators. Both Breta and Tiki considered the work of the Women's Line should be expanded to include specific acts of civil disobedience such as strikes at produce terminals, Working Parties and in fields to protest the poor quantity of food supplied to Brown Zoners. Further south they favoured factory strikes to oppose long working hours and unsafe practices that led to frequent injury and occasional death. They also envisaged transport strikes: trains loaded with produce stalled in remote regions, ships lying idle in Brown Zone ports, ferries unable to convey workers to off-shore fish farms or spotter stations. During their dialogue, Breta learned that White Zoners were totally reliant on Brown and Asian workers, even in the far south where child-carers and domestic servants were recruited from amongst the plethora of Splits found in communities close to the border. Tiki believed nationwide strikes would soon impact on the White way of life, food shortages particularly affecting those living in the Isle of Tasman, totally reliant on imported produce. According to Tiki, hungry politicians and bureaucrats would demand immediate solutions, forcing government to implement radical change, vital if Australia were ever to overcome its rogue state reputation and re-join the global community.

Privately Breta dreamed of using the Sky fleet in a concerted campaign to overthrow the White government, but at this point felt unable to share his plan with Tiki. However, he did mention it to his son on the one occasion he found Kaire alone. The prospect of participating in a confrontation that could result in countless deaths was abhorrent to Kaire, but he did concede the idea of involving Sky-ships to assist the Women's Line seemed sound.

On the second day of their short time together, Breta and Tiki set aside subversive schemes in order to cement their relationship. Promises were made to consider living together when Breta's work with the Aviation Taskforce had progressed sufficiently to allow him a protracted break. Meanwhile, Tiki would endeavour to find a medical position closer to the lakeside base, the long-distance relationship posing difficulties neither of them wished to deal with for longer than absolutely necessary.

As requested, the formal part of Pia and Kaire's partnership ceremony took place in front of the Sky-ship under a large domed sunshield. Pia wore a full-length sky blue robe fashioned by Kela from fabric woven by a group of older settlers. Blue and white silk flowers decorated Pia's curly hair, which to her relief had grown considerably in the months since the enforced cut, or 'scalping' as she referred to it, prior to the Asian Zone mission. Her Skyman dressed for the occasion in his silver bodysuit to honour his heritage, a decision he almost regretted when walking from their house to the runway in the searing heat of a midsummer afternoon.

After the ceremony, conducted by Mac in his capacity as council chairman, young and old partied into the early hours, revelling in a range of food and drink not generally available in their remote community. Mac had coordinated the refreshments, using Breta's access to aircraft to source items not grown at Kauri Haven. During the weeks preceding the partnership celebration, several trainee pilots had found flying lessons took them to unexpected places all over the country, where on landing, their instructor Breta would disembark to collect a box or two whose contents were never disclosed.

Late in the evening, a cool breeze blew in from the sea, banishing the day's heat and humidity. Settlers reacted with a flurry of activity, clearing away the remains of the food, returning tables and benches arranged in front of the main building to the dining room and fetching a variety of musical instruments from homes and school. Dancing then began in earnest, the young engaging in energetic twirls and leaps while their elders executed more sedate steps. A few chose the dances of their Polynesian ancestors, much to the delight of those who had never experienced such spectacles as the legendary Maori Haka.

It was after two before Kaire and Pia had a chance to slip away to their home. Weary and content they lay still in their bed, wrapped in each other's arms.

After a lengthy silence, Pia said wistfully, 'Not long ago I thought we'd never have the opportunity for a partnership ceremony. How I wish all Australians could live together without fear of arrest or worse.'

Kaire kissed the top of her head. 'Kauri Haven is the right place to begin our new life.'

'We need a secure beginning,' Pia agreed, then added to Kaire's surprise, 'but I'm not convinced we should spend the rest of our lives here. I think we would find it a little dull.'

'I can tolerate dull after what we've been through these past years.'

Wriggling out of his arms, she sat astride him, her brown eyes focused on the striking face she had once found so alien. 'So can I for a short time, but there are currents that will forever pull me north.'

'I understand, my love.'

'I knew you would.' She smiled and laid her hands on his smooth cheeks.

'Remind me in the morning to tell you about my father's proposal for what he calls the Sky Lines Alliance,' said Kaire, pulling her close.

'Will do, my beautiful Skyman,' she murmured, her lips sliding over his moon-pale skin.

Lovemaking seemed the obvious conclusion to their special day. Freeing her people from oppression could wait a little longer.

# ACKNOWLEDGMENTS

I wish to thank my publisher at Odyssey Books, Michelle Lovi, for her continuing faith in my writing.

Thanks also to other Odyssey authors for their encouragement and support.

# ABOUT THE AUTHOR

Sue is a fiction writer based in Mornington, Victoria. Her novel *Sannah and the Pilgrim*, the first in a trilogy of a future dystopian Australia, published by Odyssey Press in 2014, was Commended in the 2014 FAW Christina Stead Award. *Pia and the Skyman* is the sequel. Her current project, *The Sky Lines Alliance* completes the trilogy. Short stories, poetry and articles have appeared in national and international magazines and anthologies. She has also written the pilot for a TV series, based on *Sannah and the Pilgrim*, and now is seeking a producer.

www.ingramcontent.com/pod-product-compliance
Lightning Source LLC
Chambersburg PA
CBHW032121180726
48284CB00002B/646